The Abc
of
Love and War

J. M. Kent

Cover photograph *'On the Kent cliffs'* by John Gamgee

Typeset in Dante MT by Geoff Fisher

Printed by CPI Group (UK) Croydon CR0 4YY

AUTHOR'S NOTE

There is a wealth of information in historical documents, photographs and treasured personal letters about life in England over a century ago. Those of us with grandparents or great-grandparents may remember anecdotes passed down by word of mouth about schooldays, the clothes they wore or the books they read. But the conversations, thoughts, hopes and fears of young people growing up at that time are mostly not recorded and can only be imagined. In this respect, the characters and happenings in The Abc of Love and War are imaginary.

It gives me great pleasure to acknowledge the support I have enjoyed from my family and friends, old and new. No comments, words of advice, correction or amplification have been superfluous to my task. I thank you all.

When they were young . . .

The Makepeace Family and Friends

Winnie: daily help for the Makepeace family

Dora Makepeace: born 1888

Tom: Dora's father

Rosa: Dora's mother

Dr Flattery: doctor to Makepeace family

Arthur: Dora's brother, born 1897

William Bartlett: born 1885, Dora's friend in London

Miss Inkpen: Dora's primary school teacher

Mrs Brown: housekeeper at The Lions

Kitty: maid at The Lions

Evelina: born 1887, daughter of Lord and Lady
    Highton

Celia: senior prefect, Clothworkers' School for Girls

Dorothea: pupil, Clothworkers' School for Girls

Lady Alice Highton: Evelina's mother

Lord James Highton: Evelina's father

Lady Sylvia: Lord Highton's sister

George: born 1885, local boy at Brightsea

Bert: orphan, Arthur's friend

Mr Smeeth: bread delivery man

Violette: born 1899, French, London flower seller

Roland Merriman: born 1892, friend of Arthur

PART 1

CHAPTER 1

London, March 1897

There were angry noises coming from the scullery as the maid put wet washing through the mangle and emptied the bucket outside with a clang. Dora was sitting in front of the kitchen fire, a book open on her lap, too unsettled to read.

'The rain's set in for the day,' said the maid, coming into the kitchen with the clothes horse and gesturing to Dora to move out of the way. 'Things will be different from now on, you'll see.' Winnie delivered her words of foreboding with some satisfaction and placed the clothes horse in prime position in front of the fire. 'There'll be no time to sit with your head in a book.'

Reading was Dora's favourite pastime and she had no idea why she should be scolded for it. Although only nine years old, she knew, or thought she knew, the reason for the maid's irritation. She had observed that Winnie, who bustled about as if too busy to bother with such things, could not read. Ever since she had arrived to help with the housework, life at home was full of gloom. Mother had been confined to bed for weeks on doctor's orders and nothing now was as it used to be. Wash day or no wash day, come rain or shine, Winnie was not a woman to sing while she worked.

Dora left the only warm room in the house and went

upstairs to her bedroom to read in peace. She lay on the bed wishing it would not happen. She was used to her own company and was not at all sure that a baby in the house would change her life for the better.

Dora ran home along the back lane behind the houses, holding the new certificate under her coat against the rain. Neither Mother nor Dad had been there to hear her recite The Creed before the whole congregation, but she was pleased to see her friend William in the front pew, silently mouthing the words along with her. As she moved back to her seat, she overheard the vicar whisper, 'Word perfect and clear as a bell.'

There was nobody in the scullery when she let herself in through the back door. Winnie's coat was on the hook but there was no smell of cooking and the rows of shoes had not been polished. All was quiet, no noise from upstairs or from outside. She went into the kitchen, propped her wet boots up against the fender, took the Bible down from the dresser and settled herself in front of the fire to admire the certificate.

Dorothea Makepeace 1897
The Pilgrim's Award for reciting The Apostles' Creed

She ran her fingers over the blue and red edging, then turned the tissue pages of the Bible to find Psalm 23 and cast her eye over it. Her wet woollen stockings steamed and her toes itched with the heat. Six verses. If she learnt the psalm by heart, she would get a certificate edged in blue, red and gold.

Raised voices, then noises she had never heard before broke into her silence: a ghastly groaning and a beating cry. She went to the bottom of the stairs, her heart pounding, as Winnie rushed down towards her.

'Oh, you're back! Go up. Your father wants you.' She pulled on her coat. 'I'm going for the doctor. The baby's born. A boy. But it's not all over. It looks as if there might be another one. Go on up. Get a move on, girl!' The back door slammed and Winnie was gone.

The groaning had stopped but the beating cry persisted as Dora went up with silent tread, her mouth dry. She stood a long time on the landing until the wailing subsided. When Dad came out holding a bundle of blanket, he was smiling.

'It's a boy. Born while you were out,' he said, offering the baby to her. 'Take him. He's fine. Your little brother.'

She was relieved at his smile and croaked out, 'Mother?'

'She's having a hard time. Winnie's gone for the doctor. Take him. Hold him. Mother needs me.' He offered the bundle to her again, and when she had the warm weight of baby safely in her arms, he disappeared into the bedroom.

Rocking him gently, she looked in wonder at the tiny form. They were still on the top stair when Winnie came back with the doctor.

'The baby's in good hands, I see,' said Dr Flattery in his soft Irish voice, taking the boy from her to look him over. He shook him gently, smiled with satisfaction when he heard a deep gasp of breath and gave him back to her.

'Take him downstairs and keep him warm,' he said. 'I'll

take a look at him later.' Then he too disappeared into the bedroom.

A wooden drawer, laid out with blankets, was set on the floor in the kitchen. Dora sat for the rest of the day in front of the fire, watching the baby breathe, snuffle and sleep, quietly comforting him with words of the psalm. *The Lord is my shepherd; I shall not want.* A strange beginning. She read the lines through many times under her breath… *Yea, though I walk through the valley of the shadow of death…* Only when Winnie took the baby upstairs to be fed did Dora toast some bread, spread it with dripping and drink hot tea… *In the presence of my enemies…* When she went to fetch him after his feed, she took the boy willingly in her arms again, as if she possessed him. His eyes were closed, oblivious… *surely goodness and mercy shall follow me all the days of my life…*

The energetic beat of the baby's cry woke her. She was still lying in the dark when Dad came in and sat on the edge of her bed.

'No school for you this week, Dora.'

She lay under the covers in the dark. 'Why not?'

'You must help with the baby. Mother needs to rest.'

'What about school?'

'They'll understand. Will you look after him?'

'Yes.'

'We want to call him Arthur. Do you like it?'

'Yes, I like it.'

'Winnie's coming in every day this week to help out. She's already downstairs lighting the fire. One day off work is all they give me and I took that on Saturday, so I've got to go and open the shop.' He kissed her on the cheek. 'Take the baby down and keep an eye on him, will you?'

Dora carried Arthur downstairs, settling him when he cried and tucking the blankets round him when he kicked himself free. Many times a day, every day that week, she carried him upstairs to be fed and changed, then brought him down again into the warm kitchen, where he lay gurgling, sleeping and punching the air.

Mother, the lively member of the family, remained in bed. It had taken hours of hard labour for Arthur to come into the world, still, mute, bluish, until cries of triumph filled the air and a healthy pink flooded over him. The pain of that day was still with her. She greeted him anxiously whenever he was taken to her, 'Let's have a look at you, young man,' but was unable to resist smiling at him. 'You're here now, Arthur my boy, so we'd better make the best of it.'

Winnie's daily battle with the housework was a bad-tempered affair, so Dora kept out of her way as much as possible, preferring to run errands to the shops rather than help with the washing. She had to hang out sheets, pillow cases, towels and all the baby's nappies until the line was full; when it started raining, she was told to bring them all into the scullery again, where they queued up for space on the clothes horse in front of the kitchen fire. She scrubbed the hall floor on her hands and knees, reversing from the front door to the back, then laid newspaper over the wet tiles. On Friday she whitened the front step - her favourite job - and polished the letterbox, as she had seen Mother do many a time. As the long week passed, she felt the daily, hourly minute by minute pull and push of the crying baby as she lifted him out of the drawer, carried him upstairs and settled him down to sleep.

The next week she had to miss school again.

It was a fortnight before Mother came downstairs, pale and moving with difficulty. Even lifting her arms to put on her hat was an effort. They were both dressed for going out, Mother wearing her black coat that had seen better days and Dad in his Sunday suit.

'Dora,' said Mother, struggling to find the words, 'when Arthur was born he had a twin sister. She was not for this world…' Mother gave up.

It was only then Dora understood the grief within the house. She wondered whether her little sister, unseen and unheard, had a name. She waited for a sign to tell her what she should say or do, but there was no sign so she said nothing.

It was Dad who spoke. 'We're going to church. We need you to stay here and look after the baby. Will you do that with good grace, Dora?'

'Yes,' she said, taking Arthur in her arms, pleased to be spared the journey to church. 'Are you sad?'

Arthur let out such a wail her question was drowned. 'He's such a loud baby,' Mother sighed.

'Are you sad?' Dora asked again.

'Yes, we're sad,' said Dad, as they moved stiffly to the front door. 'Take your time, Rosa,' he said, taking his wife's arm, 'There's no rush.'

'Thank you, Tom,' she replied, her face white and pained.

Then they were gone, taking their sorrow out into the cold with them.

Oh, the warmth of the kitchen fire, the delicious smell and feel of Arthur's body as she held him to her. When the sadness had left the house, Dora felt the comfort of him, of his breathing beside her, of being an older sister, of being alone, yet not alone.

CHAPTER 2

After two weeks at home Dora was pleased to be back in the usual Sunday routine. Saturday night was bath night so she walked to William's house with scrubbed nails, clean hair and clean clothes. She and William always walked to and from Sunday school together and she had missed chatting to him. He was twelve years old, the oldest of six children all living in two rooms above Bartlett the Bootmaker's shop in Jelf Road, where his father worked. It was a noisy, overcrowded household with childish chatter in a mixture of two languages, because their German mother spoke to them only in her mother tongue. A new baby appeared at regular intervals in this family. William was waiting at the door for her knock.

'All the other children grow up when there's a new baby,' he said as they walked to church. 'Even Freddie behaves better since Annie was born and he's only two.'

'I never saw our baby girl,' said Dora, 'I don't even know if she had a name.'

'I'm sorry to hear that. It's awful. I remember vaguely - I must have been about five - when it happened to us. That'll be why your mother's not well. It was the first time I saw Ma crying and wearing black.'

Dora always felt better for talking to William.

'I've finished with Sunday school,' he said. 'I don't

believe in that stuff anymore. I need to concentrate on my school work. I don't want to be a cobbler and Dr Flattery says you have to be good at maths to be a doctor. Well, I am good at maths, so who knows, I might be a doctor and have my own motor car one day.'

'I want to be a teacher.'

William just laughed. 'That's no secret.'

When church was over, they walked back to Dora's house together. The terraced houses in Garden Crescent curved around a central garden, which was surrounded by railings and an iron gate. Everyone called this communal garden The Big Green. In summer it was a secluded place, green with grass, warm with sunshine and shady under the trees; the top end was laid out in allotments.

Dora and William went in through the back gate of number twenty-four and could hear Arthur's urgent cries before they had opened the scullery door.

'Do all babies cry like this?' she asked.

'All the time. There's no peace in my house day or night.'

A delicious smell of chicken broth greeted them as they went in. Dad must have made it and left it simmering on the stove.

'Mm, food,' said William, who was always hungry.

'Good. You're back,' said Dad, coming down the stairs looking weary. 'Take the baby up to be fed. Mother's just had some soup.'

'Dad,' said Dora, 'William's come to see Arthur.'

'Hello, William. How's your mother?'

'She's fine, thank you, Mr Makepeace.'

'I hear she had another girl.'

'Yes, we're calling her Annie.'

'I don't know how she does it,' said Dad, taking his cap from the hook by the back door. 'I'm off out, so help yourselves to the soup.'

'It must be grand to have this house to yourself,' said William, picking the baby up with practised hands to quieten him.

'It would be, if only Winnie would go,' said Dora, who was missing the peace and quiet that had been the rule at home before the baby arrived. If it wasn't Winnie sniffing and grumbling about housework, it was Arthur crying as if his life depended on it. She went to the front room for some books. It was always cold in there: a musty, unused room with a piano, a small bookcase and a shiny horsehair sofa. She scanned the familiar shelves, picking up *The Adventures of Sherlock Holmes* for William, unsure what to choose for herself. Her hand hovered over *Little Women*, which she had read so many times she could open it anywhere and feel at home, then she changed her mind and picked up a big leather-bound book: *A Pilgrim's Progress*. It was ages since she had looked at the pictures.

'Sherlock Holmes? Will that do?'

'Fine. I'll read one of the short stories. I forget how he works it all out.'

While Dora took Arthur up to be fed, William set two bowls of chicken soup on the kitchen table and began to read. They often sat in companionable silence together. William was easy to please.

It was with great excitement that Dora went back to school with news of the new baby. She was staying on after school to write up the lessons she had missed, while Miss Inkpen marked a pile of books. This quiet time in the warm and empty classroom was precious to Dora, who enjoyed talking to people older than herself.

'Shall I stoke the fire?'

'Yes, do. Put some more coal on.'

'Miss Inkpen,' Dora asked, attending to the fire, 'may I ask you something?'

'Yes.'

'Did you become a teacher because of your name?'

Miss Inkpen smiled. 'I think you're asking whether I had a vocation.'

'What's a vocation?'

'It's when you feel called to lead your life in a certain way. Yes, I did have a vocation. Girls are just as clever as boys and sometimes they enjoy study more.'

'How old were you when you knew you wanted to teach?'

'About eight years old. I used to watch my mother sitting at her desk writing with different coloured inks and a choice of pen nibs. The desk was an important place in our house. That's when I realised the significance of my name.

'What do you think of my name?'

Miss Inkpen smiled again. 'Dora Makepeace is an excellent name. It says in the Bible, *Blessed are the peace makers.*'

'Is the Bible true?' She had been thinking what William had said and this question just popped out. Dora sensed Miss Inkpen was considering her words carefully.

'The Bible is not one book, but a collection of books written a long time ago. The stories in the Old and New Testaments help us think about the power of God in our lives.'

11

'I'm not sure what to think when I think about God.'

'That doesn't surprise me at all. Great is the mystery of faith! And as you grow up your thoughts will change again. I was brought up a Unitarian and now I'm a Trinitarian.'

Dora was both baffled and completely satisfied with this glimpse into the adult world. She now knew that things were a lot more complicated than William thought.

'There is one thing I am certain about,' Miss Inkpen continued, 'a peacemaker is welcome everywhere.'

This pleased Dora too. 'Can you keep your own name when you get married?'

'No. You give up your maiden name and take the name of your husband. That way everyone in the family has the same name. So choose wisely! You could end up a Mrs Bucket, or worse.'

'Is that why you're not married?'

'Enough questions,' said Miss Inkpen firmly, turning back to her marking.

On the way home Dora thought how much things had changed since Arthur was born. It used to be a quiet house but Mother said she had never known such a loud baby. His name was Makepeace too.

Something was wrong. Rosa was still not better after the birth of the baby and there was a slowness in the way she walked. Tom, at a loss as to how to help his wife recover, called the doctor.

'It will take time, Mr and Mrs Makepeace,' said Dr Flattery. 'Low spirits can descend after childbirth, especially in circumstances such as these, when the little girl never drew breath and there has been neither christening nor funeral.' In this kindly way Dr Flattery acknowledged the sadness in the house but something else was definitely wrong. When Dora overheard her parents arguing after she had up gone to bed, she sat on the stairs to listen.

'Just wait until next month, Rosa. There's a manager's position coming up at Boots the Chemist and Dr Flattery has put in a good word for me. Something will turn up.'

'But Tom, this scrimping and saving has been going on long enough.'

'We'll have to economise, that's the answer.'

'We can do without Winnie for a start.'

'Are you sure you can manage?'

'Yes. Dora will have to do more. She's willing enough. Anything to get rid of Winnie.'

Dora had no idea that Winnie annoyed them too.

'When I'm better, I can go back to work,' said Rosa.

'Not that again. It's early days and I'm just not having it,' said Tom.

'They need a seamstress at The Lions and Lady Highton has particularly asked for me. It's an opportunity to work for a good family.'

'Let me look at the housekeeping books once more.' Tom was rarely angry but he was angry now.

'I can take Arthur with me,' Rosa persisted. 'Dora can have her own key and come on after school.'

The back door opened, slammed shut and Tom's foot-steps disappeared down the back lane.

Dora slipped back into her room and saw the lamp light pass by as her mother climbed the stairs with a heavy tread.

In the dark, the situation became clearer. Bread and dripping had been a treat at first, but they had been eating it every day. Even on Sundays they only had chicken soup followed by rice pudding. She thought the simple food was because Winnie had no idea what to buy. Did Mother say she was taking Arthur away? What must she do after school? Something about a key... And then she slept.

CHAPTER 3

By the beginning of beautiful May, Rosa was up and about and Winnie dismissed.

'Thanks to you, Dora, we can do without her,' said Tom, who was up early, doing his Sunday job of polishing shoes in the scullery. His black work boots, the black shoes to go with his Sunday suit, Rosa's black everyday shoes, her best brown pair and Dora's black lace-up boots were all laid out in a row.

'Are your boots too small for you?'

'Yes, they are a bit. There are holes in both of them.'

'I know about the holes, but there's no point in getting them soled and heeled if they're too small. I'll put the cardboard in again. You won't need heavy boots now summer's coming.'

On the day of the Christening, Rosa came downstairs in a new green outfit with the scent of lavender water about her. She had powdered her face, put rouge on her cheeks and colour on her lips. It was the first time for a long while she had put curling irons in the fire and curled her thick brown hair back off her face. She went to the coat stand in the hall to secure her old felt hat with a pin and admire herself in the glass. On went the newly polished brown shoes, brown leather gloves and she was ready for church.

'Right, Arthur, my boy,' said Rosa to the wriggling baby,

as Tom manoeuvred the pram out of the front door. 'Behave yourself. Try to sleep through it.'

'Arthur Ernest Makepeace, I baptise thee in the name of the Father and of the Son and of the Holy Ghost. Amen.'

The joy of spring was all too brief. Rosa's low mood persisted and daily economies continued. Bars of soap were used to the slither end and the Sunday roast was made to stretch the rest of the week. By Wednesday the housekeeping money in the red tin box on the dresser was all gone. Tom was still out of work and down-hearted, finding even dead-end jobs hard to come by. He liked to be busy so he took an allotment in the Big Green, where he passed the time digging and planting vegetables. Indoors, he took over most of the housework, taking care to keep out of sight of the neighbours.

'I'll do it, Dad,' said Dora, more than happy to help out. 'I'm better at it than you are.'

Tom had been mulling over in his mind a way to thank Dora for all she had done since Arthur was born. He decided to take her up to London to see the Queen! It would be an outing for them both, one that he needed and she deserved. He had chosen the day well. On Tuesday 22nd June 1897, which had been declared a public holiday, they travelled into London on the top of a bus, looking down on streets packed with Londoners celebrating Queen Victoria's Diamond Jubilee. What a day they had, laughing and cheering! They saw nothing at all of the Queen, because of the jostling crowds, but they did see the royal procession of fine horses and carriages on its way through

16

the streets from Buckingham Palace to St Paul's Cathedral.

'There'll be close-up pictures of the Queen in the newspapers tomorrow,' said Tom, in case Dora was disappointed. He delighted in agreeing to every treat his daughter could think of. A currant bun? Certainly, with icing on the top. Ice cream? Yes. Cheap at the price and worth every penny.

As summer turned into winter, Tom watched Arthur grow sturdy as a lamb, pushing himself up, falling down, pushing himself up again, stumbling about like a drunkard and trying to walk before he could crawl. The boy was so like his mother. Tom remembered how cautiously Dora had learnt to crawl, with one hand in front to check the step up or down. Her delicate complexion, blue eyes and fair hair were all his own. He watched her at the kitchen table, pencil, rubber and ruler to hand, writing up the housekeeping accounts, calculating the horizontal total in the right-hand margin and producing a vertical total at the bottom of each page. She did everything just as he had shown her and took obvious pride in it. Tom's main satisfaction had always been to put money on the table every week and see the housekeeping books balance, but it was plain for all to see that the household accounts did not balance and a holiday was out of the question.

When there was no more coal in the cellar, Tom pawned the pocket watch he had inherited from his father. What else was he to do? He could not abide debt. 'It's too precious to use every day,' he said, taking a last look at it and snapping it shut. 'I might as well pawn it.'

Then Rosa's gold necklace, the long one, had to go. She found solace playing the piano in the front room at odd times of the day. She could play a few tunes by ear and there was considerable satisfaction throughout the house that she was playing again. Dora began to pick out a few tunes and there was the occasional sound of laughter coming from the cold front room.

Mother and daughter always had their heads together these days, knitting, sewing, mending, darning. A place for everything and everything in its place was the rule for the sewing box: the thimble had its own little compartment, needles were inserted according to size in the needle case, coloured threads were set apart from the black and white cotton reels and buttons were stored in a separate metal box. Rosa marvelled at the way her ten-year-old daughter learnt to turn a collar and machine it back on securely. Dora enjoyed whirring away on the treadle sewing machine, putting sides to middle of worn-out sheets with a straight French seam. She was good at hand-sewing too and could let down the hem of her skirt and hem it back up again with neat stitches. With all this help at home, Rosa was able to take in sewing from outside and before long they were relying on her earnings. There may not have been much time in Rosa's day for little Arthur, but he climbed onto his father's lap for comfort and stretched out his arms out to Dora when she came back from school.

The day the piano was taken away by three strong men and loaded onto a cart was a black day indeed. Later that evening, Dora overheard her parents arguing again. She sat on the stairs to listen.

'We're behind with the rent. We'll have to give up the top rooms,' Tom said. 'Dora and Arthur can share a room. Plenty of people do it.'

'The time has come for me to take that position at The Lions,' said Rosa. 'Debt is making us miserable. Lady Highton wants me back and has offered me work in the afternoons. It's manageable. Arthur can come with me and Dora can pick him up on her way home from school.'

She had thought it all out and Tom had no answer for her. Even though he had found work at last, Rosa was adamant. Dora heard the back door slam.

The bar lady began to pull Tom's pint of mild as soon as he entered the pub. He put the exact money down on the counter and took his drink to a quiet table in the corner. It was infuriating. Just when he had been offered and accepted a permanent position as manager at the grocer's in the High Street, Rosa was going back to work. If it makes her happy, he thought, but he was bitter about it. Strangely enough it was Arthur, toddling about, falling over, making people laugh and demanding to be picked up, who was changing life at 24 Garden Crescent for the better.

CHAPTER 4

The Lions, London, December 1899

When the clock chimed the half hour, Mrs Brown stirred after her nap. Even her sleep obeyed the clock. It took her a while to return to the world after twenty minutes or so of oblivion. She was in her usual armchair by the fire in the parlour, and stretched forward to shovel some coal on the embers and watch the black dust flare satisfactorily in the grate. Mrs Brown organised the downstairs household from this chair: the housekeeping book open on a pastry board across her lap, a lead pencil in her hand and an india rubber at the ready in her pocket.

There was half an hour before Rosa was due to arrive to reintroduce herself and run over the duties required of her. I expect she's aged, thought Mrs Brown, it's been more than ten years. They fell on hard times, so I've been told. She had a girl not so long after Miss Evelina was born, then a lad quite a few years later. Mistakes happen, I suppose, but people get over them. Rosa always was a lively one with quite a temper when you least expect it. Still, it'll be good to have her back here for a few hours a day. I hope she realises times have changed and it's not just sewing she's here for. Rosa always was a dab hand with the iron. It'll be a bit of company for me and she can help with the afternoon teas when young

Kitty has her break. The poor girl's as thin as a stick, up and down stairs all day long, on call from early till late. She deserves a few hours off in the afternoon.

Mrs Brown lumbered from the parlour through the kitchen to her room just off the scullery. Years of ample food and limited activity were taking their toll. She no longer struggled to do what was beyond her and that included going upstairs. The most strenuous part of her day was putting on her black stockings in the morning and fixing them with garters: lisle in summer, woollen in winter, always black. Kitty slept right up at the top above Miss Evelina's room. All the other work was done by means of daily help, which took some organising; there was the woman who attended to the upstairs early fires and beds, the scullery maid downstairs washing up all day, the cook, the laundry woman and the man who did the garden, took up the coal and brought in the deliveries. Then there was Robins, the driver, who took no orders from her and who considered himself too grand to come downstairs, until Lord or Lady Highton kept him waiting out in the cold, when he condescended to accept a mug of tea and a bacon sandwich to pass the time.

Mrs Brown looked in the glass, tidied her hair with a few more hair pins and took a clean apron from the linen cupboard. Rosa must see her standards had not slipped.

'Put the kettle on, Kitty, straighten your cap and find a clean apron. They'll be here soon. And remember, I might call her Rosa but she's Mrs Makepeace to you.'

*

Mother and daughter walked the mile from Garden Crescent to Villa Road at the end of December, the darkest time of the year. Rosa was conscious of looking dowdy and aware that Dora's coat was tight under the arms and too short, even though the hem had been let down to the limit. But Rosa had won the argument and was to take up the position as seamstress at The Lions, where she had worked before she was married. Lady Highton was paying a more than fair wage to have her back, after a succession of other women had proved no good at all. Lord Highton himself had put in a good word for her, saying that a woman with common sense and a ready smile deserved a helping hand.

The Lions was an imposing three storey, double-fronted, detached house set back from the road. A flight of whitened steps led up to the front door and on either side of the steps was a magnificent lion in smooth black stone. These two lions with manes and large heads were lying down, paws outstretched. Dora thought she caught sight of a face at one of the long windows on the first floor as they approached.

'Someone's watching us,' she whispered.

'That'll be Miss Evelina. She's about your age.'

'Do we knock?' asked Dora.

'Yes,' said Rosa, bypassing the steps up to the front door. 'We knock downstairs. They're expecting us.'

'Who lives down there?'

'Mrs Brown, the housekeeper, and Kitty, the maid. I've never met her, she's new since my day.'

Rosa opened the iron gate and led the way down the spiral steps to the basement. It was over ten years since she was last there but it was all coming back to her now. A girl about fifteen years old, wearing a black dress, white cap and apron opened the door. 'Good afternoon, Mrs Makepeace. Please come in.'

This is how Dora first set eyes on The Lions, to which she would walk every day after school to pick up Arthur. It was a very grand house indeed. They sat with Mrs Brown at a large table in the middle of the parlour, a spacious room with a coal fire blazing in the grate and two deep armchairs on either side of the hearth. Kitty came in with the tea things just as the clock on the mantelpiece was striking the hour. (Those four silvery chimes brought it all back to Rosa as if it were yesterday, but my word, she thought, how Mrs Brown had aged!) Above the parlour door was a row of bells to summon the servants. Under the skylight on the street side of the room was a treadle sewing machine ready for use, where Rosa would work from two until six, five days a week. Arthur could play about on the floor or sleep in a wooden playpen in the corner of the room until Dora picked him up on her way home from school. Even Tom was in favour of the arrangement now that he was Manager at the shop. His early mornings meant that he would be able to look after Arthur when Dora brought him home after school. It was all most satisfactory.

The century was on the turn and change was in the air. Dora had secured a scholarship to the Clothworkers' School for Girls and her first school day was Monday 1st January 1900. Thanks to Miss Inkpen, she already had the uniform.

CHAPTER 5

Dora had lost count of the times she had stood outside the gates of the Clothworkers' School for Girls to watch the girls file in and out. Over the wrought iron gate was a gilded crest, with the school motto:

My trust is in God alone.

On this day, the first of the twentieth century, she walked through the gates and up the stone steps, her eyes shining with nervous excitement.

The girls were shown into the hushed classroom one by one. Dora was allocated a desk on the back row, next to a girl with a blond plait over her right shoulder, the only girl in the room not wearing school uniform. When every desk was taken, a woman standing at the front addressed the class.

'Welcome to the Clothworkers' School for Girls. My name is Celia, and I'm a Senior Prefect.'

Could this composed, calm, woman with a captivating voice be a pupil? The Senior Prefect, who looked for all the world like a teacher, continued:

'This is a happy place, and to keep it that way we all agree to abide by the school rules. You will find a General Work Book and a pencil on your desk. Put your name on the front and write down the rules in the book as I dictate them.'

The girl on Dora's left was looking around nervously, not knowing what to do.

'The rules are to help you to fit in to the school and its ways.

1. Stand whenever a teacher comes into the room.
2. Address every teacher by name.
3. Walk in single file in the corridors, keeping to the left.
4. Silence from the time the bell is rung for morning assembly until you are back in the classroom and silence from the time the bell is rung for luncheon until after Grace has been said.
5. Hair must be short or tied well back off the face.
6. Wear school uniform at all times in school and on all journeys to and from school.
7. Be punctual.
8. Never eat in the street and never walk more than two abreast on the pavements.
9. On a bus or train offer your place to any person without a seat.
10. Any breach of common sense or of consideration for others is a breach of a School Rule.

This last rule is the most important of all, for obvious reasons,' said Celia, as if she knew they would all agree with her.

Dora noticed that the girl with the plait had written nothing at all and was close to tears, when, unannounced, the door opened and a teacher entered the room. They sprang to their feet, as one.

'Good morning, girls. I am Miss Craze, your form teacher.'

'Good morning, Miss Craze,' they answered in half voices.

'Please sit down.' The girls scrutinised the intimidating presence for clues as to what might be in store. Thin, middle aged, with brown hair coiled in plaits behind her head, her clothes were brown and neat but otherwise unremarkable. 'I am the Classics mistress. I shall be teaching you all Latin and some of you will learn Greek when you are older.' A slight smile suggested she might be pleased about it. 'You will receive a timetable, a Bible and a hymn book. The books are yours to keep, so take them home, put your name inside and cover them in brown paper. At the nine o'clock bell we assemble in the hall for prayers. After morning break you will be shown around the school. I hope you enjoy the day.'

To Dora's surprise Miss Craze then walked towards her, looked at the name on her General Work Book and spoke directly to her. 'Dora, this is Dorothea.' She was introducing the girl with the plait. 'She has come from Germany with her family to live in London. Will you look after her and make her feel welcome?'

'Yes, Miss Craze.' What random seating arrangement placed her next to a girl with the same name? By means of hand gestures, smiles and mime Dora explained that she had to put her name on the books and cover them. She watched as the German girl wrote Dorothea Keller in an unusually florid script. In this way, on that day, with few words exchanged, the two girls felt an amiable kinship that pleased them both.

*

Dora ran up Villa Road, her satchel thumping on her back, aware that she had undergone something of a transformation. Nothing about crossing the school threshold had disappointed her. As she approached The Lions, a pale figure offered a tentative wave from the long window on the first floor. Dora had not yet spoken to Evelina, the daughter of the house, but with the confidence the new school had bestowed on her, she waved back before turning down the spiral steps to the basement.

'My, oh my, what have we here?' said Kitty, as she opened the door. 'New school, new uniform, whatever next?'

Arthur stopped banging a saucepan with a wooden spoon and held up his arms, demanding to be picked up, before Dora had uttered a word. She took off her hat, dropped her bag and settled him on her lap.

'I've been to my new school, little brother,' said Dora, pleased to see his delight at her arrival.

'Well, how was it?' asked Rosa, putting down her sewing and looking over the spectacles she needed for close work.

'Just fine, thank you,' said Dora, as calmly as you like, cuddling Artie and enjoying the familiarity of him. 'I didn't know a soul. But I've made a new friend. A German girl, whose name is...Guess what her name is.'

'Gretel,' said Kitty.

'Dorothea,' said Dora, still in disbelief.

'Fancy that! Do they call her Dora too?' Mother wanted to know.

'No. Dorothea.'

'Can she speak English?'

'No, not a word. But we're all new and I'll help her.'

'Miss Evelina would like you to go up to her room,' said Kitty, pulling a face at how high and mighty Dora was becoming.

'What, now? Like this? I could do with washing my hands and having a bite to eat. Or a cup of tea, perhaps?'

'Why don't you go straight up? Leave your outdoor shoes down here.' Kitty wanted things to go right for Evelina, who was fed up with being kept indoors. 'She's over the worst of it and there's no risk of infection. She's been leading me a right dance these last few days, keeping me from my work and asking me to put rags in her hair. All through boredom.'

'Shall I go up, Mother?'

'Yes, why not if she's asked for you? I've just finished moving the buttons on this sash. Take it up, will you? She's lost so much weight since she's been ill nothing fits her anymore. She's strong-minded, I'll say that for her. I think she's just getting back to her normal self.'

Dora went up in her stockinged feet.

Evelina was waiting by the bedroom door in a dark blue dressing gown and slippers. Her auburn ringlets and translucent complexion were so magnificent that Dora's confidence took a knock as she stood in her school uniform, her hair dishevelled from her day, holding a purple sash. There were no twelve-year-old girls at her school who looked like that.

'What was it like at school?' said Evelina at the very same moment that Dora asked, 'How are you feeling, Evelina?'

and the confusion made them laugh. There was no more than a year between them in age, but they were so different in every other way that the prospect of becoming acquainted was daunting to them both. Yet curiosity prevailed.

Dora swallowed hard when she stepped into the room and looked about her. It was not like a bedroom at all. The wallpaper had a complicated pattern of flowers, birds and ladies in oriental costume, on a deep red background. There was a pleasant smell of soap and burning coal.

'No governess, no lessons and all meals in my room for three weeks might sound good, but I'm so bored I'm even looking forward to going to church on Sunday morning,' said Evelina, sitting on the floor by the fire so that Dora could sit in the armchair.

'Is that good or bad?' asked Dora, laughing.

'A sign of desperation,' replied Evelina, as quick as a flash.

'This bedroom is wonderful,' said Dora, who had spotted a portable writing desk out of the corner of her eye. 'I can't imagine being bored here.'

'I'm making a necklace. Just something to keep me occupied,' said Evelina fetching the box of beads from the bed. 'You can make a matching bracelet if you like,' she added, sensing that sharing the repetitive task would make it easier to talk. 'What was it like at school?'

'It was good,' said Dora, finding it difficult for some reason to give account of her day. 'Our form mistress teaches Classics. She'll teach us Latin and Greek one day. She's called Miss Craze.'

'Poor woman! Do you call her crazy?'

'No! We would never do that.' How do you explain to a girl, who has never been to school, just how exciting it is? Dora needed to change the subject. 'What do you study with the governess?' Apart from the ghastly lives of fictional governesses living in the north of England, she had little idea what went on when girls were educated at home.

Evelina was similarly reluctant to talk about her lessons, all of which she loathed, but a direct question deserved a direct answer. 'French mainly, because she is French,' she began. 'But I also have to do arithmetic and English with another tutor, who is far from my idea of an ideal companion. Then there's the dreaded piano lesson, simply torture.'

'We had a piano…' Dora stopped mid-sentence, mortified at what she might reveal.

'I'm trying to persuade Mother to let me have singing lessons instead,' Evelina went on, noticing nothing untoward. 'It's got to be more fun than the piano.' Kitty knocked and came in with a tray. 'Oh, good, it's hot chocolate.'

Dora sipped the hot chocolate and waited until Kitty had left the room to carry on their conversation. 'Are you feeling better after your illness?'

'Yes, thank goodness, no temperature, no rash and no more spots, but I have to stay indoors for another week. I hope you'll come up and tell me more about the school. It intrigues me. Do you like the uniform?'

'Yes, I like it. We all look the same, with our black stockings, navy skirts and smocks. The older girls wear longer skirts, blouses and jackets. They don't look like girls at all, they look grown up.' She wanted to talk about the bits that had impressed her most. 'There's a stage in the hall, a small church organ and stained-glass windows. It's very splendid. There are four hundred of us there for assembly and the hymns sound wonderful.'

'Do the girls curl their hair?'

'I've no idea.' Dora had never curled her hair. 'Do you mean with tongs or with rags?'

'Rags. I'm not allowed to use tongs. It burns your hair.'

'How long do you need to leave the rags in? Your hair is a mass of curls.'

Evelina's hair was indeed beautifully thick and artfully arranged, off the forehead without a fringe, some of the ringlets pinned up and others left to fall down her back.

'Kitty put them in yesterday, when my hair was wet. They stayed in overnight and have been in until this afternoon. The only thing I have done all day is to thread beads and wait for the rags to be taken out. I'm bored out of my mind.'

'May I look at your writing desk?'

'Yes, try what you like.'

The rosewood box, small enough to put on a table top, had **Evelina Highton** engraved on a brass plate on the lid. Inside was an array of pens, nibs, ink, pencils and thick sheets of creamy writing paper, all unused. This would normally be an irresistible attraction for Dora, but she was acutely aware of her grubby, ink-stained fingers.

'I need to wash my hands first.'

'Oh, that's easy,' said Evelina moving to the washstand to pour lukewarm water from a blue patterned jug into a bowl. 'Forget the writing box. I've got some new hand cream for you to try.'

Dora scrubbed her hands with lemon scented soap to remove the grime of her school day. She looked at herself in the large mirror and adjusted the two hinged side mirrors to get a view of the back of her head, hating the sight of her hair, that Mother had cut straight across the back with the kitchen scissors. This dressing table is just the thing if you have long auburn ringlets, she thought, rubbing rose-scented cream into her hands and making a decision there and then to grow her hair. A leather manicure set was open on the washstand displaying a fine selection of files, scissors, a pot of abrasive cream and chamois leather buffers. Evelina was just about to show Dora how to apply the cream and buff up her nails to a sheen when Kitty knocked on the door.

'Arthur's demanding to be taken home,' she said, putting the cups on a tray. 'In fact, he's screaming the place down. Mrs Brown's had enough of him.'

'I'm coming,' said Dora, making a mental note to make her voice sound more like Evelina's than Kitty's.

'He's such a loud baby,' Evelina laughed. 'I can hear him crying from up here.'

Dora took her leave in a daze: two new friends in one day.

CHAPTER 6

London, 1902

Arthur did not stay in the playpen for long. His early years at The Lions were spent either out in the garden in summer, playing with anything he could lay his hands on, or getting under everyone's feet in the parlour in winter. Whatever the season, he liked to watch Kitty light the fire by laying thin sticks of wood crisscross on scrunched up newspaper and placing small lumps of coal on top.

'Me. I can do it.'

'No, you'll get it everywhere, just wait.'

He was at her elbow waiting to put the lighted taper to the kindling and watch the flames devour her work. If the fire refused to catch, because the wood was damp, Kitty held a sheet of newspaper across the fireplace to cause a draught and draw the flames.

'Stand well back,' she said firmly, as the fire began to roar and she let go of the newspaper, which flew up the chimney.

'Me,' he urged her.

'No. It's dangerous.'

'Me,' he insisted, to no avail.

What was the fascination with coal? He even liked the smell of it. Time and again Rosa had to stand him in the stone sink to wash his hands and knees, black from the coal scuttle.

'Mm, you smell of Pears soap, Artie,' said Evelina, giving him a cuddle when he was clean and wrapped in a big towel. She hated her lessons upstairs and invariably found her way down to the parlour around four o'clock, when Dora arrived from school. Then it was time for the buttered toast ritual, the highlight of Arthur's day. He was mastering the art of toasting a thick slice of bread on the end of a long-handled toasting fork, holding it neither too close nor too far away from the hot coals to brown. Woe betide anyone who tried to take the fork away from him.

Dora found him most endearing when he was sitting in the armchair pretending to read. Mrs Brown let him look at the pictures in the big black Bible she took down from the dresser. David and Goliath was his favourite.

'He'll be reading soon,' said Dora, pleased to see him with a book.

'Not long now,' said Rosa, not looking up from her sewing, but leaving Arthur in no doubt she was talking to him. 'I'll be glad when you go to school.' He was five years old and his time had come.

'Why?'

'You won't be able run riot at school.'

'What's that?'

'Make a noise and play with guns and catapults.'

'Why not?'

'You'll soon find out.'

'Find out what?'

'You'll see.'

Talking to Dora baffled him too. He knew she liked going to school but he had little idea what went on there.

'What do you do at school?'

'You learn to read and write.'

'Is it easy?'

'Yes.'

'Mother says I can't take my toys.'

'That's right. You don't play there. You have to be good, Arthur, or you'll get punished.'

'How?'

'You have to stand on your chair in front of the class with your hands on your head.'

'That's easy. I can do it.'

'But it's awful, Arthur. Everyone pities you.'

The day before he went to school, Rosa, for some reason bad tempered and deaf to his screams, took him outside the back door and cut his hair brutally short with the kitchen scissors. Why? When Tom came home he asked the same question. Why? Getting no answer, he took his son on his knee and comforted him. 'Your hair will grow. It never stops growing. You'll make friends at school. Just you wait and see.' Tom prayed it would be so.

Dora looked on appalled, remembering the humiliation of the day Mother cut her hair straight across the back before she went to the Clothworkers' School. Why? She shuddered at the memory. Now she was fourteen, her hair was long enough to tie back with a ribbon and she was determined to keep it that way. That's the last time you do that, she thought, seeing Arthur's misery. The omens were not good.

'Come on, quick march,' said Mother, offering her hand, which Arthur refused, his hands firmly in his pockets. It was a cruel, blustery morning early in September and they were on the way to Park Road School. He pulled his cap down over his head and lagged behind; he hated his hair and he hated her. 'Come on, pick your feet up.' She spoke and walked briskly, holding on to her hat, not wanting him to be late on his first day. 'Brrr, I loathe wind.'

Arthur had mixed feelings as they went through the iron gates to join the crowd of mothers and children. He saw a tree in the middle of the playground, tall with high, spreading branches in late summer leaf. It was surrounded by a low brick wall, where the mothers sat, waiting for school to begin. A teacher opened the doors, smiled in an authoritative way and rang a handbell.

'Be good, Arthur. Do as you are told. I want to hear all about it when you get home.' Mother bent to kiss him but he dodged out of her way. Then she was gone.

Some of the girls, and even some of the boys, were crying. They had to make two lines, girls and boys, and file through the doors together. Hold hands? With a girl? Arthur had waited anxiously for this day and it was not beginning well.

Inside the classroom individual wooden desks were arranged in rows, a cardboard box of chalks and a slate on each one. Arthur chose a desk at the front, right under the teacher's nose. Her name was Miss. The morning was long and confusing, chanting nonsense about Ay Bee See, counting their fingers and looking at the blackboard. It all took a long time. Then someone rang a hand bell and they went out into the playground.

Arthur ran immediately to the tree, determined to get to the top before anyone else. He need not have worried as none of the other children even tried to climb it. But they watched. With practised eye, he assessed the climb. Up he went, his hands feeling the familiar roughness of the branches, his feet secure on the ridges of the trunk. The leaves, at their dark September fullest, had grown their all and not yet dropped. At the top in minutes, Arthur looked with satisfaction at the spreading canopy, the branch he had chosen as a seat firm under his weight. From this comfortable vantage point, he had a bird's-eye view of the playground and the upturned faces of the children. Hidden in his green bower, the exhilaration of the climb made him feel good, free, more like himself. He had been practising tree climbing in the Big Green all summer. At the sound of the bell, he saw two lines of children ready to file into school again. All his buoyancy of spirit vanished in an instant. Arthur could not, would not, go back into the classroom. It was just not his sort of place.

'Arthur. Arthur Makepeace. Come down this instant.'

It was an angry man's voice. Why was everything he wanted to do, and could do, always wrong?

'Come down this instant.'

As Arthur considered his options he felt a surge of power, just enough to allow him to descend with dignity. He chose his route and set about it, concentrating hard on making it look easy. He hung from the top branch, moved his hands sideways to the end of the branch, where his weight caused it to bend. Then he jumped his hands to the branch below that, and dropped down again, and so on, until he landed on the playground in front of the Headmaster.

Back in the classroom all eyes were on him as Miss told him that climbing the tree was forbidden; it was dangerous and he must not show off. Then he was up on his chair, hands on his head, taking a good look at his classmates. He knew some of them from playing out. One boy, thin, smelly, coughing, had boots with the toes cut out and his clothes were all misfits; none of the children wanted to sit next to him. The teacher picked on the miserable lad, telling him he must wash and learn to use a handkerchief. Then, using a special voice that sent a chill through the classroom, she made the snivelling, coughing, and now crying boy sit in the wastepaper basket. The room went deathly quiet. Arthur, still on the chair, looked down at the boy, whose legs were hanging over the edge of the wicker basket, displaying his outgrown boots and no socks for all to see. Sickening pity hit his stomach, tears stung his eyes and fury raged throughout his body. When the bell went and the class was let out into the playground, Arthur said to the boy, 'You live near me. Let's go home.'

'I can't,' his voice was choked with tears.

'Let's go and play somewhere.'

'I got nowhere to go,' he said, looking desolate.

'I'm getting out,' said Arthur, climbing up and over the school gate, ready to run. 'What's your name?'

'Bert Farthing.'

'Come on, Bert.'

'I can't.'

'Don't say you can't. It's easy. Follow me.'

Arthur left the wretched boy inside the school railings and ran free. He had found out what school was like and it was not for him.

But what now? He jumped on a bus, went upstairs, came down and jumped off again before the conductor came for his fare. Where was he? Nothing looked familiar. He was lost, wandering about, hungry, anxious. A policeman struck up a conversation with him, brief and to the point.

'What's the matter, lad?'

'I want to go home.'

'Where's home?'

'Garden Crescent.'

'I'll take you.'

At the first familiar street, Arthur ran off as fast as his legs would carry him. He went straight to the Big Green and climbed a familiar tree, only coming down when he saw Dora put her key in the lock and it was time go home.

'What happened at school today, Artie?'

He struggled to explain. They had not taught him to read. He had climbed the tree and had to stand on the chair.

'Oh, Arthur, how could you?' said Dora, who listened with dismay to the sorry tale.

'You'll have to learn to do as you are told. No more nonsense and disobedience,' said Rosa, who had feared the worst.

'That's how it is in school,' said Tom kindly. 'It's not all play.'

'I only climbed a tree.'

'I've told you before it's dangerous to climb trees,' Mother went on.

'I like danger.'

'Enough. Bedtime. You've got school in the morning.'

'I hate it. I don't want to go.'

'If it's good enough for the other children, it's good enough for you.'

'They all wanted to go home. But I did it.'

'You'll get used to it.'

'I'm not going back there.'

'Oh yes, you are.'

'I hate this day.'

His tears spluttered hot and fast. He could do so much and try so hard but not there. Why could nobody understand he was not a school type of boy?

'You'll start reading soon,' said Dora kindly. 'I'll come in and read you a story.'

Arthur went to bed hot with misery.

'What's your teacher's name?' asked Dora, sitting on the side of his bed with a book.

'Miss.'

'Miss what?'

'Miss Summers.'

'That's a nice name.'

'She's horrible.'

'Why?'

'She's horrible to Bert.'

'Who's Bert?'

All he could do was snuggle closer to her, his mind on

his misery. She was reading but he was only half listening...about a boy, called something Nelson... twelve years old...he went to sea...a great sailor... he'd find a way...his way...Dora would teach him to read...he'd ring the handbell and set all the children free ...Then he drifted into the trouble-free world of sleep.

CHAPTER 7

The Lions, London, 1902

'It's impossible, but how would you know?' said Evelina, dipping her pen into the turquoise ink and carefully removing the excess. Being left-handed, writing could be a dispiriting affair but the sea-blue-green ink she had chosen pleased her eye. There were days when she chose purple.

'It may be a disadvantage, but people manage,' said her tutor, unhelpfully. 'It's a matter of perseverance.'

The nib scratched and faltered as she laboured to form the many loops and tails required to copy out the text, smudging even the most perfectly formed words with her fist as she travelled from left to right.

> *All the world's a stage,*
> *And all the men and women merely players;*
> *They have their exits and their entrances,*
> *And one man in his time plays many parts,*
> *His acts being seven ages.*

Lady Highton, whose copperplate handwriting displayed no irregularities, did not help matters. She was often present in her daughter's lessons and liked to make helpful comments from the other side of the room.

'If you were to use your right hand, Evelina,' she said, without looking up from her embroidery, 'you would find it easier to drag the nib across the paper.'

This was clearly nonsense, as Evelina and her tutor knew all too well. 'I'll write in pencil next time,' she replied, packing away her work in protest.

Her daydreams were leading her nowhere. She could never be a teacher, a Florence Nightingale, or travel to the heart of Africa like Mrs Livingstone. Or could she? There was no putting sheets sides to middle for Evelina, but what was she to do? Decorative embroidery was just another exasperating annoyance. How enticing it sounded when Dora talked about life at school, the friends she had made, the plays they read, the chemistry experiments in the laboratory and physical exercises in the gymnasium. Not that Dora excelled at everything by any means; she hated gymnastics and was always grumbling about the pushing and shoving involved in team games. But poor Evelina very much wanted to turn a somersault, climb a rope, vault over a horse and be part of a team.

There was no denying that the Clothworkers' School for Girls was the making of Dora, who now wore her long hair neatly coiled on the top of her head. Her school reports were good, she was learning to play the piano and had settled into a comfortable routine with her friend Dorothea, with whom she had more in common than she first thought. They often went to each other's houses and Dora was getting used to hearing the German language, speaking it a little, eating black rye bread and drinking sparkling apple juice.

Evelina was envious and it was not a pleasant feeling. 'It's not fair, Mama,' she said, 'I'm kept in all the time.'

These ill-chosen words exasperated Lady Highton, who regularly went with her husband and daughter to the theatre, where they had seats in the front row of the stalls. They had seen nearly all the operas by Gilbert and Sullivan as well as some of the modern plays. Thrilled by the smell of the scenery, the larger-than-life costumes and the illuminated world revealed when the curtain went up, Evelina's enthusiasm for the stage was becoming a passion she shared with her father; they exchanged excited glances at the sound of the orchestra tuning just before curtain up. She put her case to him, thinking, quite rightly as it turned out, that he would have sympathy for her cause.

'Papa, is it right to keep me at home? It's the twentieth century. Do you think I could have a life in the theatre? The stage is respectable now.'

'I've no doubt you would make a good job of it, my dear,' he replied, making a mental note to persuade his wife to arrange drama lessons for their daughter.

Prompted by Evelina, he spoke up when all three were together at breakfast next morning.

'Alice, my dear, shall we come to a decision about Evelina's wish to prepare for the stage? I'm all for it,' he continued, undaunted by his wife's cold stare. 'She might surprise us all and study something with vim and gusto. Goodness knows, she's got enough of both.'

'Not now, James,' was the far from satisfactory reply.

'Mama,' said Evelina, digging her heels in, 'what plans have you for my future?'

'All will become clear in time, my dear. It won't be long before you'll be out in society. Let me hear how you're getting on with the Chopin Prelude.'

'Dora will play it for you if you are that keen to hear it,' said Evelina, who never touched the piano if she could help it. Dora had been given permission to practise the piano upstairs at The Lions, in the hope that it would set a good example. That permission was immediately withdrawn by Lady Highton and Evelina's piano lessons stopped.

It was not long before both tutors were dismissed; only the tiresome French governess remained.

'French is important,' her mother insisted.

'Can't you see? I'm bored to death at home.'

'Evelina, you must not be so ungrateful. Work at your French. We'll be in Paris in May.'

This instruction, like so many others, fell on deaf ears. Many trips to Paris had convinced Evelina that an English accent and a tiny waist were her best assets. As far as she was concerned, the less attention she paid to speaking French like the French the better.

'I prefer going to Aunt Sylvia's,' said Evelina, rebelling against everything, even Paris, if she had to be chaperoned. Then she had an idea, and changed her tone of voice noticeably. 'I'd like to go to Brightsea with Dora, if I may, please, dear Mama.'

Lady Highton was instinctively against it. 'You go downstairs to the parlour every day, Evelina. It's inappropriate and must stop. Too much mixing with the servants is never a good thing.'

45

'Dora isn't a servant.' The sweet tone had gone from Evelina's voice.

'Even so,' said her mother, doggedly.

'Kitty came with me last time I went to Brightsea, if you remember and she really is a servant. It was far from satisfactory. She spent most of her day off with George and his family, leaving me on my own.' Evelina could be quite determined if she set her mind to it, even if it involved minor untruths such as this one. 'Dora and I will be able to go about together quite respectably. A girl must have friends, Mama.'

'Let her go, my dear,' said James, infuriating his wife once again when they were discussing it in private. 'Sylvia is all for it.'

Fortunately, in the summer of 1903, when Evelina was sixteen years old, Aunt Sylvia came to the rescue by inviting her to Brightsea. Even better, Dora received an invitation too.

CHAPTER 8

Brightsea, Essex, August 1903

Evelina released the leather strap to let down the window and lean out. The regular chugging of the steam engine and the rattle of the wheels on the track filled her ears, the wind was in her hair and her eyes squinted in the sunlight. She enjoyed every stage of the journey to Brightsea but especially this bit. The wide sky and flat salt marshes directed her eyes towards the horizon. There it was.

'The sea!' she exclaimed, turning to smile at Dora.

As the train curved around the track to pull in at the station, Dora had her first glimpse of the bluey grey horizon, where the vast expanse of sea merged with the sky.

London was now three hours and three train journeys away. The two girls were alone in the compartment as Puffing Billy, as the little steam train was known by the locals, came to a grinding halt at the final station on the branch line. The heavy door was opened from the outside. Evelina stepped out and Dora, picking up her hat box and small travelling bag, climbed down after her. She had kept an eye on the hat box throughout the journey because it contained her portable writing desk.

'Leave the bags, Dora, Edwards will bring them.' The mild

air and bright sunlight made them both smile as they stood on the platform. 'What did I tell you? This is the driest place in England. It's like being abroad.' Evelina's excitement stemmed from a succession of August holidays in Brightsea.

'Good afternoon, Miss Eva,' said the man who had opened the door.

'Thank you, Edwards. This is Miss Dora, my friend from London.'

'Welcome to Brightsea.'

'Are we going in the pony cart?'

'Yes, Miss Eva. The cart is outside waiting for you.'

'Perfect.'

The ride in the pony cart was the best possible way of getting to Jacob's Hall. It was like going back in time. Evelina went to greet Mussels by stroking his neck and to her delight he nuzzled her in recognition. How was it possible that the same pony could be pulling the cart from the station after all these years? He set off at his own pace, ambling along as he had always done, needing no twitch of the reins to determine either the speed or the route he would take. The girls looked about them, breathing the sea air and watching the seagulls swooping and calling over the salt marshes.

'What's your Aunt like?' asked Dora. She had been told little about Jacob's Hall.

'You'll soon find out,' laughed Evelina, giving nothing away.

'Does your Aunt call you Eva?'

'Yes. Everyone calls me Eva here. It's only my parents who insist on my full name.'

'How do you spell Mussels? Is he Mussels or Muscles?'

'What a question! I've never thought about it. Are you going to write to him?'

'I promised I'd write to Arthur. He'll want to know all about the steam train and the pony.' Dora was still thinking of him, his face a mixture of excitement and confusion as he waved goodbye from the platform at Liverpool Street station.

The pony cart turned into the High Street and came to a halt outside Jacob's Hall, a large white house with a timber frame, a thatched roof and all the beauty of age. News of Evelina's arrival by the afternoon train had spread. As the cart approached, three boys and two girls sitting on the wall opposite, turned and stared. Evelina was about to jump down and greet them but checked herself. George's brothers and sisters, her playmates of last year, seemed shy, awkward, taller and, well, older. And where was George? This summer things would clearly have to be different. She composed herself, smiled in a slightly aloof manner, got down from the cart with care and walked up the path to the front door. Dora followed, looking straight ahead.

'Welcome to Jacob's Hall, both of you,' said Lady Sylvia, standing at the open door to greet them.

'Aunt, this is Dora. We're so excited to be here.'

'Welcome, Dora. How lovely to see you. Welcome to Brightsea.'

'How d'you do, Lady Sylvia.'

'Please call me Lady V. It's nice to be informal when we're out of town.'

'Thank you, Lady V.'

'Goodness, Eva, how tall you are! Edwards will bring in your bags. Your trunk arrived three days ago, Eva, so why don't you both go upstairs to your room? There's tea at four o'clock in the garden room, so come down if you would like some. You're both in the bedroom at the back. Show Dora how to light the gas lamp and explain about our primitive night time arrangements, Eva. The stairs are too steep to come down in the night.'

'Yes, Aunt. I've told Dora how strict you are,' said Evelina, laughing as she spoke, because Lady Sylvia allowed almost everything. She was wearing a long purple skirt, a white silk blouse with a high neck and had draped a patterned crimson shawl around her shoulders. Her feet were bare inside her shoes and Dora noticed that her hair, piled high on her head, had an unnatural reddish tinge.

'You'll get used to Aunt,' said Evelina, leading Dora up a narrow flight of stairs. 'She has her own rules and often breaks even those. We can do just what we like here. My parents call her a Bohemian. I think it's because she lives alone, likes to paint and holds strong views about religion and politics. Father said before I left this morning that he trusted me to look after you. So we had better be sensible, or we won't be allowed to come again.'

As she said all this, Eva noticed how uneasy her friend looked. A seaside holiday, which she herself had enjoyed every year since childhood, was unknown to Dora, who had never been away from home, never swum in the sea, rowed a boat, smelled seaweed or caught a crab. A whole month away from London lay before them and there was much fun to be had, but Eva realised she would have to be kind.

The bedroom was simply furnished with two single beds, a chest of drawers, and a washstand with jug and bowl. There were clothes hooks on the wall, two upright chairs, watery seascapes on the walls and a gas lamp over the fireplace. The bookcase was full of books.

Evelina threw open the window overlooking the Colne Estuary. 'Come and look at the view. That's the creek. The tide is out now, but when it comes in, it comes in fast. We'll go there tomorrow.'

Dora had no idea what 'the creek' was but just now she had lost her tongue. She turned her attention to unpacking the small writing desk, a present from Evelina for her fifteenth birthday and her most treasured possession. It was a small leather-bound box, ten inches by eight, and three inches high, with her name engraved on a brass plate under the carrying handle. It was far from grand but it contained all the writing implements she needed and she could take it everywhere.

Evelina's trunk was full to the brim, a treasure chest of summer cottons in all patterns and colours. 'I threw them all in. My clothes from last year should fit you perfectly and there are some new ones for me. My shape has changed, I'm pleased to say.' She was tall and slim, with curves above and below her tiny waist. 'Take your pick. Whatever you fancy.' This pastime pleased both of them, the one offering the clothes and the one receiving the hand-me-downs. After all, everyone did it.

'I'm warning you, Dora, it is rather old fashioned here. The privy is downstairs behind the scullery door so there are chamber pots under the bed. Aunt has no live-in servants, just Edwards and Mary, the maid, who comes in every day. These beds are blissfully comfortable. Look, two mattresses, a horsehair one and a feather one on top. We make our own beds. I love plumping up the feather mattress in the mornings. See? Lavender bags under the pillows, smelling of summer. Which bed would you like?'

Dora, who had listened and looked but said nothing, pointed to the bed by the window. Making her own bed was no hardship at all and she preferred life without servants.

'Fine. It's yours,' said Evelina. 'I'm just going to get out of these travelling clothes, then we can go down for tea. I'm starving.'

Dora went downstairs to find the privy, which was outside the house by way of the scullery. It had been a long while since they stopped at the ladies' conveniences in Wivenhoe station.

Tea was laid out informally on a large table in the middle of the garden room; the plates, cups and saucers were all of different patterns, colours and sizes. South-facing French windows opened onto a patch of grass, kept short up near the house but left to grow long at the bottom of the garden, where it merged with the salt marshes along the creek. There was an odd selection of furniture, a day bed here and an armchair there, a footstool, a writing desk and a wicker steamer chair out on the lawn.

'Please help yourself, Dora,' said Lady V, pouring herself a cup from a silver teapot. 'It's China tea, silver tip. Milk curdles horribly in August, so we drink tea without. There's no cake, but there are shrimps, fresh today, with brown bread and butter and I have prepared some cucumber sandwiches.' She carried her choice of cup and saucer out into the garden and sat on the wicker chair on the lawn.

A wave of anxiety overtook Dora as she poured herself some tea. Everything here was strange. The light and the very air she breathed seem different. Arthur had cried when she left London that morning. How do you explain to a six-year-old how long a month is? She missed him already. At that moment, a month seemed a very long time indeed.

Eva stepped out into the sunshine, throwing her hands out wide, 'The sea. I can smell it.' She pulled off some flower heads from the lavender bush, rubbing them in her hands and sniffing them. 'Summer, at last.'

Lady Sylvia took this opportunity of taking a close look at her niece, who had made an impressive entrance when she arrived at Jacob's Hall. She was certainly taller, and more womanly, now she was sixteen. Her skin was white, her hands elegant and her movements quick and impulsive. She was sitting on the grass in a loose cotton skirt, which reached mid-calf, her legs and feet bare, her blouse open at the neck and the sleeves pushed up above the elbows. She was busy removing hairpins. 'That's better,' she said, shaking her hair loose over her shoulders. 'We're on holiday.'

Lady Sylvia politely avoided scrutinizing Dora, who, unused to changing her clothes three times a day, went out to sit on the lawn still in her travelling clothes. Dora had helped herself to a deliciously appetising cucumber sand-wich, made with thick white bread, well buttered. She would give the shrimps a miss. The delicious food and fragrant tea revived her spirits.

Evelina jumped up to answer a knock at the door. It was George, who had been waiting to hear from the lads and lasses on the wall that Eva had arrived. Cap in hand, he said, with a strong voice, 'Good afternoon, Miss Eva. Would you like to go to the Hard? It's a grand afternoon.' There are many ways for a young man of nineteen to show how grown-up he is and in the split second available to her, Eva observed that George had mastered most of them. She was standing opposite a good-looking man, whose shoulders were broad and his arms strong, the blue kerchief around his neck matched his eyes and his fair beard was trimmed neither too long nor too short. He was recognizably George, but there was little of the country boy about him. Just the Essex voice remained. They had always gone over to the Hard together as soon as she arrived. What should she say?

'Er…Thank you, George. One moment, please.' As she turned to consult Dora, George called after her.

'Is Kitty with you?'

'No, I'm afraid not. But I have a friend with me. I'll ask her.'

'Righto. I understand.' He turned and walked down the front path to wait with his younger siblings, who had come to watch the whole encounter.

'Aunt. What should we do? He looks different.'

'So do you,' Aunt Sylvia replied, amused at her observation. 'Very. Yes, you can walk down to the Hard. There's time to do that and be back for dinner.'

'What do you think, Dora?'

Dora had no idea where or what the Hard was but she

did not feel ready to go out again, and certainly not with a man like that. 'Let's do it tomorrow,' she said, when she had found her tongue.

'I'm off, then,' said Eva, running upstairs to pick up her sling purse. 'I'll go as I am.' She knew the attractions of dishevelment in her dress as Dora did not. 'It's only George.' She pulled on her canvas shoes and was gone.

'Would you prepare the runner beans, my dear?' asked Lady Sylvia, seeing Dora's confusion. 'They're just the perfect size, picked this morning, no thicker than my little finger. We'll have them with new potatoes, a few peas, some fresh mint and a knob of butter.'

With practised skill, Dora set to stringing the beans and slicing them diagonally, eating one or two in the process.

'I'm glad you like them,' said Lady Sylvia. 'Runner beans, peas, spinach and marrows are available all summer. Mr Peck supplies all our vegetables. Fresh eggs and fresh fish too. We keep all our perishable food on the marble slab in the larder on the north side of the house to keep it cool. You'll soon find your way around so just go to the larder and help yourself if ever you feel peckish.'

After the simple meal, which they shared together with easy conversation, Dora went up to the bedroom, keen to cast her eye over the books crammed in the bookcase. The selection was enticing. The clothes in the trunk could wait until tomorrow. It was with great satisfaction that she set out her writing box on the washstand table, mixed the light blue ink powder with a little water, laid a sheet of paper on the sloping surface, fitted a nib to the penholder, and began a letter to Arthur. He would be missing his bedtime story.

Jacob's Hall, High Street, Brightsea, Essex
Monday, 3rd August 1903

Dear Artie,

I saw you running along the platform to wave goodbye.
My goodness, you can run fast! Did you like the steam
trains? Evelina and I went in a pony cart from
Brightsea station to Jacob's Hall. The pony's name is
Mussels. When I look out of the bedroom window I
can see the sea. You will get lots of letters from me.
Remember to say your prayers before you go to sleep,
the way we always do.

With love from Dora.

With a bookcase on one side of the bed and her writing
desk on the other, perhaps she would be able to last the
month away from home after all.

CHAPTER 9

Brightsea

The rowing boat was rocking on a greenish-grey sea when Dora stepped aboard. The old sailor held out his leathery hand to steady her as she moved towards the stern. The girls had come to the Hard to go over the water to the beach hut.

'It's choppy today,' the man said, his Essex voice quite without expression.

'Should we go, if it's choppy like this?' Dora asked, gripping the sides of the boat.

'Oh, this is nothing. It'll be fine once we get over to the beach,' said Eva, dangling her fingers over the side, all set to enjoy the morning. A whole day of unknown adventures stretched out before them but Dora had yet to smile. They were each carrying a string bag with provisions for the morning: swimming costume, towel, a small rubber kneeling mat for sitting on the shingle, a flask of water and some cream crackers. She had packed a book, as she never went anywhere without one, whereas Evelina had put in a sketchpad and pencils, with no real expectation of using them. Dora had no intention whatsoever of going for a swim.

The sailor untied the rope and sat facing them wearing

long waterproof boots over his trousers and a dark blue heavily oiled jumper, as old as his boat. The peak of his cap was set low against both sun and rain, while he rowed silently with slow, rhythmic strokes, a habit maintained in fair weather and foul, with or against the tide.

'It's always breezy on the water,' said Evelina, as the waves splashed cold and uninviting against the sides of the boat. The crossing took ten long minutes and Dora wished with every stroke of the oars that she had never agreed to go to the beach. Evelina's smiling face did not reassure her.

'Twelve o'clock back,' said the boatman. 'If we leave it past noon you'll have to walk over mud.' He held the boat close to the jetty for Eva to jump out in her white canvas shoes. Dora waited to be helped out, relieved to feel dry land under her brown leather boots.

Evelina handed over some coppers from her sling purse. 'For both of us, there and back.'

'That's just right, Miss, thank you. Same as last year.'

'Twelve o'clock, we'll be here.'

She set off in the direction of a row of wooden huts on stilts, a little further down the beach. Good, thought Dora, following a few paces behind, a place to sit and read. I am not swimming in this sea.

'This is it,' said Evelina, with obvious pride, going straight up the steps of *Seaborne*, the first hut in the row, to open the door with an iron key. 'Welcome to the doll's house. Aunt has used it lots of times this summer already, so everything's here. Let's put the chairs out on the verandah.'

Dora was entranced. It really was a delightful hideaway, equipped with a day bed, folding wicker chairs, footstools, cushions, two woollen blankets, cupboards, shelves and net curtains at the windows. She scanned the books, the packs of cards, halma and cribbage board, then looked out to sea to get her bearings. The land they had left on the other side of the water was clearly visible and the shingle beach before them was golden now the sun had broken through.

'What a wonderful place,' she said, smiling at last, pleased at how sheltered and private it was on the verandah. 'I'm going to read for a bit.' She found her book, the water and the brown paper bag of buttered cream crackers. 'This is bliss.'

Evelina tied her hair high on her head with a ribbon and set off along the sea shore to the jetty, carrying her swimming costume, the rubber mat, an enamel bucket from the hut, a ball of string, a sharp knife and a bag of bacon rinds, even though part of her was feeling too old to go crabbing. She turned to wave but Dora was already deep in her book, munching biscuits.

At noon the two girls climbed into the boat to be rowed back over the water. One of them had a sunburnt face and wet hair. 'I must bring my hat tomorrow,' said Evelina. The other, who had spent the morning in the shade of the hut with her feet up reading and watching the sea shore, was cool, calm and collected. She had seen a rowing boat pull up on the shingle and a young man get out. She had observed that Evelina had not been alone for long.

An appetising smell coming from the kitchen of Jacob's Hall made the girls realise how hungry they were. Lady Sylvia asked no questions as she came from her studio to greet them.

'You both look better for some fresh air,' she said. 'Lunch is nearly ready. Mary came in to prepare it. Lamb with carrots and onions is in the oven and the potatoes are on. All you have to do is shell and boil the peas. Pop some mint in the saucepan.' In half an hour the meal was on the table.

'George called here at about ten o'clock,' Lady Sylvia said, as if she had just remembered. 'I told him you had left early to catch the tide. He was going to row over to find you.'

'He must have missed us,' said Evelina, making the lie sound just like the truth.

Later that evening, Evelina suggested a walk along the prom, which Dora declined, having no idea what such an outing might involve. She had been thinking of Arthur at home expecting his bedtime story and a wave of homesickness hit her, so she went upstairs to read in bed, as she often did in times of trouble. Then she had a brainwave; she would bring him here one day. The steam train, the sea, crabbing, the country boys, boats, swimming, rowing…she would bring him when he was ten …she would take some sea shells home for him…seaweed … Without reading a word, much cheered, she fell asleep, only to be disturbed by Evelina climbing into the other bed.

'Is that you?' Dora mumbled, half asleep.

'Yes, who else would it be?'

'Did you go to the prom?'

'Yes. We had fried potatoes wrapped in newspaper, smothered in salt and vinegar.'

'Who's we?'

★

Dora pulled on her clothes and went downstairs to the privy without waking the sleeping mound in the other bed. The garden was coming to life in the quick morning light, making the path leading from the bottom of the garden out to the salt marshes impossible to resist. She climbed over the stile in the fence, brushing the lavender bush with her skirt and rubbing the flower heads between her hands to release its reviving scent. On she walked, drawn towards the mysterious terrain of the estuary, where sea water gushed in perpetual motion between the clumps of grass beneath her feet, finding inlets and outlets with the suck and pull of the tide; all the while the birds calling. She turned back, wary of its power.

Evelina, a habitual late riser, was walking round the garden in her night clothes, eating a slice of toast. She seemed pleased with something. 'You're up early. But you don't look very summery. Help yourself to clothes from the trunk,' she said. 'Take your pick. And don't you think it's time to abandon your stockings? It's going to be hot today and the tide will be high in an hour or so. I fancy another swim.' Eva liked to dress simply on holiday, no stockings, no corsets, no hat apart from the sun hat and certainly no gloves. She wanted the freedom to walk along the prom, climb in and out of a boat, or ride George's boneshaker of a bicycle should the opportunity arise.

Dora took her time choosing from the selection of blouses, skirts, dresses, jackets and scarves on offer from Evelina's wardrobe. She noticed immediately how well made they were and once she had made her choice, how good they felt next to her skin. She was unable to resist a blue seersucker flared skirt and a full sleeved white cotton blouse.

'Just the perfect combination for the seaside,' said Lady Sylvia encouragingly. 'You might like a parasol. There's one by the front door.'

Dora took it from the stand in the hall and was just deciding on the angle at which to hold it, when she heard music far in the distance, getting ever louder, wafting in through the open windows.

'It's the Sally Army,' cried Evelina, running down the stairs. 'The hymns come to us in Brightsea, we don't even have to go to church.' Dora followed her out into the High Street in her new hand-me-down summer clothes, holding the parasol at the perfect angle, which she had verified in the full-length looking glass in the hall.

The Salvation Army brass band was marching down the High Street in full uniform, playing the hymn *Eternal Father Strong to Save*. People were gathering on both sides of the street outside Jacob's Hall, where the band came to a halt. There was the usual Sunday crowd, who enjoyed the hymn singing, and there were newcomers, curious to see what it was all about. After three hymns, sung from hymn sheets by a bold few, the band struck up *Onward Christian Soldiers*, the signal that the Army women in their black bonnets were coming round with the collection bag before the band moved on. Evelina had her money ready. Lady Sylvia slipped a sixpence into Dora's hand.

'You must have a sling purse, my dear,' she said, as they went back into the house. 'Ready money can nearly always get one out of trouble.'

'We're off to the hut, Aunt. Going for a swim.'

Dora was prepared for the walk to the Hard and for the boat crossing but not for the swim, not under any circumstances. She walked alongside her friend, enjoying the pleasant holiday feel of the light cotton skirt cool and airy on her legs (stockings were compulsory at school in winter and summer) and her feet bare inside the canvas shoes.

Dora settled down to read on the verandah of the hut while Evelina went for her swim. She was half watching and half reading when she heard Evelina shriek with exhilaration as the gasping cold enveloped her body and she took her first frantic strokes.

'Morning.' George stood beside her, his eyes darting towards the sea and the screams. 'Is Eva here?'

'Yes. Enjoying her dip by the sound of it. The thrill of the sea never fails her.'

They watched the water nymph frolic about and then get into her stride. She swam towards a boat moored off shore and clung to the anchor rope, waved and set off again.

'She shouldn't swim alone. The tide has turned. It's dangerous,' said George, his eyes on her every movement. 'She's heading for the buoy and there are rocks underneath. I'll have to go and get her.'

He ripped off his clothes at high speed and ran across the shingle in his swimwear and shoes, kicking the shoes off just as he plunged in. Even for Dora's long-sighted eyes the drama in the water was a blur. Both were smiling as they walked back up the beach to the hut, Evelina wrapped in her towel and George carrying his clothes.

'Marvellous,' said Evelina, glowing, not shivering.

'You took a risk,' said George, going behind the hut to change. 'It's dangerous when the tide's on the turn.'

'You're right,' she said going into the hut. 'I couldn't see the beach at all. It's one thing having to wear spectacles in the theatre but it would be ridiculous to wear them in the sea. George gave me the shock of my life.'

She shook her hair when she came out and gave George a sharp look. 'You were early.'

'Good thing I was. It's always risky to swim alone. Don't take risks in the sea.'

It was apparent that their meeting had been arranged the previous evening, while they were eating chips on the prom. Dora decided to leave them to it. She took the ferry boat back on her own.

CHAPTER 10

Brightsea

It was a relief to be back at Jacob's Hall. Dora was feeling unwell and knew she was in for hours of pain. At times like this there was only one place to be and that was home. Lady Sylvia was rinsing paint brushes at the stone sink.

'You're back early,' she said, taking off her painting smock and wiping her hands on it. 'Another beautiful day. I think I need some sun.' She had spent the morning in the north facing studio and craved the summer air. 'Tea? Marvellous. I was just about to make a pot.'

'I'll get it.'

'Oh, thank you,' she said, moving back into the garden room. 'I'll stretch out in this patch of sunlight and you can tell me about your morning.' She lay on her back on the floor by the open window, arms outstretched, knees crooked, breathing slowly and deeply.

'What have you two been up to?' she asked, when Dora came in with the tray.

'We were at the hut. I was watching Evelina swim.'

'Not alone, I hope.'

'No, George is with her. What have you been painting this morning?'

'Seascapes. There's more water on the paper than paint.'

Lady Sylvia was still lying on her back, her eyes half closed. 'It's lightning quick work. My seas and skies are getting increasingly wet the more I paint them. In winter, it's oils, a completely different process.'

'I'd like to see them.'

Lady Sylvia turned to take a good look at her. 'What's the matter? Are you unwell?'

'I'm indisposed.' This was the accepted word at school if one of the girls had monthly pains and had to go to the medical room to lie down. 'I'll be better tomorrow.'

Lady Sylvia understood. 'I'll bring you an aspirin and a cup of strong tea with sugar in it. I used to find it helped. Curl up on the day bed, or maybe you'd prefer to go up and rest. No point in working through it if you don't have to. There are plenty of days when rest in these circumstances is just not possible. Indulge yourself. You're on holiday.'

Dora relaxed and swallowed the two aspirins Lady V brought her and drank the strong, sweet tea. She had no wish to go upstairs to rest, preferring this engaging company. 'You're different from other women in so many ways. Free. You seem to live how you choose.'

'Only up to a point. My circumstances were thrust upon me. I live alone because I'm a widow and have no children. That was not my choice, although there are some advantages. My money is my own. When you marry, your money becomes that of your husband; when you are widowed, the money is your own again. I'm fortunate to be able to live as I choose.'

'Were you born to this?'

'Yes, I was. Lady is the courtesy title I am able to use because my father was an earl and I was the only daughter. It's the same with Evelina, but she has decided not to use her title.'

'Really? She never told me.'

'Her mother would prefer her to use it, of course. She may use it later. When she comes out in society.'

'She never told me that either!'

'Eva is still finding her way.'

'But you? I thought you had to take your husband's name when you marry.'

'That's right. My name is Mrs Sylvia Nightingale, but those who knew me before I was married still call me Lady V sometimes! I was sixteen and Marcus was twenty when we married in 1864. Things were different then. But we were in love and our life together was one great adventure. He was dead within a year.'

'Sixteen? That's Eva's age now. I'm so sorry. You've been alone so long.'

'Yes, indeed. But it's lovely to have your company. It fascinates me to see you and Eva going your different ways, she trying to free herself from the conventions of her upbringing and you wanting to adopt them.'

'The first thing I wanted to do when I went to school was change my speaking voice. There was a Senior Prefect at school, she's left now, with a lovely voice. And she could play the piano! I copied everything about her.'

'Your voice is just right. It will take you anywhere.'

This was a boost to Dora's confidence. Lady Sylvia was the sort of woman who rolled both Rs in the word 'library', as they were instructed to do by Miss Swithin in elocution lessons at school, which set the girls giggling.

'You can learn almost anything, I suppose.'

'Certainly,' said Lady Sylvia leaning back in the armchair. 'The point of good manners is to make other people feel comfortable. Posture is important too. Walk tall, sit up straight and move gracefully.'

Dora had noticed that wearing a corset helped with this. She would certainly wear one when she was standing in front of a class as a teacher.

'A good tip is to lie on the floor for a quarter of an hour every day, just as I was doing earlier. Any time, any place and your posture will improve. The trick is to feel the small of your back sink flat onto the floor. It might be fun to walk about trying to balance a book on your head but nothing is as beneficial as lying flat.'

This amused Dora, who was unable to imagine her straight-backed school mistresses lying on the floor every day for the sake of their posture.

'If I start on table manners we'll never finish. But I do suggest you never eat out of doors. We are all tempted. Queen Victoria was photographed eating at a picnic once; it never happened a second time. Just keep a mint in your bag for emergencies.'

Dora thought of George and Evelina enjoying fried potatoes covered in salt and vinegar out of newspaper on the prom. 'That is a school rule too,' was all she said.

'The rules are intricate and many. No elbows on the table, tip your soup spoon away from you, never speak with your mouth full –'

'I never do that,' Dora interrupted.

'Of course, you don't. That's enough of that.'

'No, please, go on.' Dora was all ears. Where else would she be given tips like these?

'I've noticed that Evelina needs to be reminded of a few things. She seems, metaphorically speaking, to be casting off her corset just when you're beginning to wear one.'

'What about clothes?'

'I wear whatever I fancy here in Brightsea, where everybody knows me and accepts me as I am. I dress quite differently in London. But as for fashion, ask Eva!'

'Not fashion, general rules.'

'Dress modestly, not necessarily soberly. Bright colours, feathers and fans are fine. Hem lengths may go up and down with the fashion, but stockings are *de rigueur* in town. Out of doors, arms and legs must always be covered. Hats are useful as well as fashionable throughout the year, gloves are a nuisance in summer, because you can't pick anything up, but I advise gloves in winter. In hot weather, and it has been hot recently, dress protectors are essential to prevent a show of underarm perspiration.'

Dora looked horrified.

'I offer these words of advice to give you confidence, Dora. In no way am I reprimanding you.'

At this moment Evelina made an entrance, clutching her skirt at the waist, her hair tangled and loose, her arms and legs bare, her hands bloody and her knees grazed. She was either laughing or crying, and sucking hard on a sweet. 'Thank goodness, I'm back.'

'What on earth has happened?' asked Sylvia.

'I fell off the bicycle.'

'Whose bicycle?'

'George's old bone-shaker.'

'Are you hurt?'

'Yes. My hands and knees are bleeding. There are tiny stones in them.'

'Your skirt is ripped.'

'I know. The gathers pulled out of the waistband when I fell off.'

'How did you get home?'

'George brought me back.'

'Sit in the armchair,' said Sylvia, 'I'll bathe your hands with warm salt water and paint on some iodine.'

'Thank you, Aunt.'

'I'll put the kettle on,' said Dora going into the kitchen, 'Camomile tea will make you feel better.'

'Thank you, both of you. Mama never pampers me like this.'

'Perhaps your Mama sees these things differently,' said Sylvia, going to fetch the iodine.

'It was all my fault,' Evelina whispered to Dora, while they were waiting for the kettle to boil. 'George was wheeling his bicycle and I was walking along beside him. I wanted to feel his arms around me, the way he had clasped me to him in the sea, so I asked to ride on the crossbar. "You can try," he said, so I jumped on, sitting side saddle, and the next thing we're hurtling down the grassy slope from the prom to the path, landing in a heap at the bottom. My skirt got caught on the handlebars and the gathers ripped out at the back. It was impossible to hide the damage. He saw my drawers. Can you imagine? I was mortified, but decided to make light of it, so I composed myself and said, 'Have you got a safety pin in your pocket by any chance?' He was the perfect gentleman, rummaging in his pockets as if he might find one, but there was only a folding pocket-knife, some cigarette papers and tobacco in one pocket, some rather dusty tiger nuts and two sweets in the other. No safety pin. But he offered me the sweets, fortunately wrapped in paper, and walked me home, one hand steering the bicycle and the other around my shoulders. It was almost worth the indignity of the situation to see this caring side of him.'

'Perhaps I should add,' said Lady Sylvia, coming in with the camomile tea and the iodine but addressing her words to Dora, 'that the advice about bare arms and legs does not apply on holiday. When Marcus and I were abroad all those years ago, we wore just whatever we liked. That was freedom.'

Eva looked baffled. 'Have I missed something?'

'Let this be a lesson to us all,' Lady Sylvia went on as she gently bathed Evelina's grazed knees. 'A safety pin attached to undergarments comes in useful on occasions like this. It could have been the bloomer elastic that broke. Where would you have been then?'

That message certainly hit home.

It was just before bedtime when Dora finished writing her letter to Arthur. She could imagine Dad reading it aloud at the kitchen table.

17th August, 1903

Dear Artie

I hope you like the shells I sent you. It's easy to catch crabs by tying bacon rind onto a piece of string and dangling the string into the sea. Crabs are greenish brown when they are alive but when they are cooked they turn pink. Have you seen them in the fishmongers? It won't be long before I'm home. Are you crossing the days off on the calendar in the kitchen? I think of you playing on the Big Green and climbing trees. I'll bring you with me on the train to Brightsea one day.

With love from Dora.

Eva came in and flopped down on her bed, with more to tell.

'He picked me up off the grass, put his arms around me and kissed me as you would a child who had fallen over. I kissed him back.'

'Will you kiss him again?'

'No idea,' Evelina replied with a smile in her voice.

CHAPTER 11

Brightsea

George was on his way to leave a small bunch of lavender on the front step at Jacob's Hall, when he saw Dora on her way to post a letter in the pillar box further down the High Street. He had hardly slept, going over in his mind the events of the day before. Why on earth had he let Eva sit on the crossbar? If only he could turn the clock back. After she fell, she had clung to him the same way she had clung to him in the sea. He should not have kissed her but he would never forget how she kissed him back.

'Morning, Dora.' He fell in step beside her. 'How is she?'

'She's fine. No harm done.'

His relief was palpable. 'Thank goodness.'

'There's nothing to worry about.'

'I wouldn't hurt her for the world.'

'It was clearly an accident.'

'I wish things hadn't gone wrong.'

'There's nothing wrong. She likes the way you laugh together.'

'We certainly do that. Will you tell her I'm out on the trawler all this week fishing?'

'I will.'

'I'll see you before you go back to London.'

Dora was in the studio looking at seascapes. There were paintings, finished and unfinished, propped up everywhere, an easel in the corner and a large table under the window. Painting took place at the table, as is the way with water colourists, amid a muddle of jars, palettes and brushes on every surface. Half a dozen experimental displays of blue and aquamarine were laid out on the floor to dry. She chose one and took it to Lady V in the garden room. 'I love it. A beautiful pattern of light and water, transparent and full of movement.'

'How kind you are! That's how I see Greece in my mind's eye.' She was sitting in the armchair, looking far into the past. 'The Aegean. I first saw it forty years ago when Marcus and I were on our honeymoon. We went by horse-drawn coach, journeying for three months across France, down through Italy and over the sea to Greece. What a journey that was! We wore a ridiculous amount of clothes for travelling in those days, most of them uncomfortable. As it got hotter the further south we went, we shed layer after layer. For all the marvels of Michelangelo and Raphael we saw in Italy, and they are truly marvellous, not one painting affected my senses as did the sea in Greece. We discovered a paradise island, as if by magic. Up against the rocks, lapping the beach, blue, green, silver in the light, the water is soft to the touch, irresistible. We basked in the sea, the air a balm for the skin.' She looked down at her hands (it was only her hands that betrayed her age), her face set, resigned. 'It was a lifetime ago,' she sighed. 'The North Sea is iron grey, with only occasional hints of blue and green far in the distance. When I paint an English seascape, the picture is all sky.' At this her face brightened. 'Pinks, mauves, blues, England excels in skies.'

'Did you live at Jacob's Hall when you were married?'

'No, nor in London. All our time together was abroad. My marriage was brutally short. A matter of months. Marcus and I fell in love when I was fifteen and he nineteen. I married at sixteen. He was amusing, well-educated, loving and I was captivated. It went wrong all of a sudden, when a terrible sickness overpowered him while we were still in Greece. He had a fever, became delirious and there was nothing I could do except stay by his side. He was gone, dead and buried in ten days. I made the journey home alone, seventeen years old, a widow. This house, the house he had inherited, was waiting for me on my return. I spent a full year here before I could face London society.' She forced a smile. 'Now I go where I wish and live where I wish. My freedom is unconfined.'

Dora posed no more questions. This was a life the like of which she could never imagine.

In the last week of the holiday, the girls spent a lot of time beautifying themselves, washing their hair, rinsing it in beer and letting it dry in the open air. Poor Dora had come to accept that her thin hair never would curl, no matter how long the rags were left in. Their bare arms and legs had turned golden brown and they liked to apply cooling glycerine and rose water lotion in copious amounts. Aunt Sylvia watched with a mixture of amusement and concern.

'You may think this is an old wives' tale but stay out of the sun! When Marcus and I spent our summer months travelling south, we were out in the sun at every opportunity. Just look at me now,' she said holding out her hands, palms down, to reveal wrinkled skin with brown patches. 'It's too late for me, but take my advice. Gloves are the answer. I wear them now to hide my hands but you young things should wear them to keep your skin unblemished.' She was not surprised they took no notice. For them old age was a lifetime away.

In the early evening, with just enough light left to read, all three women were sitting in the garden room chatting and sipping peppermint tea, as had become their custom, when Eva put a loaded question to her Aunt.

'I want to work in the theatre. Doing anything. Acting, moving scenery, applying make-up. Father has almost agreed to it, but Mama is resisting, saying it would be a frivolous life. What do you think?'

'I can't agree with her there. Not that I know much about it. You have the right personality, that's for sure.'

'Are you good at learning by heart?' asked Dora.

'I'm not bad,' said Eve, who had practised Juliet's balcony scene a few times in her bedroom. 'But I'd like to be part of a team. I'm always on my own.'

'Let's do some readings together,' suggested Lady Sylvia. 'Let's do it now.'

'We can each choose our favourites,' said Eva.

'Even if you never go on the stage, our time will not be wasted,' said her Aunt. With no fuss and bother she went to the bookshelf for a selection of poetry books and plays and the readings were under way. Anybody else would have said, let's begin tomorrow.

On their last evening together the conversation turned to women's suffrage, the burning issue of the day.

'We never question it at school,' said Dora. 'Our teachers are educated and work hard. They deserve to vote.'

'Educated or not, women make up half the population. Isn't that enough reason?' asked Lady Sylvia. 'Besides, women have been allowed to vote in New Zealand since the end of the last century.'

'Really?' Dora was amazed.

'I have no property, I'm not working and haven't been away to school. I don't suppose I deserve to vote,' said Eva.

'Oh yes you do,' said Lady Sylvia and Dora together.

'Does acting count as working?'

'Of course, it does!' they replied in unison again. Dora was amazed at how in tune she was with Lady Sylvia after these few weeks.

'Well, I hope my parents will agree to it,' Eva said, turning the conversation round to where it began.

'And shouldn't there be women representing us in the government too?' asked Lady Sylvia, who knew a few women campaigning for this.

At times like this Dora discovered that she no longer missed London at all.

Then summer was at an end, peas dry in their pods, lavender grey on the bush, the sun lower in the sky. Dora was first up, making breakfast, her bare feet comfortable in her canvas shoes, her limbs free and loose. The holiday had surpassed her expectations and to her great delight Lady Sylvia had invited her to come back with Arthur one day.

'Oh, thank you. Yes, he'd love it here.'

The trunk, a muddle of worn clothes, scuffed shoes, shells, seaweed and not a little sand, was already on its way back to London.

Edwards was at the door with the pony and cart. The girls sat on the wooden seat of the cart in their travelling clothes, taking in the scenery for the last time, their bodies rocking towards each other and away again, as Mussels ambled the familiar road to the station. Lady Sylvia waved them off and arranged to see them in London.

George was there on the platform, wanting to say goodbye. 'I hope you have a good journey back,' he said, rather formally, as he lifted the bags onto the train. He was determined to put pipe dreams of London women out of his mind, yet he added, in spite of himself, 'Please give my regards to Kitty,' as he and Eva exchanged a few last words through the train window.

Eva waved until both he and the station had disappeared around the bay. The slant of autumn sunlight came in the carriage window. Brightsea would be a distant memory by the time blackberries were ripe in the hedgerows.

'What a lovely holiday,' said Dora wistfully, looking down at the soft leather sling purse, a present from Lady Sylvia.

'It really was,' Evelina agreed, pulling a small hand mirror out of her bag to powder her nose and check her London smile. 'Thanks to you and my dalliance with

George.' She dabbed her cheeks with rouge. 'London, here we come,' adding, as if an idea had just occurred to her, 'Shall we go to Paris next time?'

Dora looked at her friend in disbelief.

'Aunt Sylvia has lodgings there.'

London, September 1903

'I'm home!' Dora dropped her bag on the step and rushed up to Arthur. 'Come here, little brother. Give me a hug.' She took him by the hand and set him on her lap to feel his loveable weight against her body. 'Oh, Artie, how I've missed you.' A month was the longest they had ever been apart. 'How you've grown. You look so big and strong. Have you been climbing trees?'

As she smiled, the misery of her long absence overwhelmed him and no words came. He leant in against her as she rocked him to her. To him she seemed different, taller, thinner, her skin brown from the summer sea air.

Rosa could not deny that her daughter, who was just fifteen when she went away, seemed to have come home fully grown up. Tom said she even sounded different. Dora had changed, there was no denying it. It took a while for things to settle.

CHAPTER 12

Happy days at the Clothworkers' School for Girls were nearly over for Dora and Dorothea. There's something about school that will always bind us, Dora thought, as her friend, now fluent in English and accustomed to English ways, prepared to return to Germany with her family. They had shared so much and promised to keep in touch across the miles by writing regularly.

Dora was about to begin her training as a pupil teacher, but she was apprehensive, because Celia, who was already teaching, had found the training hard. They had spoken about it before the summer holidays, when they met by chance at the bus stop. Dora saw Celia approach the back of the queue and moved out of her place to join her. Schoolgirl adoration had turned into deep friendship. They were alike in many ways and both felt the comfort of it. As for the age difference that had once seemed unbridgeable, it no longer mattered a jot.

'It's never easy to admit you've made a mistake, but I think I've made one,' said Celia, sounding fed up.

'What's going wrong?' Dora asked as they climbed aboard and found seats side by side.

'It's exhausting. Day after day, talking slowly and loudly, saying the same things over and over again.'

'Was it like that in training?'

'The training was worse! Miss Grace watching and finding fault all the time.'

'What were you doing wrong?'

'Oh, just about everything. I speak too quietly, I stand when I should sit and sit when I should stand. And my attire needs attention.'

'Why on earth is she like that?'

'Don't ask me! I'm no good at teaching, I suppose.'

'I can't believe that. You always wanted to do it.'

'Did I? I wonder whether it was because I couldn't think of anything else.'

'Our teachers seemed to manage.'

'The Clothworkers' School is completely different! We had no idea how lucky we were. Where I teach there's noise and chaos all day.'

'What will you do?'

'I'm planning to give it all up as soon as I can. I'd like to get married, so I can stay at home!'

'Really? Have you met someone?'

'No, unfortunately not. So for the time being, I've got to keep my nose to the grindstone.'

'How ghastly!' Dora was incensed that the friend she had idolised should be in this position. 'But you're clever. Could you find something better?'

'Perhaps. I could become a bus conductress, I suppose.'

'Couldn't you write? Or type?'

'Yes. I could do both those and get married.' She laughed as Dora stood up to get off the bus. 'Am I putting you off?'

'Yes. No. I don't know!'

Dora was unnerved by this report on life as a teacher,

but decided to go ahead with her plans, telling herself that forewarned is forearmed. Apart from anything else, she was worried about Arthur, who invariably pushed her away whenever she tried to help him with his school work. He still liked her to read to him but went rigid with frustration when pen and paper were involved. If there was a way to help him, she needed to find it. So she made no mention of the conversation with Celia to her parents, who were all encouragement on the subject of her training.

'It'll be regular work, well paid, with a good pension,' said Tom, relieved that his daughter would be entering a respectable profession. 'You've always wanted it, so I'm pleased for you.'

'Thanks, Dad.'

Arthur ignored these conversations, playing with happy abandon now that Dora was home and things were returning to normal. But after only a few days, Rosa reminded him firmly, too firmly for his liking, that he had to go to school again. The very word made him sick to the stomach.

'It may be better this year,' said Dora kindly, on his first morning back. 'You'll have a new teacher. I hope she's nice. Tell me about it this evening.'

The first few days were not so bad. They were asked to take in things to show what they had done in the summer, so Arthur took the shells, crabs' claws, seaweed and coloured beach pebbles Dora had brought back from Brightsea. He took them to school in the special box for secret things he kept under his bed and they were given pride of place in a tank of water on the Nature Table. The seaweed floated.

'Where d'you get 'em, Artie?' asked Bert, who had turned up again in the same class.

'At the seaside, of course.'

'Where?'

'Brightsea.'

'Where's that?'

'You have to go on three steam trains to get there.'

They all thought he had been on holiday.

Then it was the same miserable experience. Try as he might to explain that writing was not for him, he was overruled at every turn. Would there never be an end to it? Locked up in a classroom behind locked gates, he became anxious and fidgety. The best he could do was look out of the window and daydream about the trees he would climb on his route home. Sometimes he put his hand up and asked to be excused, just to get into the playground. He rarely went back. How do you explain to people that the teacher has a horrible smile? That it's all boring? That playtime is too short?

Arthur was right about Bert, the lad with his toes sticking out of his shoes; he did live nearby. They bumped into each other a few times in the streets around Garden Crescent, but if Bert had a home life it remained a mystery. He was away from school more than he was there, turning up only on cold winter days, when there was a coal fire in the classroom and a chance of getting a hot school dinner. Arthur wondered how he got away with it, so one day, when he saw him sitting on the pavement tootling on his tin whistle, he tried to find out.

'Do you live near here?'

'No. I'm just 'ere for a bit.'

'Where?'

'In the awful 'ome.'

'Are you staying there?' asked Arthur, not knowing what or where it was.

'No.'

'Why not?'

'There's too many boys there.'

'You talk funny.'

'No, I don't.'

'Where were you before?'

'Manchester.'

'Where's that?'

'Long way away.'

'So why are you here?'

'A lady brought me 'ere. I'm not staying. She 'ates me.'

'Are you coming to school any more?'

'No. The teacher 'ates me.'

'She hates me too but I've got out loads of times. My Ma makes me go back.'

'I've got no Ma.'

'Why not?'

'They took her away.'

Arthur had that horrible sick feeling he had when the teacher put Bert in the waste paper basket. He was thinking fast…They could go to the park…

Bert interrupted his plans. 'Have you got anything to eat?'

'No. But we'll get something.'

Spending his childhood down in the parlour at The

Lions, Arthur had never been really hungry. He ate every-thing put in front of him and second helpings when they were on offer, as if planning for the times when he would be out on adventures and unable to eat. He was a strong lad, who could go without food if he had to. They walked to The Lions and Arthur went round the side to knock on the scullery door, while Bert hung back in the shadows. Kitty answered his knock and Arthur whispered, 'Can we have some food? We're both starving. School finished early and…' his voice trailed off as he indicated Bert behind him.

Kitty took one look at Bert, a starving lad if ever there was one, and returned with a loaf of bread, two hunks of cheese, two apples and two slices of fruit cake.

'Thanks, Kitty,' said Arthur, pleased to help Bert out. 'And don't tell Mother.'

It would be wrong to say that the two boys became friends because Bert was hardly ever at school, but when their paths crossed, they picked up where they had left off.

CHAPTER 13

London, 1904

'Good afternoon, girls.'

Dora stood facing a class of fifty girls. At the back of the room sat Miss Grace, notebook at the ready. Why did a woman with such a beautiful name disgrace herself by looking so hostile? Forewarned is forearmed, thought Dora, not for the first time.

A hand went up at the front. 'Are you being tested this afternoon, Miss?'

'No, Aggie, I am not. I am teaching Scripture,' whispered Dora.

'We can't hear you at the back,' Miss Grace enunciated, more clearly than was necessary.

'Today's Bible story is from the Old Testament,' said Dora in her gentlest voice, determined not to be intimidated. She had chosen to begin with the picture of Daniel in the Lion's Den that each girl had in her Bible. It was Arthur's favourite. 'What sort of animal is a lion?' Hands went up and she turned to write a selection of words on the blackboard: wild, carnivorous, mammal… 'And what is a den?' She wrote a selection of these suggestions too and so she proceeded, not unlike the way she had been teaching at Sunday school since the age of fourteen.

Miss Grace watched stony-faced throughout. When the lesson was over and the girls had left the room, her bony finger beckoned.

'I am disappointed in you. See me in my room.'

Miss Grace was at her desk.

'Miss Makepeace, you are weak,' she said, with a menacing smile. 'You are here to teach, not to ask the girls questions. Do not allow yourself to be led by them.'

Don't go to pieces, Celia had said and Dora remained in one piece.

'You were supposed to be giving a lesson in scripture, not nature study, geography or art appreciation.'

They had discussed mammals, the habitat of lions, natural aggression in the wild and the plight of Daniel in the face of false accusations.

'Daniel's plight and how God came to the rescue of a good man is the theme.'

'Quite so, Miss Grace,' said Dora, wishing that someone would come to her rescue.

'Do not turn your back on the class to write on the blackboard. Anything could happen and today it did. Giggling, talking, yawning, passing sweets and copying from each other's books. I am amazed you didn't notice.'

Let it be water off a duck's back.

'Are you able to do better than this, Miss Makepeace?'

'Yes, Miss Grace.'

Dora thought of Arthur's misery. What made people behave like this?

*

Locked in the classroom, he looked at the clock, then away, then back at the clock to find the big hand had moved half way round and the small hand not at all.

'Has your mind absented itself again, Arthur?' asked Miss Summers, when she saw him gazing out of the window. His mind was busy planning his escape, so he heard his name but not what she said.

'Yes, Miss.'

'If you don't want to join in with the class, you must stand and face the wall.'

'I haven't done anything, Miss.'

'Precisely.'

The two fifteen-minute interludes in the day when Arthur came into his own began and ended with the school bell. That precious breathing space, when his blood was up, fighting a battle with wooden guns and all the boys wanted him on their side, was all ruined, time and time again, by the sound of the bell. In they went, except for Arthur, who sat in the corner of the playground, his frustration at crisis point, his tears copious and unstoppable. His only way of surviving school was to turn up for morning register then make a dash for it. He had lost count of the times he had been given a good hiding. The torment, which began when he was six years old, continued unabated for four long years. It felt like the whole of his life.

In and out of work and out of spirits since the day Arthur was born, Tom searched in his mind for ways to turn things around for his son and came up with nothing. Dora had tried many times to help but Arthur would not, or could not sit still to listen. Week after week, month after month, year after year, Tom saw and shared his daily misery. On the rare occasions Arthur allowed it, Tom would take him on his knee to comfort him.

'Bad things don't last for ever.'

'Why can't I do it like the other children?' His face was hot and wet.

'I don't know, Artie.'

'Do I have to go?'

'Yes, you do. But don't look so glum. It's not for ever. Go and get the pack of cards from the dresser. We'll have a game and I show you a new way to shuffle the pack.'

Tom saw the misery lift from his son's face, if only for a moment. 'School will be over one day. That's a promise.'

Another assessment was due. In the intervening weeks Miss Makepeace and her girls had come to an understanding. We shall all do our best. If we do our best we can be satisfied. To do better, we try again. Arithmetic was Dora's strong point and she enjoyed revealing how many different ways the same problem could be solved. But on the morning of her assessment she was not feeling well. Painful abdominal cramps were making it difficult for her to walk up and down the rows of desks to help those girls unable to remember the method for long multiplication. Begin on the right with the units was the only advice she was able to offer that morning. Under the circumstances she handed out cards of multiplication tables to those who were struggling and retired to her desk at the front.

Miss Airs-and-no-Graces stared over the top of her glasses

from her seat at the back. The minutes crawled by and the pain got worse. Unable to proceed, Dora brought the lesson to an end, releasing the girls for an early mid- morning break. Once they had believed their ears, there was a stampede to the door.

The bony finger beckoned. 'Have you given up, Miss Makepeace?'

'I am unable to continue. I ask to be excused.'

'You have a black mark.'

By the end of the training, by means of perseverance, laughter and ridicule, Dora and most of her fellow pupil teachers had survived and qualified. It was team spirit that saw them through. The few who failed had no regrets, convinced there must be easier ways of earning a living. In Dora's case, her pupils thanked her with smiles on their faces. Reward enough.

CHAPTER 14

London, May, 1907

One heaven-sent day Arthur overheard a snippet of conversation that put a spring in his step.

'He'll be leaving soon.' Mother and Dad were talking about school again.

Life instantly took a turn for the better. He was ten years old, too old for school and he made plans there and then to walk out at a time of his own choosing and never go back.

The opportunity presented itself one clear blue day in May. The girls were practising country dancing in the hall and the boys were outside in the sunshine, marching round the playground. Arthur was taking instructions from the Headmaster to lead his men round the four edges of the playground, down the middle, skirting round the tree and finishing at the school gate. He marched rhythmically, swinging his arms, his shoulders back, head held high. Marching drill took place every morning that week, the Headmaster shouting himself hoarse. Whenever they stopped, he said to Arthur under his breath, 'Good lad, that's right, you show them.'

On Friday 24th May, before he left for school in the morning, Arthur announced, 'It's Empire Day and I'm carrying the flag. You can come and watch if you want.'

'Oh, no! What a pity, I'll miss it,' wailed Dora. 'I'm teaching all day.'

'What time do we have to be there, Arthur?' asked Mother.

'Dinner time. Half past twelve in the playground. Then we all go home early.'

'I'll be there,' said Tom, without hesitation. He was always thrilled when Arthur showed his mettle and would find a way to leave work early.

'Thanks, Dad.'

'That's good, we'll both come.'

Things were looking up.

'Why did they choose you, Artie?'

He knew why. After the final marching drill, the Headmaster had called him into his room and pinned a medal onto his shirt with great solemnity. It was the school badge, made of metal, about the size of a penny, with the school tree embossed on the front and three words on the back.

'For good work,' said the Headmaster and they were the only words that were spoken before Arthur left the room.

But Arthur said nothing of this.

'All the boys want to do it but I'm doing it,' was all he said.

Parents began arriving at the school gates well before noon. Some gathered by the railings and others sat on the wall around the tree. A brass band was already playing a medley of folk tunes and the younger children were handing out small Union Jacks to the onlookers. Twenty-four girls in red crêpe-paper skirts and black felt boleros came dancing out of the school in two immaculate lines, taking everybody by surprise so nimble on their feet were they, swirling in circles to the left and to the right, weaving in and out of rows and swinging their partners round to their starting places. The little ones clapped in time to the music, hoping their time in the spotlight would come one day.

A march is not a dance; it is a different thing altogether. The opening bars of *The British Grenadiers* were Arthur's cue. Holding the Union Jack high before him, his arms steady, the route secure in his mind, he stepped out to lead the hundred marching boys through their paces. Along four sides of the playground they marched, then, as the music changed to *The Men of Harlech*, they turned up the middle to skirt around the tree, then down the other side of the playground without missing a beat, arriving at the school gate to the tune of *The Farmer's Boy*. At the spontaneous applause, the Headmaster stood tall, as pleased as punch. 'At ease, lad, at ease,' he said to Arthur, who was still standing to attention. 'School's out. Go and ring the bell.'

The dancing girls curtsied, Miss Summers was beaming, Rosa was wiping her eyes, Tom's heart was bursting and all the parents were congratulating each other. Arthur rang the hand bell and set the children free. Then he walked out, satisfied. He was ten years old and had done with school forever.

CHAPTER 15

Summer, 1907

An invitation in Lady Sylvia's generous handwriting for Dora and Arthur to spend August at Brightsea lay on the kitchen table for all to see. Both parents were against it at first.

'I'm not at all sure about this,' said Tom, who had not taken his family on holiday since Arthur was born.

'Don't worry, Dad,' said Dora. 'I've been saving up for the train fares. I'm earning now I'm qualified, don't forget.'

'He's such a handful,' said Rosa.

'How will you manage?' asked Tom.

Dora laughed. 'I'm trained to manage. A class of fifty girls can be hair-raisingly badly behaved sometimes. Brightsea's the perfect place to recover. Besides, you two deserve some peace and quiet at home.' She was nurturing an unspoken hope that they might go away for a day or two by themselves, even though money was tight. Nothing would deter her. When Arthur was six years old, she had set him on her lap and said, 'I'll take you to Brightsea one day.' It was a promise neither he nor she forgot and at long last it was going to happen.

After three days of packing and looking at the map of England, Arthur found himself at Liverpool Street Station amongst the bustle of porters, departing passengers and the hiss of steam. He even liked the smell of it. Rosa was working, but Tom was there to wave them off.

'Don't worry, Dad,' said Dora. 'I'll write.'

'Look after her, Arthur,' said Tom, wishing he could go with her to do just that.

'Yes, Dad. When are we leaving?'

Tom was already feeling the desolation he knew he would feel when the train had gone. August was going to be a long month. He had planned a few days away at the seaside but Rosa had refused to go point blank. They had agreed on a day trip to Broadstairs but the date had not been fixed. On the rare occasions they were alone in the house, at the meal table or in bed at night, both were ill at ease. When she wasn't busying herself about the house, she was knitting. The constant clicking of the needles irritated him.

'Five minutes,' he said to his son, who was more than ready to go.

Arthur ran up and down the platform in his new cap to find an empty third-class compartment, lifting not only his but Dora's case onto the train and letting down the window to wave as the steam engine hauled them out of London. Dora resisted the temptation to remind him for the umpteenth time to be on his best behaviour. She felt in her bones that he was perfectly ready for this adventure.

Three hours and two changes of train later, they were on the final leg of the journey, almost the only passengers on Puffing Billy, the little steam train chugging its way into Brightsea Station. The thrill Dora felt at her first view of the bluish-grey horizon was enhanced by Arthur's wide-eyed excitement. 'The sea! I can see the sea.'

Edwards was there to greet them with a motor car.

'Where's Mussels, Mr Edwards?' asked Arthur, remembering every detail from Dora's letters, which Rosa had read and reread to him when he was six.

'Mussels is no more,' said Edwards, gravely, opening the door for them to climb aboard. 'It's motor cars now. And it's a devil of a job to get them started in the winter mornings, I can tell you.'

'I like travelling in motor cars,' said Arthur, disappointed at nothing.

News of the date and time of their arrival had reached the town, because Dora and George had exchanged letters, tentatively lining up his younger brothers and sisters as playmates for the London boy. Three of them, two boys and a girl, were sitting on the wall outside Jacob's Hall waiting. Arthur took a good look at them from the back seat of the car.

Lady Sylvia was at the door smiling her greeting and happy to dispense with all formalities. In no time at all, Arthur was taking his bag up to the bedroom, changing out of his travelling clothes, and accepting everything he was offered to eat and drink so he could go out into the street to meet his new friends.

'Can I go out to play now?'

Lady Sylvia looked at Dora, who was looking disapprovingly at Arthur.

'Please, is it convenient...' Arthur began the sentence Dora had made him practise on the train.

'Yes, you may,' said Lady Sylvia, delighted at his enthusiasm. 'The rough energy of the boy,' she said, when he was gone.

'He sleeps long and deep, I expect that's why,' said Dora, equally delighted to see him on holiday at last, away from school and out of London.

Four years had changed both women but it was an affectionate reunion.

'You were just dreaming of becoming a teacher when you were here last and now you are one. I think this calls for a celebration. How about a glass of champagne this evening with our meal?'

'That would be a lovely treat. I've never tasted champagne! I'll cook this evening. I remember exactly what you like.'

'Thank you, my dear. Agreed. You'll find food on the marble slab in the larder. I don't cook as much as I used to and I've never enjoyed it.'

'Are you still painting?' Dora had noticed that Lady Sylvia had aged, though she looked pleasantly summery in a yellow silk blouse and green cotton skirt. Her hair was now white at the temples and grey at the back, though still piled up high on her head.

'Yes, fortunately,' she said, as they went into her studio, 'in spite of my arthritic hands. More abstract than before, as you can see. All water colours. I've stopped painting in oil.'

Dora cast her eye round the studio with genuine enthusiasm. She liked visiting art galleries in London and was getting her eye in. Lady Sylvia's paintings were even more delicate than she remembered, and certainly more abstract, a painterly wash of light infused colour. 'I think they're wonderful.'

When they were talking over tea, Dora blurted out, 'Arthur hates school. He thinks he's left for good. He can't accept he has to go on to the boys' school. I haven't the heart to tell him. I've seen him every night for years, distraught, dreading the next school day.' Her voice was cracking. 'It breaks my heart to see him crushed like this day after day.' It was good to confide her concerns to someone outside the family but she was surprised at how readily tears overcame her when the subject was Arthur.

Lady Sylvia had listened sympathetically and she paused for Dora to collect herself before she spoke. 'Arthur reminds me of James, my twin brother. In our childhood he regularly went white with fear every time he was sent away to school. I was taught at home, of course. It upset me to see him trying to be brave when he was going back to a place he hated. I have no idea what went on at his school. He has never spoken about it. I'm not sure they taught him much.' Dora felt the pure relief of being understood. 'At home, James was the life and soul of the party,' Lady Sylvia went on, 'and his confidence developed quite naturally as soon as he left school and went to work in the City. His title helped, I suppose. I think that's why Eva was educated at home. Her father wanted to spare her the misery of school.'

'Artie is extremely capable at some things but completely stuck in the mud at school. I often think of the lines:

"But to go to school in a summer morn,
O! it drives all joy away."'

'Is it Blake?' asked Lady Sylvia.

'Yes. *The Schoolboy.*'

'I remember now:

> *"How can the bird that is born for joy,*
> *Sit in a cage and sing?"*

Blake hated school too. Arthur's not the first.'

'I know. I see it every day in the classroom. Some children find reading unfathomable and others take to it like ducks to water.'

'Certainly. You are bookish and he is not. It's as simple as that. Now he has four weeks of summer freedom ahead of him. Believe me, it's a real tonic to have him here.'

The whole blessed month, come rain or shine, Arthur was in his element. No pen, paper or book in sight, out of doors all day earning a few coppers here and there, he made himself useful wherever he went. His new friends, most of them George's siblings and their friends, were all outdoor boys and girls, who liked to spend their days swimming, eating plums from the trees and peas raw from the pods, and buying ice cream whenever they got the chance. He liked their mumbling voices and was soon imitating the Essex accent.

'I like it,' he said, when Dora asked him about it. 'They sound like pirates.'

Learning to swim was a must. He watched the others and when he had made up his mind the type of swimming trunks he wanted, he asked Dora to buy them for him, presenting her with the perfect excuse to have a word with George.

'You can buy them in the general stores on the High Street,' George said. 'But we've a vast selection at home in all sizes if he wants to have a look.'

So Artie went to George's house and made friends with all the pirates. He chose swimming trunks from the faded hand-me-downs on offer (a new one would not look right at all) and set his mind to the task. All the Brightsea boys and girls could do it, so he knew it was only a matter of time, but this London boy was in a hurry. He found a quiet place by the water's edge, where he lay on his back in the shallows. The waves lapped his body, coaxing first one foot, then an arm to rise and fall with the tide. He felt his limbs waft gently this way and that until he was rocking, swaying, rising and falling. He moved in deeper, absorbing the salty buoyancy as if by osmosis, until he was lying on the watery cushion four inches off the shingle. 'I'm floating!' he cried. He went in deeper still, sculling with his hands and kicking his legs until the task was done.

'What have you been up to?' asked Lady Sylvia when he returned to Jacob's Hall.

'Swimming,' he replied as he passed through the room, nonchalant, triumphant.

'Already? How marvellous.'

'It's not that hard. The water holds you up.'

'Be careful of the tide,' she said. 'Nobody can swim against a tide, Artie. Ask George, if you don't believe me.'

'I believe you. You're the type of person that knows things.'

'Have you had lunch?' asked Lady Sylvia, amused at the compliment.

'Yes. At George's house.'

'What did you have?'

'We only had marra.'

'What's marra?'

'Pale green, never had it before, tastes of nothing much. I had to have three pieces.'

'Go into the larder and cut yourself a piece of cake,' she said, knowing from experience that swimming could make you ravenous.

A week later he was swimming along with the rest of them, on his back, on his front and jumping in off the jetty.

These weeks, carefree and time free, out playing pirates, were the best of Arthur's life. Occasionally Dora found herself saying, 'It's bedtime, Artie.'

'Impossible! I'm going out on the bicycle to meet the others on the prom. Bye.'

'Back before dark, please,' said Dora. 'And don't fall off.'

'I've fallen off loads of times,' he said disappearing out of the door.

'He seems to get back on straight away,' observed Lady Sylvia. 'It's a delight to see him living life to the full. Mr Peck was telling me only the other day how much he appreciates the help Arthur gives him picking runner beans. Mr Peck's days of stretching and bending are over.'

Aha! So that's where he gets money for chips and ice cream, thought Dora, content to hear he was helping others and being rewarded for it.

George surpassed her expectations. He was a full-time fisherman now, either away at sea for a week at a time or out on the small fishing smacks in local waters. Dora was instantly at ease with him, a man in his element, confident in his knowledge of the sea and its power.

'How's Kitty?' he asked, with some hesitation. He had never been to London.

'Fine. Still working at The Lions.'

'Remind her of me, will you?'

'I will, George.'

'It's a while since she came here with Miss Evelina, but I remember her well.'

'Artie wants to learn to row. Would you have a moment to show him?'

'I can teach him the rudiments, but it takes more than a few days.'

'He'll take instruction from you, I'm sure.'

George was as good as his word. Arthur pulled his cap low over his eyes against the sun, set the oars in the rowlocks and learnt to slant the blades as they dipped and rose through the water, feeling the weight of the tide and the power of the wind as he pulled and pushed. At the end of the morning, he secured the boat to an upright post with a clove hitch, which George had shown him only once.

'How do you feel about coming sea fishing for a day or two, Artie?'

Arthur nodded.

'On a boat like that one over there.' He pointed to a small fishing smack with red ochre sails, gliding silently out to sea from the estuary. 'It needs two men and we'll be out for two days, so ask Dora if you can come.'

'I'm going fishing with George tomorrow,' said Arthur

when he got back to Jacob's Hall, relying on his tried and trusted way of asking permission. 'We'll be away two days. It's all arranged.'

'Two men means two experienced men, not one skipper and a novice,' George explained to Dora, when they were talking it over.

'If you know how to fish you'll always get work,' said George, as Arthur climbed aboard. 'Meet Ted. He'll show you the ropes.'

For two magical days and nights Arthur helped the two men with their work. Ted, who had been on boats all his life, was a man of few words; his orders were made clear by hand signals, short commands and rhythmical body movements. Throughout the two days it was Arthur's responsibility to keep the coal fire burning down in the galley stove, to boil water in the kettle swinging from the hook and to make the tea. Up and down all day, fetching and carrying, hauling in the sails and letting them out again, if this was work, he thrilled to it. It was here that he learnt the meaning of the word shipshape. They sailed, dropped anchor, hauled nets, mended nets, caught fish, gutted fish, cooked fish, ate and drank together, taking turns to enjoy the bliss of sleep. At night, rocking on the inky sea, they looked up at another world: the Milky Way, the Great Bear, the Pole star. What names, what a sight!

'What do you think, Ted? Will he do?' George asked when they were on dry land again, where Dora was standing to greet them.

'He'll do,' said Ted. They were almost the only words Ted had uttered over two days. George's verdict on the expedition was more cheering. 'Willing and able. He'll get work anywhere, any time.' Dora glowed.

Arthur had decided. 'When I'm twelve I'm going to run away to sea like Nelson.'

CHAPTER 16

London, September 1907

'Good morning, girls,' said Miss Dora Makepeace, standing in front of a class of fifty girls at Kennington Elementary School. She looked at the empty chair at the back of the room and rejoiced. They were her girls, her class and her responsibility. She would do it all with kindness. Never at ease in showy clothes, Dora had set her sights on a look of quiet distinction. The bus journey to and from work in all weathers meant that she had to have two pairs of polished shoes with a comfortable low heel; the old black pair for travelling and the new black pair to change into once she had arrived. Two warm woollen skirts, one black, the other navy, were both home-made on Rosa's sewing machine; the decorative pale blue braid on the blue skirt was six inches from the hem to prevent it from becoming dirty. Six pearl buttons decorated the cuffs of her blouses, every one of which had a white detachable collar that could be changed every day. A home-knitted cardigan in grey Shetland wool with deep pockets and a warm shawl collar completed the outfit. She wore a new wrist watch, given to her by Mother and Dad on the day she qualified, and wound it every morning. In this guise, wearing a corset underneath for warmth, comfort and posture, she stood tall. Miss Inkpen, her first teacher, was much in her mind as she faced the challenge of her new class. Come on, Dora, you're nineteen, the time has come, you can do this.

The three Rs in this school were rules, routine and respect, all strictly enforced. As Celia had warned her, lessons here were a far cry from those at the Clothworkers' School for Girls. Few pupils were able to take dictation, so the first task of the day was to copy from the blackboard. Thanks to Arthur, Miss Makepeace brought with her a special understanding of the torment school could be for pupils who struggled to read and write. Surely these girls would not push her away as Arthur had done. Thanks to Evelina, left-handed pupils had her understanding too. Any girl misbehaving was sent out of the room to explain herself to the Headmistress, who would give her a black mark. Three black marks and the girl was seen no more. Discipline was strict, but Miss Makepeace's pupils found the school a forgiving place. Most of them were destined to become maids, shop girls or factory workers and many who ran joyfully out of school the minute they turned fourteen were later heard to regret it.

Every day began with prayers and hymns in the assembly hall. Then classroom work began, with English before the mid-morning break and arithmetic before the dinner hour. The morning routine was unchanging, and always finished with monotonous, sing-song chanting:

Monday it was measures: *twelve inches one foot, three feet one yard, twenty-two yards one chain, ten chains one furlong, eight furlongs one mile.*

Tuesday, weights: *sixteen ounces one pound, fourteen pounds one stone, eight stone one hundredweight, twenty hundredweight one ton.*

Wednesday, money: *two farthings one ha'penny, two ha'pennies one penny, twelve pennies one shilling, twenty shillings one pound, twenty-one shillings one guinea.*

Thursday, the Kings and Queens of England:

Willie, Willie, Harry, Ste,
Harry, Dick, John, Harry three,
One two three Neds, Richard two,
Henry four five six, then who?
Edward four five, Dick the Bad,
Harrys twain and Ned the Lad,
Mary, Bessie, James the Vain,
Charlie, Charlie, James again,
William and Mary, Anna Gloria,
Four Georges, William and Victoria.

Friday, the months of the year: *thirty days hath September, April June and November, all the rest have thirty-one, except February alone, which has twenty-eight days clear and twenty-nine in each leap year.*

Afternoons were for all the other subjects, of which there were many, in rotation throughout the year. Text books and props were few and far between but Dora found enough in the school cupboards to teach History - her favourite subject - Geography with maps and a globe, Nature Study with fresh flowers, insects and pets, Scripture (her Sunday school teaching made this an easy option), needlework, art and music. Physical exercises in a cold playground she gladly passed to another teacher.

'If a subject does not interest you, sit patiently and it will soon end,' she told her girls, unperturbed if a few needed to stare out of the window or rest their heads on the desk. Consequently, there was an air of concentration mixed with bored yawns and forbearance in all her lessons. When the girls were forced to go outside for a breath of London air, thick though it was with fog, smoke and coal dust, the energetic ones ran about the playground, while others huddled together talking, sharing sweets and shivering until it was time to go back inside. The day ended with 'quiet time', when they pulled their chairs forward to gather round or put their heads on their desks, while Miss Makepeace read a story aloud in a calm, slow voice, against a background of muffled, fidgety silence.

The days were long and exhausting but teaching was her chosen profession and a job for life, or at least until she was married. Marriage. How could that ever come about when she was living at home, teaching all day and marking books at night?

CHAPTER 17

'It's a chance to start again, Arthur,' said Mother, her words
a clear warning. 'You can start with a clean slate.'

'I don't want a clean slate.'

'It's pen and paper this time. You'll have to try harder.'

The suggestion that he did not try made him seethe. 'I've
left,' he said. He was eleven years old. 'I'm going to be
working. There's always work on the trawlers.'

How did he know that? 'You have to go to school to
learn to read and write, then you go to work. It's the
law.'

Arthur groaned at the opposition he was facing. 'I'm not
going.'

'You've got a quick brain for some things,' Mother went
on. 'You're going to have to find a way to get on at school.
Your own way.'

Nothing she said made him feel any better. Out of doors
he was strong, bold, fearless even, but indoors, especially
in school, the obstacles were insuperable. It was as natural
for him to be this school-hating boy as it was for Dora to
have her head in a book. He lay in bed that night troubled
by his mother's words of doom. Next day, it was more of
the same.

'I've spoken to Mr Hartman. He said he'll sort you out.
But you must do as you're told. And stop talking like a

pirate.' Arthur shrank inside, miserable. It was as if he had never been to Brightsea.

Tom sat in the pub thinking about his son with a heavy heart. He was not in his local, preferring to vary the places he went to drown his sorrows. Out of the corner of his eye, he saw a lanky lad, no more than twelve years old and a weak specimen at that, collecting empty beer glasses from the tables and drinking the dregs. More than once the poor boy missed his footing. Not in school and on the drink, thought Tom. Spare my son this.

An image of Arthur's face came clearly into his mind: a happy, laughing boy, having fun playing cards, quick and competitive, doing something he enjoyed. Yes! It was time to teach him how to play cribbage: fifteen two, fifteen four, two for a pair is six and a run of three is nine. Artie would learn his fifteens and keep score on the peg board. Tom ordered another pint and drank it with good cheer.

Arthur dragged his feet to the new school and found a desk at the back. No girls now, just boys.

'Good morning, boys.'

'Good morning, Sir.'

'My name is Mr Hartman. Some boys call me Mr Hardman, because I am... strict.'

Snigger. Arthur looked around the room. There was Bert Farthing and some new faces too. All were uneasy.

'In this desk is a slipper.' The schoolmaster banged the slipper on the desk. 'Boys who misbehave are beaten with the slipper. In this cupboard is a cane.' He whacked the desk with the cane, a noise like no other. 'Boys who misbehave a second time, are beaten with this cane.' Whack! The room was scared quiet.

'Some of you boys are unable to read or to write. You are here to learn and learn you will. It's for your own good.'

At this Arthur pricked up his ears. Perhaps his time had come to learn to read. Bert looked different, older and wiser, full of stories about the Boy Scouts. He had been sent away on a summer camp and returned about a foot taller, bragging about how he could play umpteen tunes on the tin whistle and cook over a camp fire. They had much to share about their summer adventures, but when Bert produced a book about knots it was clear he could read. Arthur had that hopeless feeling again.

'Makepeace.'

He jumped. 'Yes, Sir.'

'Stand up, when I talk to you.'

'Yes, Sir.'

'I have heard about you.'

'Yes, Sir.'

'Are you a dunce or a half-wit?'

'No, sir.'

'We shall see.'

'Yes, Sir.'

Every day that week, Mr Hartman failed to teach Arthur to read or write. Letters made no sense, were all mixed up, the wrong way round or in the wrong order, their secret hidden from his sharp eyes as if by obscure glass.

'Write on the blackboard, Arthur Makepeace is a dunce.'

Arthur stood stock still, focusing directly in front of him.

'No, Sir.'

'Do as I say.'

'I can't, Sir.'

'Can't or won't?'

'Can't, Sir.'

'We shall see. Write on the board, Arthur Makepeace is a dunce.'

'No, Sir.'

'Do you refuse?'

'Yes, Sir.'

Arthur was beaten for disobedience. He did not flinch. Apart from the noise of the slipper there was silence in the room.

'I can't put brains where there are none. Go home and tell your mother you are illiterate, belligerent and refractory,' said Mr Hartman.

Arthur had been pushed to his limit. He had to find a way. His way.

'Morning, Mr Smeeth. Can I give you a hand?'

Arthur was up and out of the house early, waiting on the front step of The Lions for the sound of the horse and cart as it turned into Villa Road. Mr Smeeth, the bread man, was holding the reins, looking bad-tempered.

'Yes, you can, lad. That lazy so-and-so 'ain't turned up again and I'm all behind. Take these two loaves to number twelve and be sure to knock. Wait for the maid.'

That is how it started. When news had reached him that the bread man needed a lad, Arthur decided he had done with school and was ready for work.

''Ow old are you, lad?'

'Thirteen,' said Artie, impatient to reach his twelfth birthday in a week or two. If Nelson could leave school at twelve, why couldn't he?

The more running about he did the more Mr Smeeth appreciated him. He charged through the day with boundless energy, a breath of fresh air to everybody he met and he was never short of something to eat, the housemaids made sure of that.

''Ere you are, lad, a nice sausage for you. This'll keep you going.'

Even Mr Smeeth was whistling now, hardly believing his good fortune at finding a lad such as this, who had the good sense to think on his feet and make himself indispensable. Whenever Mr Smeeth disappeared into the local public house for 'a couple of pints,' he asked his new helper to take care of the old shire horse. It was all new to Arthur, but man and beast soon got used to the routine of brushing, feeding and mucking out the stable. Thunder enjoyed the attention and listened without complaint to Arthur's grumbling when they got soaked to the skin in a downpour or failed to deliver to the right house. Keeping out of sight of the school inspector bothered Arthur at first but not for long. Thinking of the boys shut up in that schoolroom was guaranteed to cheer him up. How time had dragged when he was confined to the same classroom, with the same teacher, the same children, doing, or in his case not doing, the same senseless tasks over and over.

Compared to that, working or loitering on the streets was different, with money surprisingly easy to come by. Coins that had been dropped were there for the taking, in the kerb, under a park bench, in shop doorways, on the ground in the market place, and Arthur's sharp eyes spotted every one. He was putting it all in the secret box where he kept his school medal. The man in the bath chair beckoned to him each morning to fetch his newspaper and ten Woodbines from the shop on the corner. That was a farthing without fail and sometimes a bag of tiger nuts on top. He could make a few coppers by shovelling up horse manure from the road, and a few coppers more if he was willing to take it round the back for the vegetable garden. He was looking forward to the day when he would give his wages to his mother.

After a few weeks, he was beginning to feel at home on the streets of London. His quick legs had the uncanny knack of remembering routes he had taken only once, which made him an invaluable errand boy and not only to Mr Smeeth. When the bread rounds were finished, Arthur went into public houses, churches, hospitals, schools - well not exactly into schools - delivering, helping people out and earning money. Window cleaning was his speciality, going up ladders as quick as lightning and sitting out on high window ledges. He liked the danger and the round of applause from the appreciative onlookers below. The time would come when he would have to explain to his parents what was going on, but that day had not yet come.

Dora, however, was becoming suspicious. Her young brother had changed; he was shooting up fast and asking questions.

'Why are there twelve pennies in a shilling?' he asked,

producing a selection of coins he was polishing with a soft cloth.

'There just are, Arthur.'

'Why are there twenty shillings in a pound?'

'It's always been like that.'

'What's a guinea?'

'One shilling more than a pound. It's just a way of talking. People use guineas for expensive things.'

Arthur had no difficulty in identifying a sovereign, crown, half-crown, florin, shilling, sixpence, a thruppenny piece, penny, ha'penny and the little farthing with the wren on the back. They all felt familiar in his hands but he needed to be able to add them up.

'How many pennies in a pound?'

'Two hundred and forty.'

'What?' he groaned.

'But Arthur, that's not the way to add up pennies. I'll show you. First you find out how many shillings you have and then how many pounds.' She produced a chart from her teaching bag.

Arthur groaned once more. 'Can everyone do this?'

'Not everybody, no, but you have to be able to do it if you want to keep an eye on your money.'

'Why isn't it all in tens? We count in tens and we've got ten fingers.'

Dora laughed. 'There are some politicians who agree with you. But decimalisation will never happen in England. Pounds, shillings and pence are known all over the world.'

Arthur was getting impatient. She was not answering his question, so he asked another one.

'Do they use our money all over the world?'

'Well, yes and no. They have their money too.'

'I need to know about our money.'

'I think you need to learn your twelve times table.'

'Don't start all that again,' he shouted. 'I'm doing all right as I am.'

'How much money have you got?'

'Come upstairs and I'll show you.'

Arthur dragged his secret box out from under the bed. Dora gasped at the sovereigns, florins, shillings, sixpences and lots of coppers, many of which Arthur had polished with brass cleaner and a soft cloth. He tipped the coins onto the floor with a satisfying clinking noise. Together they piled the coppers in groups of twelve pennies and the shillings in groups of twenty. He had a staggering £2..16s..3d.

'Arthur! Where did you get all this money?'

Arthur averted his eyes, put the money back in the box and the box back under the bed before owning up. 'I'm working. Doing errands. I find money too. People drop it. Sometimes I ask for what I want and sometimes they just give it to me.'

'You're not begging!'

'No. I'm working. Mr Smeeth needs me for his bread round.'

Dora was impressed. She had been adept at balancing household accounts for a long while, but in the art of finding money on the streets she was a novice.

'I hate school.' Arthur was still angry. 'The teacher calls me names.'

'What names?'

'Rude names. Something about litter and a factory.

'What?'

'I hate him. I don't need him.'

Dora did not protest. In that moment, he grew up. Under no pressure, he was able to add, 'I'm not going back. Ever.' At last, he had persuaded her.

Dora thought long and hard about Arthur's truancy. As a teacher she disapproved, but since he had left school of his own accord there was a noticeable improvement in his mood. When they played cribbage, he found it easy enough to beat her. If he had to count on his fingers, so be it. A royal card or a ten plus five made fifteen, so did a nine plus a six or a seven plus an eight. 'Fifteen two, fifteen four, shut the box and say no more.' He counted in fives moving the pegs along the cribbage board and, more often than not, reached home first. All he needed was a good hand.

Dora showed him how to work out the change from a pound for items costing six shillings and nine pence three farthings. She watched him count it back into her hand: one farthing makes ten pence, plus two pence makes seven shillings, plus three shillings makes ten shillings, plus ten shillings makes a pound. Thirteen shillings and tuppence farthing change. Easy, when you know how. Arthur was learning more on the streets than he had ever learnt in school, so she kept his secret.

PART 2

CHAPTER 18

London, March 1911

Arthur considered his fourteenth birthday to be the day he grew up. He had been getting noticeably taller with every month that passed, he was shaving every morning and he felt different. On his birthday morning he was up and out of bed early, as was his habit, waiting outside The Lions for old Mr Smeeth to arrive with the bread cart, when Kitty rushed out looking flustered.

'Thank goodness, you're still here. When did you get so tall? Can you do me a favour? Take this to Jubilee Market, will you?' She was holding an envelope in her hand.

'I'll take it after work,' said Arthur, in a new deep voice, always pleased to help Kitty out.

'It's gotta go now,' Kitty insisted, taking a second look at him when she heard him speak.

'I've got the bread round to do.'

Kitty would not take no for an answer. Lord Highton was always most insistent that the envelope reached the flower market first thing in the morning. Some men were like that. 'It's important,' she said. 'I'd take it myself but I just can't go today.'

'Right you are. The old man's late again this morning. I

could be waiting here all day. He might be dead for all I know, I'll take it.'

'Thanks, Artie, you'll be well rewarded, I know that. Hand it to Violette, the French girl, on stall 20. She's only young. Nobody else, mind. I'm run off my feet here.'

The Jubilee flower market was one of Arthur's favourite places, always bustling at this time of the morning, bursting with colour and scent. Standing by stall 20 was a girl with her back to him, a small black and brown spaniel dozing in a basket at her feet. She was wearing an old apron over her long blue skirt and muddy clogs on her feet, but her poise and the elegance of her hair coiled up on her head stopped him in his tracks. He watched her for a while as she tended the blooms with unhurried movements. When he held out the envelope to her, she turned and smiled as if both surprised and pleased to see him.

'From Kitty?' Her voice was young, pretty, French.

'Yes,' was all he could say; she looked just perfect to him.

She set to her task of selecting flowers from buckets of water, taking her time to mix and match the colours and lengths into a colourful display of eye-catching simplicity. Without any sign of rush or fluster, she twirled the bouquet in paper and tied it with green ribbon, cleverly curling the ends with a knife. He watched transfixed as she hid the envelope in amongst the flowers, then looked up at him rather shyly from under her lashes. The whole process was a ballet lasting a few minutes.

'28 'annover Square,' was all she said, the few words delivered with an entrancing pursing of the lips. The dog shifted comfortably in its basket at her voice and opened one eye as if to check on the proceedings. To share the secret of the envelope with Violette and her dog was pure delight for Arthur, who was fast becoming one of the London boys in the know. So far so good.

But where was 'annover Square? Right at the pub, left at the church, straight down Hallem Street. Alan Street? He was mortified at repeatedly having to ask the way. Which street? His sole intent was to deliver the flowers, be rewarded for his efforts and return to Mr Smeeth as quickly as possible. He had learnt to take the ups and downs of living by his wits in his stride but on this particular day he was up against it. His luck went from bad to worse when he arrived at the correct address, only to be told the lady was not at home and there was no payment for late delivery. He left the flowers anyway, praying that neither Violette nor Kitty would find out about it. To make matters worse, Mr Smeeth was fuming when he got back south of the river, wanting to know where he had been all morning.

'I was five minutes late picking you up on the corner and you'd 'opped it. Gone. You're gonna 'ave to be more patient, my lad, or I'll 'ave no use for you. Me and Thunder aren't getting any younger.'

Even the thought of losing his job with Mr Smeeth filled him with dread. The time had come for Arthur to take his future into his own hands. He knew what he had to do. He could put it off no longer.

When Dora had finished marking the pile of school books on the kitchen table, Tom was out at the pub and Rosa not yet back from The Lions, Arthur took a deep breath and asked the question that had troubled him ever since he could remember.

'Why can't I read?' The question nearly suffocated him.

'I don't know, Artie. Perhaps your brain works differently from mine.' She said it kindly.

'I just want to be able to read the street names.'

'I'm sure you'll be able to do that. They're all in capital letters. Let's do it together. But you must be patient and not get angry with me.'

'You'd get angry if you couldn't do something everyone else can do.'

'Trust me. I am a teacher.'

'I hate teachers. You don't understand. Nobody understands. I can't learn like other people.'

'I'll teach you in a special way, just for you. Once we begin, we must do it every day.'

'Starting tomorrow.'

'No, Arthur. Starting now.' She looked at him, willing him to agree. 'Agreed?'

Arthur groaned with pain. Why now? Why must it be now? He hesitated. His earning power depended on it. And what would Violette think if she found out? Still he hesitated. 'Agreed.'

Right there and then she got out the box of wooden letters she had been using with her class. She tumbled the capital letters out onto the kitchen table. The consonants were a pale wood, but the five vowels A E I O U and the Y she had painted the rainbow colours: red, yellow, orange, green, blue and indigo/violet. Each group contained one coloured letter and there was a gap at the halfway point.

She laid the twenty-six letters out in a rainbow arch, slowly, evenly and deliberately. There were six groups with a gap at the halfway point:

ABCD EFGH IJKLM   NOPQ RSTU VWXYZ

Arthur watched with trepidation, relieved only that nobody was there to witness this humiliating process. Then Dora sang an alphabet tune, quietly and gently under her breath, with a low and steady voice pointing to each letter as she went, so that Arthur heard the names of the letters and the tune simultaneously. Then she collected the letters together, still in order, and asked Arthur to lay them out again. He had to remember the rainbow shape, remember that each group had a coloured letter in it, remember the break after the third group and, bit by bit, remember the letter names that matched the tune. This was the process that Dora and Arthur repeated at five o'clock every evening for a week before Rosa got home from The Lions. He fingered the letters, held the smooth wooden shapes in his hands and made an identical pattern every time he laid them out. As the days went by, Arthur was laying out the letters with increasing speed and confidence, even when they were mixed up. He liked this private time spent together, he liked the shape of the rainbow arch and he was breathing more easily.

Dora's eyes were opened to the mystery of Arthur's predicament one evening, when she was marking Emily Lipscombe's Scripture homework about The Wisdom of Solomon. Emily, the most talented eleven-year-old in her class, could produce evenly spaced, elegant copperplate handwriting that was a pleasure to the eye. Every capital letter was separate from the small letter following it, whereas all the small letters were joined together evenly at the same height. There was uniformity in the writing but it nevertheless displayed its own style. Every pupil's handwriting was different, some more and some less legible than others. Seeing this variety through Arthur's eyes was a revelation. To him it was all confusion: there were as many different rearrangements of the alphabet as there were words and as many writing styles as there were writers. His burden was heavy and it was Dora's ardent wish to see the weight fall from his back. She decided not to trouble him with the curly script he had been made to write at school, by dipping a pen nib in watery ink and scratching it over the paper.

Not long after his failure to deliver the flowers, Arthur went back to the flower market to watch Violette from afar. JUBILEE MARKET. The capital letters caught his eye, but Violette was nowhere to be seen. She had already left for the day.

That evening he was ready with his questions for Dora.

'How do you spell Market? Piccadilly? Billingsgate? Daffodil?'

'Slow down, Artie. One letter at a time,' said Dora, determined to do things methodically, by making sure he remembered the name and the sound of every letter. 'MARKET'. What's the sound of the first letter?' In this painstaking way, Arthur solved the clues to the sounds of initial letters. Then it was three letter words in all configurations, which took not very long at all. Gradually two initial consonants, then two final consonants were added to the pattern. 'You'll be able to find your way around London in no time at all,' she said encouragingly, even though experience told her it would take many months.

'Why didn't they teach me like this in school?' he asked crossly, not understanding why something so easy had defeated him for so long. When order finally emerged out of chaos, Arthur was seeing place names everywhere.

'What? All this time? Hopping the wag? Arthur, say something!'

Rosa had found out that Arthur was working, as she was bound to do, and demanded an explanation.

'Lord Nelson left school and went to sea at twelve years old,' was his considered response.

'How do you know that?' Rosa almost screamed.

'I just do,' he shouted back.

She was flabbergasted, dumbfounded and far from speechless. 'How long has this been going on?' Was this the price she paid for going back to work? To be kept in the dark? She turned to Dora accusingly. 'And you? You knew all about it?'

Both Dora and Arthur were silent, waiting for the moment to pass. Rosa was pacified only because Tom knew nothing about it either. Tom had been watching Arthur of late and had mentioned to Dora he seemed happier. If she was in on it, she had given nothing away to him. Tom took the news in his stride. 'He's fourteen, Rosa. His schooldays are behind him now.'

When the time came for Arthur to tip out the coins from his money box and hand over his earnings, it was a moment of great pride. Dora was relieved everything was out in the open. 'Before you ask, Mother, yes, it is all honestly earned,' she added, just to be on the safe side.

Tom made every effort to hide the glow of pride that warmed his heart. He decided to give Artie a special cash box, which could be locked with a key. He would hand it over one day when the two of them were alone together.

There was a spring in Arthur's step as London opened before his eyes. Street names he had heard spoken so many times became instantly recognisable. FLEET STREET. What was difficult about that? PICCADILLY could be muddled with no other place. PALL MALL just jumped out at him. In the weeks and months that followed, he was deciphering pub names, destination boards on buses, labels on boxes, street names and shops, all with ease. Long words were just short words put together. He felt good. The misery of school was behind him. Nothing could stop him now.

CHAPTER 19

London, 1912

The bread round finished at midday, when Mr Smeeth took what he called 'a breather'. He needed it in winter, when his chest was bad, and insisted on it in summer, when he got hot and bothered. Either way, he went for a drink or two at noon. If Thunder was back in his stable, brushed, fed and watered by six o'clock, when Mr Smeeth staggered out of the pub very much the worse for wear, Arthur was tipped a bob and the whole of London was his oyster.

Thunder rested for an hour or so in the middle of the day and more often than not Arthur had forty winks on the stable floor to make up for the early morning starts. A carrot was enough to entice the old horse out in the afternoon for an amble to the park. He established a slow plod around the lake, past the bandstand, coming to a stop by the railings near the refreshment hut. His days carrying heavy loads were over, his time nearly up.

The twosome became quite a talking point, 'Here they come, in training for the Derby,' and Thunder got sugar lumps and lots of attention. There was some shire horse in his ancestry, evident from the shaggy hair around his hooves, the rest of him was a mixture of black, brown, white and grey. Arthur liked to describe him as dappled, a word he had heard used for horses with many patches and colours, and those in earshot nodded politely.

'More like a pile of old bones, I'd say,' came a voice from nowhere. Arthur was affronted. Anger took him like a gust of wind, his fist found its target and the impudent young upstart was on the ground, to a round of applause from the park regulars.

'Go back to school,' said Arthur, at ease with himself for being anywhere in the world except in a classroom.

The coppers added up, a bit here and there as the work came in. 'Here, lad. My legs aren't what they were, let me sit on the back of the cart as far as the pub on the corner.' And sometimes silver coins too. 'This mangle needs to be dropped off at my daughter's. She can't keep up with the nappies.'

'That'll be sixpence including loading and unloading,' Arthur replied, without pausing for breath.

'You're a smart one, you are.'

'They don't call me Smartie for nothing.'

A horse and cart at his disposal for the afternoon and Mr Smeeth oblivious to everything was a chance too good to miss. Wearing a clean shirt, cap, leather braces, polished boots and a muffler round his neck, Arthur set off, determined to right a wrong. He tied up the reins outside the Jubilee flower market and went in search of Violette, who had been in his mind ever since he first saw her far too long ago. He had mistimed it badly again. She was nowhere to be seen and it was beginning to rain.

'Was Violette here today?' he asked a woman as old as her shawl, almost the last to pack up and leave.

'Why do you want her?'

'I owe her a favour.'

'Do you indeed? Are you sure she wants a favour from you?'

'Most girls do.' Arthur could talk barrow boy.

'She's not that type of girl.'

'Do you know where she is?'

'I might. But does she want to see you?'

'She can decide that for herself, if you tell me where she is.'

'Help me with this crate. It goes on the top of that pile over there.'

Three crates and an annoying dirty mark on his clean shirt later, he asked the old woman once again. 'Where can I find her?'

'Drury Lane. Outside the theatre. But you'll have to be quick. Once the show has started she goes off home. She's here by four in the morning so I can't blame her. I'm too old to work the afternoons. Those days are gone.'

Arthur asked Thunder by means of several 'Gee ups' and twitches of the reins to attempt a trot to Drury Lane. Trot he would not, not in this rain, which was coming down with a vengeance. A slow amble was all the old horse could muster, so they took shelter under a bridge on the Embankment out of the rain.

'Whoa, there,' came an echoing voice out of the gloom. 'My, you look grand. Smart cart.' It was his old pal Bert, who had also put school behind him, sheltering from the weather.

'Shut up, Bert,' said Arthur, always sensitive when Thunder was derided.

Bert was sitting on a wooden crate, next to what looked to Artie like a parrot in a very small cage. Red, green, blue in patches with an ageing yellow beak, it looked very much under the weather.

'Who's your friend?'

'Sooty.'

'Eh?

'Someone was throwing him out.' Bert was always picking up possessions here and there and getting rid of them because he had nowhere to keep them.

'Does he talk?'

'No.' Bert took a roll-up from behind his ear, lit one for himself and offered another to Artie. There's nothing like a smoke when you're waiting for the rain to stop. 'What are you up to?' he asked. It was a while since he had seen Arthur.

'I'm looking for someone.'

'I'll find him, if you give us a ride.'

'Her. I need to find her.'

Bert knew a lot of people. He had to. In a few words, French, pretty, flower market, dog, Drury Lane, Arthur had put him in the picture.

'I'll take you right to her,' said Bert, miraculously producing a gentleman's umbrella capacious enough to keep both them and the parrot dry in the downpour. He climbed up alongside Arthur on the driving seat and the search for Violette was underway.

'Where d'you get it?'

'The umbrella? I found it. On a bench in Vauxhall Gardens. I know who left it. I'm minding it for him.'

It was chaos outside the theatre, crowds pushing and shoving in queues for cabs, motor cars and buses. Arthur drew Thunder to a halt and looked where Bert was pointing. Violette was soaked to the skin, clutching a few bedraggled roses. With minimum instruction to Bert, 'Hold the reins!' he grabbed the umbrella and made a dash through the throng towards her. 'Violette,' was all he managed to say. Her face, wet with rain and tears, showed some recognition, which was all he needed. He put one arm around her, held the umbrella over her with the other and jostled through the crowd towards the cart.

'Tomorrow, Bert. I'll give you the umbrella back tomorrow. Three o'clock under the bridge. I owe you a favour without a doubt. I'll be there.' Bert and his parrot were dismissed without the umbrella and without ceremony.

Violette sat shivering and chilled to the bone beside him on the driving seat. How light and thin she felt when he put his arm round her to share the shelter of the umbrella, while they waited their turn to get out of the throng of the traffic.

'I'll take you home.' She shook her head. 'What's the matter?' Still she did not speak. 'Where's your dog?'

A torrent of tears and precious few words, some French, some English, most incomprehensible said it all. 'My dog. She is gone.'

'Since when?' But all he got was tears from the girl pining for the smell and touch of her dog's wet fur. 'She'll be sheltering somewhere. We'll find her. Tell me. Where do you live? I'll take you home.'

'The market.'

'You live in the flower market?'

'Yes.'

What was she hiding? Arthur hated the idea of leaving her there, cold, hungry and alone. He tried another tack. 'What's the dog's name?'

'Belle.'

'Bell?'

'Yes.'

'Small, black and brown?

'Yes.'

'Long ears?'

Just a nod.

'Let me take you home.'

'No. I go alone.'

He handed her the umbrella. 'We'll find her. I'll come here tomorrow, early.'

'Yes.'

They parted, each knowing it was only for a few hours, both now living in hope of a happy reunion.

He put his arm around her again and kissed her cheek before driving off.

Mr Smeeth would have to do without him. It might make him appreciate the help a bit more and up his wages. Arthur went on foot to the market at first light to find Violette already unpacking boxes of flowers onto her own stall and onto the stall of the old lady next to her. She brightened when she saw him and handed him the umbrella. He got straight down to the business.

'When did you see Bell last?'

'Saturday. Last week.' That captivating accent.

'What time?'

'Afternoon.'

'Where?'

'In zhe basket.'

'Did the old lady here see anyone strange come near your stall?'

'Yes. In a car.'

'I'll speak to her.'

'Zhey took my dog. I have only zhis.' Violette was clutching a scrap of red blanket.

'Does she come when you call her?'

'Sometimes.'

'Does she come when anybody calls her?'

'Sometimes.'

Arthur could see this was not going to be easy. 'Does she know her way home from here?'

'Yes.'

'Where do you live?' Still she would not say. It was time to interrogate the old woman on the next stall. 'Did you see anything suspicious in the market the day the dog went missing.'

'What's it to you?'

Arthur persevered, undeterred by the way she looked him up and down. 'Come on. You remember me. I want to find Bell.'

'A motor car drove up. A dodgy-looking geezer was at the wheel and a woman, a bit shabby in spite of her large hat, got out and asked me for some flowers. Distracting me. I see it all now. I was packing up the stall and told her she was too late. By the time they had driven off, the dog was gone. In seconds. When Violette saw the empty basket, she ran after the car but it was too late. She's been everywhere calling that dog. Worn herself out crying. She's been looking for over a week. We all have.'

'Are you saying she was stolen?'

'You're a bright spark. Are you a policeman?'

'What did he look like?'

'Rough. Nothing special.'

'What colour was the car?'

'Black. All cars are black, aren't they?'

'Do you know where Violette lives?'

'What's it to you?'

'The dog might be there.'

'If the dog was there she wouldn't be lost, would she?'

'Ta very much.'

Arthur spent the morning on a wild goose chase looking round the market and the narrow streets back streets around the theatre. No luck. In the afternoon, he went to the bridge, arriving on the stroke of three.

Bert was clearly angry, but chose to feign indifference. He lit a cigarette without offering one to Arthur. 'What's your game?'

'No game. Everything went wrong.'

'Oh no, it didn't. I took you right to her.'

'Yeah, you did.'

'You took the umbrella, not one word of thanks, then scarpered.'

Arthur handed over the umbrella but knew he was cornered. 'I owe you. I know I do.'

'I'm still waiting.'

'Thanks, Bert.'

'I'm still waiting.'

'She's lost her dog. We've got to find it.'

'*We*, is it now?'

'Bert, I'm sorry.'

'At last. An apology.' Arthur offered his hand, which Bert refused. 'What's in it for me?'

'Blimey, Bert, we're mates.'

'Not good enough.' Bert was genuinely hurt. 'Can you bring Sooty back to life?'

'Oh, no! The parrot. Is it dead?'

'You took my umbrella, it got wet and died of cold.'

'I'm sorry, mate. How can I make it up to you?'

Bert took his time before saying, 'Fifty-fifty on all your takings for week.'

'Deal. If you find the dog.'

'Dead or alive?'

Arthur gasped. Please don't let the dog be dead. 'Yes.'

It was Bert's turn to come up trumps. 'Black and brown? Small? Long ears?'

Arthur nodded in astonishment. 'Have you seen it?'

Bert was enjoying taking his time. 'I might have.'

'Where?'

'Is it sweet? A lady's dog?'

'Believe me, Bert, it's sweet.'

'Are we a team?'

'Bert, we are.'

'From now?'

'From now.'

'Deal,' said Bert, as they shook hands. 'As it happens,' he added, pausing to good effect, 'I've found it.'

'Where?'

'Vauxhall Gardens. Be there, two o'clock, tomorrow. Bring the girl. She can pay me too.'

CHAPTER 20

'I've found it.'

Did Bert really say those spellbinding words? Artie was still daydreaming about the moment when Violette and her dog would be reunited and her delight would turn to love and gratitude, when he realised that Mr Smeeth had still not arrived for work, putting his master plan in jeopardy. Why did the old man have to be late this morning of all mornings? If the bread deliveries were not finished by noon, he would not be able to pick Violette up from the flower market and take her to Vauxhall Gardens for two o'clock. He walked to the yard behind the bakery to find out the state of play.

The baker's boy was outside having a smoke, surrounded by the baskets of bread and cakes that had to be loaded every morning.

'Where the heck is he?' asked the boy, fed up with being kept waiting.

'No idea,' said Arthur, setting off for the stable to check on the horse, who had been refusing to trot. It would be just like Mr Smeeth, more drunk than sober these days, to forget to take him to the farrier. Arthur felt a stab of conscience about the number of times he had taken Thunder into town, rather than leaving him to rest in the afternoons. Goodness knows how old that horse was.

The stable door was open; both man and beast were on the floor. Thunder was on his side, his coat dull, threadbare in patches, his breath shallow and rasping, his teeth brown, loose or missing. Mr Smeeth was on his knees, his breathing more like a gasping cry as he struggled in his inexpert way to diagnose Thunder's infirmity by inspecting his hooves. Arthur was hit by a wave of compassion for the poor old horse in these his last hours. He got down on the floor to pat and stroke his neck with gentle caresses, making a soothing, moaning, whoaing sound. Mr Smeeth straightened up, his joints creaking. He faced the open stable door and slowly pronounced his verdict.

'His ears are down. He's going. He's old. I'm old. It'll be the workhouse for me.'

'How old is he?'

'Old. I got 'im for comp'ny when the Missus died. He was a good 'un. A lifeline. Now 'e's gone too.'

'No, he's not. Look, his nostrils move when he breathes, and I can feel his heart beating. I'll stay with him.' No sooner had he spoken than he thought of his two o'clock rendezvous with Violette. 'I'll go and tell the baker we can't deliver the bread today. Then I'll sit with him.'

'Right.'

Arthur was thinking ahead. 'Come back at midday and take over from me.'

'Yes, lad, whatever you say.'

'Shall I get the horse doctor?'

'No.' Mr Smeeth was adamant. 'I'll call 'im when the time comes. To take 'is bones away.'

It was common knowledge that the so-called horse

doctor shot horses to relieve their suffering, as he liked to put it. No, they would take turns to look after Thunder by watching and waiting.

Mr Smeeth was squeezing water onto the horse's mouth from a sponge when Arthur took over the vigil.

'Come back at twelve o'clock,' he urged the old man, whose hunched back and unsteady steps as he made his way to the pub alarmed Arthur. Was this the end of their working partnership? Would he be able to manage on his own? Bert. Yes, Bert was the answer. He'd do it with Bert. They'd work alongside each other. Violette could work with them...then his daydreams were interrupted by a coughing and twitching from poor old Thunder, who had noticed his presence. Arthur inched closer, his conscience troubling him. Was it the downpour outside the theatre that had finished him off?

Arthur whispered gently to his old friend, dispensing words like balm. 'This is better than being on the streets, eh, old fella? Just the two of us. In your stable. Safe and sound. We're admired wherever we go. Think how many people we've helped since we've been working together. Hundreds. And before I climbed aboard, it's hundreds more.'

At noon, when Mr Smeeth made no appearance, Arthur left Thunder's side to fetch him. Swaying diagonally along the pavement, the old man came towards him, his eyes red, his speech incoherent. Arthur led him to the stable and, with a thousand misgivings, left them together. They've known each other for years, he reasoned to himself, I'd be in the way, two's company, three's a crowd: useless stuff like that.

He got to the flower market, just in time to find Violette packing up.

'Artie!'

It was the first time she had called him by his name! He had to weigh his words carefully, no longer daring to expect anything to go right on a day as black as this. 'Come with me. I know, or I think I know, a good place to look for Bell at two o'clock this afternoon.'

Her eyes opened wide. 'You 'ave found 'er?'

'We'll see,' he said, unsure of everything. They set off at a fast walk towards Vauxhall Gardens, Violette almost running, asking endless questions all of which he was unable to answer, so she asked Bert, who was sitting on a bench with the umbrella.

'Does she 'ave a collar with a bell?'

'No idea,' he said. 'A woman walks a dog here every day about this time. She has done for the past week or ten days. She shows it off to her friends.'

Violette was beginning to believe him.

'She lets it off the lead,' Bert went on, 'and calls it back, tempting it with a titbit.'

'Does she call her Belle?'

'Er, no idea.'

'Does she come when she is called?'

'It's a hit-and-miss affair,' said Bert.

Arthur was feeling left out of this conversation. Was this the moment to mention the events of the morning to Violette? No. To Bert? He gave it a try.

'Bert, Thunder has collapsed. I think he's at the end.'

'No surprises there, mate. He's ancient.'

'The bread man is with him. They both look as bad as each other.'

'You paint a pretty picture.'

'Shut up, Bert.'

Violette was on her feet, looking into the distance. 'Belle!'

'Wait. Are you sure?' Bert was taking over again.

'Yes. It's Belle!'

'Wait, here. You'll see. They go to the railings and sit on that bench over there.'

To Arthur's consternation, Bert was directing proceedings and Violette was doing exactly as she was told. She was all eyes and ears when Bert said, 'Watch. She'll walk down that path by the bandstand and tie it to the railings.'

'It's Belle. It's my dog. Let me go to 'er.'

'No. Wait until she lets it, sorry, her, off the lead. That's when you call her to you.'

All three waited, eyes glued to the dog, as a man, flamboyantly dressed, approached the young woman, touched his hat and sat down next to her.

'Right, the dandy's arrived. Where's my prop?' Bert had the umbrella by his side. 'I'm waiting for the right moment.'

The young woman untied the dog's lead from the railings and set the dog free. Bert was right in every particular. The little creature ran off, stopping every now and then to look in all directions. Violette ran hotfoot towards her, calling, 'Belle! Be...elle, Belle, *viens tout de suite!*' The dog stopped, instantly alert, pricking up her ears, turning this way and that.

'Katya, come to me,' called the woman sharply, springing to her feet in alarm at the unexpected turn of events.

Too late. Belle had already set off at top speed, running full pelt to arrive at Violette's feet, tail wagging, front legs pawing at her skirt.

What a lot of licking, kissing, laughing and crying went on as she swept her little darling up into her arms, cradling her precious bundle and smiling that dazzling smile that Arthur had seen only in his dreams.

'Katya! What a terrible name for my Belle!' she laughed.

The woman and the dandy were fast approaching, she in obvious distress and he with a pugnacious swagger looking for a fight.

'I'll let you deal with the formalities,' said Bert, preferring to take the rewards for his good deed by talking to Violette and sharing her delight.

Arthur set his jaw, more than ready to take out his frustrations of the day on the unpleasant man coming towards them. 'Right,' he said, through clenched teeth, spoiling for a fight. 'Where did you get this dog?'

The argument was quickly won, without a fight, by the instant rapport between Violette, joyful at her longed-for reunion with Belle, and the elegant young lady, who was now in tears. She had wished only to provide a home for a stray dog but now graciously accepted that her adorable pet belonged to another. She offered Violette her gloved hand, then removed her glove to give Belle a final stroke, while Violette thanked her over and over again.

'*Merci, Madame, merci beaucoup.*'

'She is a beautiful lapdog. I have always wanted one, ever since I first saw spaniels in paintings. Belle is the perfect name for her. She is indeed *très belle*. Please, take this lead. It's a gift.'

Arthur, excluded from this conversation too, was left to puzzle over why Bell could be the perfect name for a little dog who no longer had a bell on her collar. The unpleasant man had lost his swagger and was in a hurry to leave, brushing down his jacket as if caught in a brawl against his wishes.

'Just a moment, sir,' said Bert. 'Your umbrella. You left it here a day or so ago. I'd say it's worth a bob or two at the very least.'

'Er, thank you, young man. How honest you are. Er, please take this for your trouble,' said the dandy, handing over a few coppers from his loose change and in a hurry to go. Bert stood his ground with his hand outstretched, not releasing the umbrella until several silver coins had been handed over. Arthur was nonplussed. Would nothing go right for him today? Was he to play no part in all this? He watched the disgraced fancy man hurry after the young woman, who clearly wanted nothing more to do with him. Ever.

'Let me take you home, Violette,' Arthur pleaded, giving it one more try.

'No, zhank you. Belle and I go alone.' She bestowed her sincerest smile of gratitude on Bert, blew a kiss to Arthur, then turned, skipped, ran and jumped up and down with Belle bouncing on air beside her.

She had not kissed him, she had kissed the air.

'Thanks, Bert.' He had to say it.

'It was a pleasure,' replied Bert, failing to disguise his satisfaction.

Back at the stable, the baker's boy was outside, unwillingly guarding the door.

'Dead. They're both dead.'

CHAPTER 21

No horse, no cart, no work and no money, Arthur was in no position to refuse when the rag-and-bone man asked him to climb aboard.

'Jump on, lad. I'll try you for a week,' he said, fighting against a rumbling cough.

After a week of loading and unloading a motley collection of old household items, while the man sat on the cart smoking, it was Arthur who called it a day. He had received a better offer.

Mr Bright, lawyer at Messrs Taylor, Cooper and Bright, had been watching Arthur through the ground floor window of his office in Chancery Lane. Knowing they were short of a post boy, he went out on a whim and offered him the job.

'He's young, fleet of foot and strong as an ox,' said Mr Bright by way of explanation to his fellow solicitors.

The job was to deliver the mail throughout the building, from the post room in the basement to offices three floors up. The Head Porter made the job quite clear: 'Ninety men work here. Outside every office, and there are thirty offices, are three named inboxes and one outbox. Take the mail from the outboxes down to the post room in the basement and deliver the incoming mail to the appropriate inboxes on all three floors twice every morning and twice every afternoon.'

The rabbit warren of offices, corridors and staircases was easy for Arthur to fathom, but nobody had warned him that lawyers' clerks are incapable of writing legibly. Indecipherable sloping, looping, smudged and blotted copperplate scrawl on every envelope rendered Arthur as useless as a fish out of water.

'Another of Mr Not-So-Bright's hare-brained schemes,' said Mr Taylor to Mr Cooper at close of business, by which time Arthur had long left the building to recover his spirits with Bert and his cronies in the local pub.

'Working indoors is not for me,' was all Arthur would disclose about this experience. Down in the dumps and changing jobs all the time – oh, how he missed Thunder's slow plod - it was months since he had seen Violette. He would have to put his thinking cap on.

London, March 1912

Wearing a clean shirt and his best cap, he jumped on a bus and off again before the conductor had a chance to collect the fare, on and off another couple of buses until he came to the flower market. It was still early and a beautiful spring day into the bargain. Arthur was fifteen years old and in pursuit.

'At last,' said an old fellow unloading wooden crates of flowers from a cart to a wheelbarrow. 'Give us a hand. Daffs, roses, irises to stalls fifteen, sixteen and twenty. Three crates to each stall then report back to me and you've work for the day.'

Barrow boy now, is it? He set off with the barrow in haste and in the wrong direction.

'Strewth, lad! Stall fifteen's over there. Got it?'

Handing over three boxes of flowers to Violette at stall twenty, Arthur was rewarded with a ravishing smile of recognition and was smitten. This was the best place to be and not only because of the vibrant colours and intoxicating scents; work that offered a daily *rendez-vous* with Violette was worth its weight in gold. He decided there and then to make himself indispensable. As the weeks and months passed, he mastered the art of distinguishing between daffodils, irises, lavender, roses, pansies, lilies and geraniums and things were looking up. Luck came into it of course, like the day he rescued a bicycle from a scrap heap and had it up and running in week or so. Riding around London was child's play to him and it wasn't long before he could set a price for his flower delivery services.

Violette watched Arthur at work and liked what she saw. He knew his way around the back streets of London, had money in his pocket and always found time for her. They went to a picture house together for the first time, joining the queue for a film at the Balham Empire and they laughed all the way through it. She bewitched him when she laughed.

Afternoons they spent in theatre land, where Violette sold flowers to the theatre goers. Arthur treasured the memory of the place where he had come to the rescue when Belle had been stolen. (Or was it Bert who had found Belle? He had quite forgotten.) Thanks to time well spent with Thunder and Mr Smeeth, Arthur was a dab hand at brushing down horses, covering them against the rain and seeing to the nosebags and water buckets. He got good money for minding the horses outside the theatre and could keep an eye on Violette at the same time. His most lucrative source of income was from tips he got in teeming rain, sheltering ladies under a big umbrella as they hurried to and from their cabs and cars. A gentleman would tip an alarming amount to protect a lady's hat from the rain.

All through that year and into the next, when the London streets were paved with cold and wet, Arthur and Violette were inseparable. Gadding about from dawn to dusk as if they had no homes to go to, they strolled first side by side then arm in arm under the electric lights along the Thames Embankment. He had no idea what scent she was using but he knew he liked it. When she turned her face towards him, his kiss was tender, his embrace warm and strong. Life was good when they were together but every time he offered to walk her home, she refused him.

'Do not follow me, Artie,' she insisted.

'I won't, I promise,' he said, mystified, but determined to do nothing to spoil their happiness.

In April 1914 they moved their pitch to His Majesty's Theatre, Haymarket, where *Pygmalion* was playing. It was Violette's idea to go there in the afternoons, when her work in the market was over for the day, to pose as Eliza Dolittle, the common little flower girl.

'Won't you buy my pretty flowers?' she asked, with her delightful French accent, offering her eye-catching posies to audiences coming out of the matinée.

'A bunch of lavender, Eliza, my dear,' said one gentleman after another, every one convinced of his originality.

'*Avec plaisir, Monsieur.*'

'She's not a cockney! She's not common either. She's French. And she's dashed pretty.' Her photograph was taken more than once, for which money was dropped into the tall vase strategically placed at her feet.

The love they had for each other was no longer a secret thanks to Kitty, who told Eva, who told her Aunt Sylvia, who told her brother James. Dora, who had told William long ago, now told Rosa and Tom, who found it impossible not to be amused by the young couple who went to work diligently day after day in all weathers. There was no need for anybody to tell Bert, who had been in the know for ages.

'I wonder where she lives,' said Dora to Eva one day.

'Don't we all,' replied Eva, who had wondered the same thing with Kitty.

'Hear the news! Read all about it.' Not one word barked from the mouths of the news vendors on the street corners was intelligible but the threat was real and spreading fast. Assassination? Where? Who?

By the end of July 1914 all the talk was of war, in public houses, at school gates, on buses and in the corner shops. And not only in London. News boards were changing by the hour. War in Europe? The news was read and passed on with a mixture of ignorance and disbelief.

'Not war. Surely not.'

'We should stay out of it. It's not our quarrel.'

'Where is Serbia, anyway?'

'Archduke who?'

'Russia is coming in with France against Germany.'

'That's too close for comfort.'

'Our King won't want war with the Kaiser. They're cousins.'

'It's not the King that's to blame. I blame the politicians.'

Arthur was sitting in the Royal Academy Art Gallery deep in thought. It cost nothing to get in, and he liked to pass the odd half an hour there once in a while. His eyes were fixed on a painting of families at the seaside. Children were paddling, women under parasols, men reading newspapers, everyone was enjoying the sunshine; even the young man running about earning a bob or two renting out deckchairs was having a good time. Brightsea. Why not? They had been close for two years and he loved her. It would show everyone he was serious. Summer was always a busy time at the flower market but something told him the time was right. The Germans were going into Belgium, and France might be next. The mood in London convinced him it was now or never. He could remember every road, path, and beach as clear as yesterday. Yes, he'd take her to Brightsea.

Bursting with enthusiasm, he nevertheless decided to keep it to himself until his plans were watertight. When Violette looked enquiringly at him, he put his arm round her with a smile full of promise, kissed her more than once and said, 'Wait and see.' His brain was working overtime. He'd ask Dora to write the letter to Lady Sylvia on his behalf, he could find out the cost of the train tickets, count the money he had saved up and check that Belle was allowed to travel with them on the train. They would go away together, away from all this talk of war to a wonderful place by the sea. The lure was irresistible.

151

Chapter 22

Brightsea, July 1914

Violette arrived at Liverpool Street Station, flushed with excitement; it was her first trip out of London. She was wearing a delightful blue outfit, most of which had been passed on to her by Evelina, Kitty or Dora, who had all enjoyed the satisfaction of seeing their clothes used to such good effect.

'Please, take what you like, I haven't worn it for ages,' Eva had said.

'The colour really suits you,' said Dora, encouragingly.

'It's too small for me, but it fits you a treat,' said Kitty generously, envying her tiny waist.

Violette had not been afraid to pick and choose. She was wearing a dark blue skirt, a white blouse with a high collar, black leather shoes, rather old and shabby but sufficiently polished for it not to matter, with a light blue woollen jacket. There was nothing gaudy about Violette. A dark blue felt hat with a butter-soft, dove-grey feather curling round the brim hugged her head. She and Arthur had chosen it together, brand new, from the Bon Marché department store in Brixton. On this day, the first of their holiday, her bluey-green eyes shone with happiness.

Arthur could not take his eyes off her. The tickets safe in

his pocket and Belle temporarily hidden in a hat box, he opened the door of the third class carriage for Violette to climb aboard. As soon as the train was on the move, he breathed a sigh of relief that she had not changed her mind and Belle was released, with much tail-wagging. Violette had thought of everything; she put a woollen mat on the floor under her seat and settled her dog on it with a dry biscuit. Belle at least was travelling first class.

The second train, smaller than the first, took them into the countryside, where men and women were working in the fields.

'This reminds me of home,' said Violette, sadly.

'Where is home?' asked Arthur, for the hundredth time.

'France,' came the answer, brief and unadorned, as always.

By the time they climbed aboard Puffing Billy, Belle and Violette were jumping on and off like seasoned travellers.

There was nobody at Brightsea station to meet them, so they walked. Every breath of sea air reminded him of his childhood holiday, the smell of the salt marshes, the gulls calling and the invisible line where the sea met the sky. Arm in arm, Arthur carrying the suitcase, Belle trotting and sniffing the air beside them, never did a prouder man walk up the High Street and through the gate of Jacob's Hall.

It was the first day of August when Lady Sylvia answered a knock on the door to find the young couple waiting expectantly on the threshold, with one suitcase and a little dog between them. She had seen Arthur a few times in London at The Lions, but with Violette by his side he was a different boy. He was a man.

'Welcome, my dears. What a marvellous surprise! Oh, you little darling,' she said, bending down to stroke the silky ears of the tail-wagging dog. 'What's his name?'

'Belle.'

'Of course! Why did I ask? Come and meet my brother.' Lady Sylvia had been expecting them to stay for two weeks in August but had no idea when they might arrive. Never one to stand on ceremony, her welcome was as warm as if she had been preparing for a week. 'James, we have visitors.'

Introductions were informal but it took a while to put everyone in the picture.

'James, this is Violette, Arthur's friend,' said Lady Sylvia, to start proceedings. 'Violette, this is Lord Highton, my brother James, Evelina's father.' Violette offered her hand. 'And I am Evelina's Aunt,' said Lady Sylvia kindly, seeing the confusion on Violette's face. 'And most people call me Lady V, or Lady Sylvia.'

It was going to take a while for everybody and everything to fall into place but they all shook hands and everybody took turns to make a fuss of Belle. Lord Highton remembered Arthur as Rosa's boy, who had spent so much of his childhood downstairs in the parlour at The Lions. He looked at the young visitors with interest, with eyes that were kindly, yet keen and far-sighted. He saw a strong, good- looking young man and a charming young woman, entwined by love if not by marriage, and warmed to them at once. He had all the confidence of wealth, disliking scholarly types and fussy ways with drink and dress. Blessed with an easy-going temperament, he was generally well liked, especially by women.

Lady Sylvia had a particular liking for incongruous guests and had soon resolved sleeping arrangements. James was to remain in the guest bedroom, Arthur was up in the attic and Violette would sleep on the day bed in the garden room.

'Perfect,' said Violette, when she stepped outside to let Belle sniff around the garden. 'It will be easy to wash and dry my hair here. It's so difficult in London. I'll do it tomorrow.'

'Oh, yes, do,' said Lady Sylvia. 'I have some gentle soap. The water is very hard here.'

The impromptu gathering around the table that evening bubbled with laughter and champagne. *'Santé!'* Violette was soon made to understand that *Monsieur*, as she called him, loved everything French. They shared a meal of freshly caught fish, with an array of summer vegetables: peas, runner beans, marrow, new potatoes with fresh mint, all prepared by the maid before she left for the day. When the men went into the garden for a smoke, or 'a breath of fresh air' as they described it, Lady Sylvia and her willing helper cleared the table and stacked the plates in the scullery for the maid to deal with in the morning. Violette was proud beyond measure to see Artie and Lord Highton talking amicably together, man to man. She was quite at ease with Lady Sylvia, chattering in a mixture of French and English, drinking peppermint tea, enjoying the fragrance that hit her nose rather than the taste and cheered to hear unbridled laughter coming from the garden.

Tired from the journey but still vibrant, she was at a loss to understand how an evening of such conviviality had come about.

'How is it I am in Brightsea, talking French and drinking champagne? Is it really all because Arthur is my beau?'

Lady Sylvia was in no doubt. 'Yes, my dear. Love is at the heart of it.'

When the men came in, trailing a whiff of cigars, Violette kissed Artie goodnight, murmuring endearments he had heard many times. He dragged his feet up to the attic.

'Sleep well, Violette,' said Lady Sylvia, leading her into the garden room by candle light. Just use the garden if you need to in the night.'

'*Merci, Madame,*' Violette replied, answering on behalf of herself and Belle. '*Bonne nuit.*'

James and Sylvia, both of them approaching their three score years and ten, stayed up talking. With the threat of war unresolved and unresolvable, they spoke of other things. For the first time for many years, no doubt prompted by the arrival of the young couple, they exchanged confidences about love and marriage. Sylvia had always assumed that the tensions between James and his wife were caused by their disappointment at not having a son and heir but James explained it differently. It was after this conversation that Sylvia, who had always had a soft spot for Arthur, found a place for him in her heart.

CHAPTER 23

Brightsea, 4th August, 1914

Out of doors from morning to night, jumping from one grassy clump to another over the rushing inlets of water along by the estuary, they knew it was love. Arm in arm in the sunshine on the Brightsea promenade, no onlooker could deny it. What was happening in London was, for this young couple, out of sight and out of mind.

It is a great day when a young man has the key to his own lodgings for the first time. When Arthur opened the door of the hut, Violette's face was his reward. She stood on the verandah and looked inside, delighted by the little room set out with table and chairs, a day bed, curtains at the window, shelves with rows of cups, plates, books, a cribbage board and playing cards.

'Oh, c'est joli.' She often lapsed into French when overcome by shyness or delight. French or English, Arthur knew she liked it and was mightily relieved. His plan to impress by rowing over the water from The Hard had not gone well. Never did he row, turn and scull the little boat with such skill and care as on that morning but being on the water brought back unhappy memories of the journey from France to England for Violette. Belle was similarly unnerved, unable to fathom why the floor of the boat moved under her paws. When they got to the other side, he had to lift them both onto dry land.

It was the first time they had been completely alone together since they left London. He fetched water from the standpipe, while she set the bread, cheese and tomatoes they had brought with them on the table. As they worked and chatted together, intent on making it a home, he blurted out, 'I love you, Violette.'

She searched his eyes and was able to say, 'Yes, I know. I feel it, here, in my heart.'

It was clear to both of them, that on this day and in the intimacy of this place they were building a future of their own.

'The tide's on the turn,' he warned, when the sun was low and they were tidying up. 'We need to get going, or it will be a hard row back.' He locked the hut, lifted Violette and Belle into the boat and pushed it off the shingle.

'She couldn't walk, poor thing,' said Violette, who had tried to take Belle along the beach but had to carry her back when small stones got stuck in her paws. 'She's a town and country dog, not a seaside creature at all.'

'And I've done no fishing all day. Lady V will be wondering what we've been up to.'

'I'll tell her we've been playing cribbage,' laughed Violette.

Lady Sylvia was in no mood for conversation when they got back, having much on her mind that day. Her brother had returned to London, alarmed by the latest reports in the newspapers of crowds thronging the streets. She made no mention of the two envelopes he had left on the hall table for the young couple before leaving Jacob's Hall. Lord Highton liked to do these things. By 11pm war had been declared, crowds were gathering outside Buckingham Palace and the ghastly news was on its way around the world.

The next morning torrential rain fell over most of Britain. People muttered to each other in their homes and on the streets. There was no buoyancy in the air or on the water. Arthur went out and about to earn what money he could, while Violette stayed indoors.

'Help yourself to paper, pencils and anything you need,' said Lady Sylvia generously, waving her hand around the studio, wanting Violette to feel at ease in spite of the gloom. 'Here, take this book, it's a beauty.'

Violette had never before enjoyed the luxury of a leather-bound note book, smooth paper, soft pencils and an India rubber. She moved into the garden room, hugging them to her. Looking out at the rain, stroking Belle's silky ears abstractedly, she was lost in a daydream, when words from her childhood, words she had neither written nor spoken aloud tumbled into her mind one after another. Alone with her thoughts, she cast a cascade of memories down the page... *peur, sabots, camion, me cachant de quoi, de qui, un sac de lavandre, faim, Belle près de moi, les réligieuses, loin de mon malheur, Londres, fleurs, pleurs,* onto the next page and the next, vivid and real, in her untutored and unpractised hand. For a long time she poured out the story of her journey, her hopes and fears, her life in London, in the childlike French stored in her memory. When she had finished and cried her all, she turned to the title page and wrote *Ma Vie*. Then she closed the book, secured it with the clasp, drew Belle to her and lay down to rest, to sleep, to dream. She and Arthur would manage come what may.

That evening Violette spoke to Lady Sylvia in French, the language still teeming through her mind, *'Merci beaucoup pour le livre'* and showed her the title page. At last she had told her story of her life, but it remained her secret. *'C'est mon secret.'*

Lady Sylvia remembered the book of sorrows she had written after the death of her husband, when she was only eighteen years old. *'D'accord, Violette. I understand.'*

The outbreak of war cast its shadow everywhere. George was having a drink with Arthur in The Anchor pub down on the waterfront. He, like all the other Brightsea men, was having to decide what part to play. The enemy were just over the Channel and keen eyed the local fishermen had many a time seen foreign boats fishing in British waters. George preferred not to speculate on the reality of conflict at sea.

'This damn war. They're going mad for it in London, I hear. Our men and fishing boats will be out as usual. People have got to eat.' He had always got on well with Arthur from when he was a boy and he still liked him now. 'You're too young to go,' he said, 'Be grateful for that. Your life with Violette is just beginning.'

Arthur wanted to talk about love not war. 'I want to marry her. How do I go about it?'

'Ask the vicar. He'll tell you all you need to know. He lives next to the church. I'm walking there this afternoon for bell ringing practice at five, if you want to walk across the fields with me.'

'I'll be there.'

Wheat was being harvested that week, but the downpour of rain had left the crops sopping wet, so the field workers had either gone home early or were in the pub. George and Arthur, both in coats and caps against the rain, had some catching up to do along the way.

'How's Kitty?'

'Kitty? How do you know Kitty?'

'She came here with Miss Evelina once, a long time ago.'

'She's doing fine, still working at The Lions.'

'Give her my regards.'

'I will.'

Little more was said, because George needed to go through bell-ringing sequences in his head before the practice. He was new to ringing, which demanded all his concentration, and the obsession was bedding in. Ringers walked miles from the surrounding towns and villages for the chance of a ring.

Five o'clock turned out to be a bad time to call on the Reverend Drinkwater. A learned but short-tempered man came to the door with spectacles balanced on the end of his beak nose, because he was always reading small print. Half his mind was on the glass of port wine he always took at this time of day to sharpen his appetite, and the other half was on the bell ringing coming from the church tower. He wondered why he should spend time with a Londoner in a hurry to arrange a marriage service for which he would not be receiving payment, in the unlikely event that it took place at all. He unhelpfully answered Arthur's questions with other questions.

'How old are you?'

Arthur said eighteen, thinking it would speed things up.

'In that case you will need permission from your parents. How old is the lady?'

Arthur was only after information when all was said and done, so this question unnerved him. 'I'm not sure.'

The vicar continued to pile on complications. 'If she's under twenty-one, she will need permission from her parents.'

She had no parents.

'Or legal guardian.'

She had no legal guardian.

'Do you live in the same parish?'

Unlikely.

'Where does she live?'

Don't know.

'Religion?'

Not sure.

'How long have you known this woman?'

'Long enough, thank you, Vicar,' said Arthur, turning on his heels.

CHAPTER 24

Lady Sylvia did her best to avoid war talk with the people of the town. She had no time for tittle-tattle and craved peace and quiet. At her suggestion, the young couple booked a day trip to Sandling-on-Sea for the Saturday.

'Yes, do go!' she said, 'You'll like Sandling. It's a proper seaside resort, with sandy beaches and gardens along the promenade. You can walk out to sea on the pier. The charabanc leaves from Brightsea post office at nine and returns at six. You'll need a shawl for the ride, Violette.'

'What's a sharrabang?' asked Violette.

'No idea,' said Arthur.

'It's French, Violette! *Char-à-banc.*'

'*Ah, bon.*'

'That's clear then,' said Arthur, with a shrug.

Saturday morning was overcast, but to young lovers with money in their pockets it was a special day. Arthur was wearing a waistcoat under his best jacket, a peaked cap on his head and a muffler round his neck. August could not be relied on for weather. Violette, who had no idea what such an outing involved, was in her London travelling clothes, a shawl round her shoulders and another over her head to protect her hat while they jogged along in the open motor coach. The final stop was right on the promenade at the entrance to the pier. As Violette climbed down from the charabanc, a photographer took her picture, promising to have it ready for collection at four o'clock.

The beach was crowded with children playing on the sand and with parents and grandparents sitting in deck-chairs, keeping an eye on them. Holidaymakers of all ages were paddling at the water's edge, lifting their skirts above the sea water or rolling their trousers up but Violette was not tempted to walk on the sand in the boots she had polished that morning. She wanted to go straight onto the pier, never having seen such a thing in her life before. The distractions and amusements along the length of the pier delayed their every step, their laughter as good a tonic as a lungful of sea air and worth all the sixpences and coppers they threw away at every stall. They walked straight past the queue outside the Fortune Teller's booth, their future decided. At the end of the pier, vying for a place with the fishermen, Arthur and Violette looked out to sea at the vanishing point on the horizon, a haze of cloud, sea and sky. The murky water below gushed in and out with the waves.

On reflection, Arthur thought it was the way she held on to his arm and leant in against him that made him say it. Or perhaps it was the hat, or the chignon at the nape of her neck. When Violette looked back on the day, she was sure it was when they both looked at the horizon and then at each other at the same moment.

'Will it always be like this?' she asked, as if for them both.

'If we get married…' he stopped, realising there was a proper way to do this. 'Violette, will you marry me?' Shock jumped across her face and she put her hand to her mouth. 'Please?' he added and could do no more but wait.

'What? Today? Here? Now?' She was teasing him.

'When we get back to London. We need to find a church, get permission, arrange for banns to be read, and -'

'Stop. How do you know?' She looked alarmed, no longer teasing, but asking in earnest. 'Who must give permission?'

'We'll find out everything when we get to London.' He was still waiting. 'Did you say 'Yes'?'

'Yes, please.' She put her arms round him in gratitude and he lifted her off her feet, his arms encircling her with warmth and love. She kissed him tenderly, with Belle pawing at her skirt. She picked her up. 'We say, yes!'

They walked back to the promenade, shyly in step with one another, smiling non-stop and very hungry. They sat in a shelter to eat fish and chips covered in salt and vinegar, looking out to sea and not forgetting to say a thank you to Lord Highton for the envelopes of money.

What a photograph that was! Violette in her travelling clothes, wearing the hat with the butter-soft plume, holding her skirt in one gloved hand, Belle's lead in the other, smiling at Arthur, who was holding her by the elbow to steady her as she stepped off the charabanc. A masterpiece of French chic captured in a moment. It cost half a crown and was priceless.

By the middle of August, over one hundred thousand British men had left for Belgium. After days trying to ignore the gravity of the situation, Lady Sylvia decided they must leave Brightsea for London. She knew Arthur and Violette were in love, she had seen and admired the photograph taken at Sandling, but it was out of the question to leave them at Jacob's Hall alone and unmarried. She had real concerns over Violette's name, age, parentage, religion and place of residence but was able to extract precious little information from her.

'How old are you, Violette?'

'Fifteen.'

'What is your family name?'

Silence.

'What was your mother called? And your father's name?'

Silence.

'Were you called Violette in France?'

'No. I chose my name when I arrived in London.'

The only information Violette offered voluntarily was that she was Catholic. 'I had my first communion in France at eight years old.'

'Catholic is no obstacle,' said Lady Sylvia, by way of encouragement. 'We must all return to London. I'm in favour of young marriages,' here she smiled warmly, 'but it would not be right for you to arrive in London unchaperoned while you are in my care.'

They set off the next day, leaving Edwards and the maid to clean and lock up Jacob's Hall for the winter.

On the third train back into London, the one which took them into the smoke of Liverpool Street Station, their inward hopes and fears tormented them. Only Belle slept peacefully on her woollen rug under the seat. As they stepped onto the streets of London, it was clear that nothing would ever be the same again.

CHAPTER 25

London, August 1914

London was in a frenzy. Young unmarried men were pouring into the recruitment offices in a clamour to enlist. The front page of the Daily Express had touched a nerve.

England Expects Every Man Will Do His Duty

'We're all in it together,' was Bert's view. 'I'm a scout, remember? I've promised to do my duty to God and the King.' It was just a matter of time for him.

'Steady on, Bert,' said Arthur, with more than war on his mind. He and Violette had a future together.

'What's happening in France?' she asked, when they were sitting in a bar in Fleet Street. Neither of them read the newspapers but he had heard it from Dora.

'The Germans have marched into France.'

The colour drained from her. France was in her blood.

'If I'm needed, I'll have to go,' he said, shaken at the sight of her.

'No,' she said inaudibly, betrayed by this one utterance.

He reached for her hand, but she withdrew it and rushed away. Neither she nor Belle looked back.

*

'I'm looking for a wedding ring. Gold.' He was in Goldsmith's the Jewellers in the Burlington Arcade.

'May I suggest you choose from our selection? I can put it aside for the lady to try on for size?' The shopkeeper was politeness personified. Business was good.

'Yes. That one.'

'The twenty-two carat rose gold ring? This beautiful ring is £10.'

Arthur was tongue-tied. Is that what they cost?

'May I suggest this pretty yellow gold one, for a guinea? It's unusual, very dainty. Has the lady a small hand?'

Violette's hand, delicate fingers, cool, white skin, and how he could enclose it with his warm grasp, came straight into his mind's eye. 'Yes.'

'If you look closely, you will see an engraved decoration around the band. Very attractive.'

Arthur was thinking hard, but knew not what to say or do.

'May I suggest I put it away until tomorrow?' said the jeweller.

'I'll take it now.'

Arthur handed over the money in a state of great confusion; if they got married he could not join up.

September 1914

Dora was standing at an upstairs window looking out along the street to the pillar box on the corner, where the road curved behind the gardens of the square. It had been a hot day and the window was wide open, but she was hidden from view by the net curtain, which moved gently in the breeze. It was cool inside the house and the air from outside felt warm on her skin. A perfect day, yet all this talk of war.

Then she saw him. She shivered, her bare feet cold on the bedroom floor. It was unmistakably Arthur, in his shirtsleeves, flat cap on his head, striding towards the house. When he came in the gate, she was sitting on the bottom stair in the hall. Through the glass panes of the front door she saw him pause on the step, as if to collect himself. She too, waited a moment, then went to open the door just as he was putting his key in the lock. She looked him straight in the eye and asked the question she could not bear to have answered.

'What have you done?'

'What do you mean, what have I done?'

'I saw you this afternoon, with Bert, going into the Picture Palace.'

'Let me come in first.'

Dora saw the brown envelope under his arm and fear hit the pit of her stomach, sending a shudder over her skin.

'You know what I've done. I had to. I wanted to.'

'You're too young. They won't take you.'

'Well, they have taken me. And Bert. We're both going.'

Those words, that forced her to free herself from him. 'But you're seventeen.'

He hesitated. 'You know I'm no good with dates.'

'Arthur, you lied. You lied about your age.'

'I have to lie to do things my way. It's always been like that.'

'Why are you going?'

'It's something I can do. I'm not good at much and they wanted me.'

'When are you going?'

'I don't know. But I'll be back by Christmas.'

'I can't bear it if you go.'

'You know how I struggle here. This is war. No one can touch me in a fight.'

'Oh, Artie, no.'

'I thought you'd be proud of me.'

That chill again. She was unable to say what he wanted to hear. 'Where are they sending you?'

'I don't know.'

'Why are you going?' That same question again.

'I'll miss it if I don't go. It's a chance for me to show what I can do.' He was searching for the words to make her proud. 'I'm strong and my country needs me.'

'We need you here.'

'But I need to do this.'

He moved past her and started up the stairs. 'Come up and read these papers for me. And don't tell Mother.' She dragged her feet after him. Nothing she could say would make any difference. Her brother was going to war.

Arthur was walking around the lake in Hyde Park, deep in thought, when he saw a man with a moustache, perhaps in his fifties, sitting on a bench, with a newspaper open in front of him, which he did not read. Arthur sat down beside him and felt compelled to speak.

'I've joined up. Yesterday. I only went into the Picture Palace to see what the fuss was about. There were crowds going in. Women too, wives and girlfriends. In the interval, soldiers in uniform started setting up tables. I saw the words YOUR COUNTRY NEEDS YOU on the screen. I don't mind telling you, as I don't know you and you don't know me, that I struggle with reading. I always have done. But these words jumped out at me. A piano was playing and people started singing. Everyone, including me, joined in when it got to *Steady, boys, steady!* I don't even know it but I joined in that bit. I thought to myself, I can do this. I'll be good at it. I've seen a dead man. And a dead horse come to that. I can handle it. So up I went. I had to give my name and date of birth, which I can never remember. The chap said, "Did you say nineteen years old?" I said, "Yes," and got my papers. As quick as that.

'At school, the teacher, he looked a bit like you, was always trying to sort me out, as he put it. I'm not dim, I'm different. But he liked to shame me into doing the impossible. I told him, I can't.'

'Can't, or won't?' said the teacher, who was always ready for a fight. That's when I knew I was in for it. That whacking noise. I flinched every time. It's natural. A sort of shudder goes through you. It wasn't the pain. I couldn't write. That's what hurt. He bared his teeth when he hit boys. A sort of smile. He was getting something out of it for sure. He tried to give me the strap once. I said, "I've done nothing." He just barked back at me, "Before you do!" That was it. I legged it, off, out, over the railings.

'I can read now, of course. They don't call me Smartie for nothing. It's not that hard. Now I'm off to fight for my country. I'll do better than most. My sister said, "We need you here." Mother started crying, "What have you done? What shall I do without you?" So now I'm needed. But I won't lie to you, I'm worried. I'm leaving my girl behind.'

The man, who had a military air, nodded to Arthur, tucked his newspaper under his arm and walked away without saying a word. It was some time before he sat down on a bench beside an elegant woman in her forties, opened his newspaper but again failed to read it. His words stuttered and faltered.

'I'm too old to fight, so when they offered me the job I took it. We all want to do our bit. Some days there are a hundred new recruits here in the park. We get a lot of them from the Picture Palaces. They go up in the intermission. It's the music that pulls them in. *Hearts of Oak*, I think it is, or *Rule Britannia*. And the woman walking up and down the aisles, touching them on the shoulder. She shames them into it. Well-to-do, rough and ready, tall, short, fat, thin; we get all sorts. But to me they are all the same, toy soldiers on the scullery floor. The day I see them as individuals, I'm lost. I shout, "Stand, march, halt, at ease, charge, lunge, down, forward." If they fall, I shout, "Get up." Some say, "I can't." I parry with, "Can't or won't?" I bark at them again and up they get. Or someone drags them up. I'm training them to kill and be killed. I must admit I enjoy it. Every night I repent of my sins.'

The woman stood up and walked away. It was a long while before she, too, came to rest on the bench next to Arthur.

'Thinking about the war? What else? You look the same

age as my boy. Boy! He's twenty-four years old and down from Cambridge. It's a waste. A waste of his life. He's the brainy type, you know, short-sighted, glasses, reads poetry, hopeless at games. It was only his wits that got him through Harrow. He was bullied at first. They all are, I'm told. Fortunately, he turned it to his advantage. It wasn't long before the brutes were paying him to write Greek epigrams, parse and analyse. I've seen them here in the park undergoing training, all moving together with some idiot barking orders at them. My son was offered a post as a Recruiting Officer, which he refused for reasons of conscience. "I can't take that," he said. "Can't or won't?" I asked. "Won't," he said. Never have such words passed between us. All his advantages are now as nothing. He has as much and as little chance as all the others. Since he left, I've hardly slept.'

Arthur got up, touched his cap in acknowledgement and walked on.

CHAPTER 26

Dora and her childhood friend William were talking in the back room behind Bartlett the Bootmaker's shop. Not much had changed, the same smell of leather and boot polish pervaded the shop. But William, or Dr Bartlett as he was now professionally known, had become forthright in his political views. Dora craved his permission to stop Arthur enlisting and he did not disappoint.

'He's too young. It's not right for a seventeen-year-old to be going off to war.'

'It's not even allowed. He lied about his age.'

'You could stop him by revealing his real age.'

Dora had considered and reconsidered this many times. 'I want to stop him, but he'd feel thwarted. He likes to make his own decisions.'

'That's important to all of us. I'm not responding to this call for volunteers. And not just because my mother is German. As a Quaker, I'm against it.'

'I keep thinking of my school friend Dorothea and her family back in Germany. Are they the enemy now?'

'What made him volunteer?'

'He saw a poster. A line of soldiers in uniform and a line of onlookers. He knows where he belongs.'

'That poster did the job it was designed to do.'

'What can I say to make him think again?'

'That he's dishonest.'

'I don't want to criticise him. He's asked for my support.'

'This war is dividing families and not only yours and mine. The King and his cousins are at war with each other.'

'He wants me to be proud of him.'

'Are you proud of him?'

It was the question she dreaded. Did she feel pride? She knew she should. But if he died, in that terrible event, she also knew that pride would count as nothing. It took her a long while to come up with a reply.

'My conscience tells me I have to decide what is right for Arthur,' she said meekly. She had lost the fight and she knew it.

William was being uncharacteristically unforthcoming during this conversation for a very good reason; Arthur had been to see him only a few days before to ask a favour and had extracted from him a promise of confidentiality. So William kept his counsel.

'Mama and Papa, I deserve an explanation.' Evelina had chosen a time when both her parents were sitting in the drawing room at The Lions to speak her mind. There was a touch of theatre about the way she positioned herself between her father, who was standing with his back to the fire smoking a cigar, and her mother, who was sitting in her favourite chair preoccupied with some embroidery. Evelina delivered her prepared speech with an unmistakeable air of self-determination.

'Men are going off to fight, women are working in factories, on the buses and in hospitals and you have prevented me from becoming an actress. It's absurd. I have money of my own, no work to do and I'm still not married at the age of twenty-six.'

'It's just a matter of time, my dear,' said her mother, trying, without success, to hide her concern at the number of eligible young men disappearing from the scene. 'There are plenty of thoroughly decent young men in the city and many more in the country. You should make an effort to mix more with men of your own class.'

'Marriage seems a luxury in the present circumstances,' said her father, always more likely than his wife to see his daughter's point of view.

'Consequently,' Evelina continued, as if nothing of consequence had been said by either parent, 'I'm considering training as a nurse.'

'Whatever next?' said her mother, throwing away her sewing and clutching her head. 'Isn't there enough to worry about in our lives already? I blame you, James. You should never have agreed to her not using her title.'

'Mama, my title is irrelevant. Even the old Queen admired nurses! If I stay in England, I face hard work but no danger, so don't try to stop me.'

'Let her go, Alice, my dear,' said James. 'It's a sign of the times. She'll be safe. That's what matters.'

Evelina could not believe her ears. She had said her piece and her father had agreed! But should she do it? She needed somebody to talk to but Dora, who was working all hours and in a permanent state of exhaustion, rarely came to The Lions these days. She decided to write to her friend and ask for a meeting.

★

They met in the tea room at Waterloo Station, to which Evelina travelled on the bus unchaperoned, as was her custom these days.

'Nursing's a great thing if you've got the stomach for it,' said Dora, genuinely surprised that Eva was even considering nursing.

'There's only one way to find out if I'm up to it.'

'Where will you train?'

'No idea.'

'I wish you all the best with it. I hope you don't get a dragon of a Matron.'

'Blimey, so do I.'

'Eva! What did you say?'

'Just practising.'

'Have you heard that William is not volunteering?' Dora had so far kept this information to herself, but she shared it now with Eva. 'He says it's against his conscience.'

'But as a doctor he'll still have a part to play. That's the point about doctors and nurses. They are always needed.'

'Why don't you talk to him about it?'

'Do you think he'd be willing to tell me honestly what's involved?'

'He would be honest but I've no idea whether he's got the time. I rarely see him now. He's always out at political meetings and Women's Rights groups.

'Really?' Eva decided to be bold. 'How do I get hold of him?'

'You could write to him at the bootmakers in Jelf Road.'

'Thanks, I will.'

'I've been wondering about George, in Brightsea,' said

Dora, wanting to change the subject. 'Have you heard anything?'

'Aunt Sylvia told me he's a skipper on the trawlers now and takes his turn on one of the boats patrolling the coast of Essex round the clock.'

Dora let out a gasp of admiration. 'That's good. Our seas need to be protected.'

'And our skies.'

'Don't. The thought of being attacked from the air. I just can't bear it.'

There was standing room only in the local pub, where men were talking little and drinking too much. Arthur was at the bar, drowning his sorrows with Bert. Dora was deathly quiet at home and he wanted to do something to make her feel better.

'Something…special,' was all he could come up with.

'I've seen just the thing,' said Bert, who knew enough about Dora to come up with the idea. 'Small, lightweight, and going for a song.'

'Steady on. What is it?'

'I'll take you right there.'

'How much is it?'

'Not much for what it is.'

'I need to see it.'

'Tomorrow morning, ten o'clock, under the bridge,' said Bert, 'I'll meet you. It's a shame you've got no horse and cart because you'll want to take it away with you.'

'What is it?'

'You'll see.'

'I'll be there.'

The next morning, still very much the worse for drink, Arthur remembered, just, when and where to meet Bert. He heard him before he found him, under the bridge, tootling Polly Wolly Doodle on his tin whistle.

'Let's go,' said Arthur, with no great expectations.

Bert took him to a small furniture shop down a side street off Charing Cross Road. In pride of place in the window was a roll top desk with a plain white card on the top. Bert read the notice to him:

The perfect desk for the perfect lady.

Arthur knew at first sight it was ideal for Dora, but the notice put him off. He knew of only one perfect woman and Violette did not need a writing desk.

'How much?'

'He wants one pound ten shillings.'

'What's it worth?'

'No idea,' said Bert, already through the door.

Under the gaze of a grey-haired man, who emerged from the back room the moment the two unlikely lads entered the shop, Arthur set to with his tape measure, assessing the desk and all it had to offer. Two foot six wide, three foot six high and just over a foot deep, it was well made in light oak, with a roll top, which moved smoothly back to reveal eight compartments for stamps, pen nibs and bottles of ink. There was a small pull-out writing surface, a drawer for storing account books, paper and envelopes, and underneath were two shelves for books.

'This desk will tuck away nicely into the corner of a lady's boudoir or front parlour,' said the grey man.

'The price is high, to my certain knowledge,' said Arthur, who knew nothing at all about the price of desks but knew that Dora would love this.

The man shrugged. 'It has been in the window since yesterday and several women have come in to examine it. They pull out the drawer, roll back the top, lock it with the little key and exclaim, "I love it." This desk will be gone by end of business today.'

'How much is it?' Arthur was struggling to hide his interest.

'If you take it today, I'll let it go for one pound ten shillings.'

Arthur felt in his pocket for the gold sovereign and the shilling he had taken from his savings box that morning. He was nine shillings short. 'For a guinea, I'll take it this morning.'

'No, thank you,' said the grey man, turning away, not at all inclined to begin an unrewarding conversation.

Arthur was suddenly certain he needed to clinch this deal. 'I hope you will accept one pound five shillings, sir.'

'If you return with the money and take the desk away, I shall honour that price until noon. Until then, it will stay on sale in the window at full price.'

'Write me out a bill of sale for one pound five shillings and I'll be back,' said Arthur, who knew enough to get the price in writing.

The man disappeared into the back office and returned with a bill of sale, stating all the particulars.

'Don't look at me,' said Bert as they left the shop. 'You'll have to put your thinking cap on. I've not got that kind of money.'

'I've got an hour and a half to get it. I'll see you here at twelve.'

'Better make that ten minutes to, or you'll lose your price.'

Arthur walked away with a frown on his face as Bert called after him, 'And remember, you've got to shift it.'

He went two stops on the Underground then jumped on a bus, going upstairs to sit in the open air and have a smoke, arriving at The Lions in good time. Evelina was the only person he could approach who had ready money and Dora's interest at heart. Kitty answered the door.

'Good morning, stranger. It's a while since you called here to pass the time of day. I've heard you're going.'

'Is Evelina at home?'

'That's charming, I'm sure. Not so much as a how d'you do.'

'It's about Dora.'

'Is she in trouble?'

'No. But it's important.'

Kitty looked doubtful. 'She's going out this morning, but I'll ask if she'll see you.'

After what seemed ages, Evelina appeared, dressed ready to go out.

'What is it, Artie?'

'I've come to ask a favour. I want to buy Dora a …going away…a present. I've joined up and she can't forgive me.'

'I know. She told me. How can I help?'

'I need four shillings until next week.'

'Gladly. Anything for Dora. She's feeling miserable. We all are.'

'Thank you.' He was impatient. 'I have to be in town by twelve.'

'Where do you need to go? Robins is waiting at the front.'

'Charing Cross Road.'

'I'm going into town. We'll take you.'

Once Evelina had told the driver the destination, their conversation in the back of the car began in earnest. 'Here are two florins. What on earth is it you're buying?'

'A desk.'

'For four shillings?'

'Don't be daft.'

'Dora loves desks. I remember her reaction when she first saw my portable writing box.'

'I'll show you if you've got time. I could do with your opinion.'

By this means Arthur, who had decided to buy the desk regardless of her opinion, arrived outside the shop at a quarter to twelve in a chauffeur-driven car.

Bert was pocketing some small change he had made from playing his tin whistle when the car drew up. If this deal went through, he would get a shilling from the grey man. They had already shaken hands on it.

'What the…?' he began, seeing Arthur get out and open the car door for an elegant woman dressed for town.

'Oh, how perfect,' said Evelina, catching sight of the desk in the shop window. 'She'll love it.'

'This is Bert,' said Arthur, adding, because he had to, 'He saw the desk first.'

'What a good scout you are, Bert,' said Evelina, peering at the price ticket. 'But it's sold!'

Sure enough, a red SOLD sign was propped up next to the price ticket.

'Sold?' Arthur was aghast.

'No wonder,' said Evelina. 'One pound ten shillings is a fair price for a roll top desk like that.'

'Has it gone?' asked Arthur, looking at Bert.

'No. He's keeping it for you. It's yours.'

Arthur handed over one pound five shillings, put the key in his pocket for safe keeping and the deal was done. When the peace offering had been safely loaded into the back of the car, Arthur climbed into the front seat next to the driver and was driven to 24 Garden Crescent in style. When they had gone, the grey man slipped Bert his shilling. Everybody had done a good deed that day.

CHAPTER 27

London, October 1914

On the day before Arthur was to leave for Belgium, Dora went to work as usual. The last lesson of the afternoon was geography, a subject she normally liked to teach, but a headache pressed on her temples, robbing her of all powers of concentration. The globe was in its place on her desk and a map of the world pinned to the blackboard. She put two lumps of coal on the fire and settled the class down to the task of filling in the detail on an outline map of Africa. It was a pleasant way for the girls to finish the school day, quietly creating a picture of faraway countries, oceans, mountain ranges, rivers, deserts and jungles. A hush descended on the room, as the diligent ones laboured to get everything right, the artists created a picture of many colours and the uninspired yawned, waiting for the bell. Dora sat at her desk, her eyes fixed on the globe, her mind a sick headache.

At home in Garden Crescent, Arthur had spent the morning laboriously copying out the letter William had written for him. They were his own words expressing his wishes and he was determined to write them with his own hand. The task was arduous, taking more than one attempt. When it was done to his satisfaction, he put the sealed envelope in his secret box under the bed and burnt the evidence of the help he had received. Dad had given him a black metal cash box from the shop, with divisions in the top layer for coins and a space underneath for bank notes. It was in this underneath section that Arthur hid his letter, before locking the box with a little key tied to the handle with a length of string. It was heavy with money; Arthur did not want to be thought penniless.

Time dragged. Mother was not expected back from The Lions until after six o'clock and Dad had gone out for his usual drink. He had asked Arthur to join him but they had said all there was to say, so Arthur had refused. 'I'll wait for Dora and then get myself an early night,' he had said, by way of explanation.

'I understand,' said his father, too upset to talk any more. 'Don't worry about us. We shan't starve, whatever the Kaiser might say.'

Drained of all energy, Arthur went out for some fresh air, timing it right to meet Dora as she turned the corner of the road by the pillar box.

'What's this?' he asked unnecessarily, taking the string bag from her.

'A globe,' she answered, just as unnecessarily, relieved to have help with her many bags.

They let themselves into an empty house and Dora put the kettle on and took two aspirin for her headache. She could see how agitated he was but she also discerned his excitement.

'You'll feel better when you're off away with the other men.'

'I know.' He got the words out at last. 'I just wish one thing.'

'What is it, Artie?' She just mouthed the words and sat down at the kitchen table, her head pounding, all appetite gone.

He gave a sort of laugh. 'It may be ages before we talk again and now I don't know what to say.'

She nodded and let him take his time, while she made the tea. 'I'll write to you every week. Maybe more. You'll get lots of letters.'

'It's not the same, is it? People have telephones, don't they? But not the likes of us.'

'They couldn't have wires all over the countryside, not to every village and every place in the world. How could that ever be?'

'If you could talk to people wherever you are in the world, nobody would mind going away, would they?'

'Even the King can't do that.' Dora took out a pile of envelopes from the dresser drawer. 'I've done these envelopes for you. They're addressed to me. Twelve. One for every week till Christmas. There's a card inside every one. Just put the date and sign your name. Send them off and we'll know you're well.'

Arthur brightened, as if relieved of a heavy burden. He sat down opposite her while she sipped her tea. She was beginning to feel better. 'Maybe someone could add a message for you.'

'Impossible. I'm telling nobody.'

She moved the globe onto the table between them. 'Look, we're here. And here's Belgium. You'll be about there,' she pointed, 'just over the Channel. And that's only twenty-three miles wide.'

'I don't know what to expect. They talk another language and I don't want to struggle.'

'It's a war. Everyone will struggle. But you're good in a crisis. That's why you're going.' She took a deep breath. 'Remember how much we share.'

'What do you mean?' Arthur wanted her to go on talking.

'When you look at the moon over there, we'll see the same moon here in England. The heavens above are the same for you and for us.'

'And for the Germans,' he said, refusing to be comforted.

Dora knew he was listening, so she went on. 'The sun that warms you warms us too.' Her voice was scarcely audible. 'The scarf around your neck is knitted with the same wool as the scarf around mine. We have talked in the evenings like this since you were young. Just say the conversations over to yourself, my words and your words, and you can be sure I am doing the same. There will be lots of prayers and Bible words that will be familiar to you.'

'We'll see.'

He left next morning before it was light, aware of Tom and Rosa watching from the upstairs window. Dora was in the hall, preparing to shut the front door behind him.

'Be brave, Arthur, be brave.'

There was an unmistakeable spring in his step as he set off through the autumn mist towards the centre of London with one thing only on his mind: the ring in his breast pocket. He had been awake since the early hours buffing it

187

with the soft cloth inside the leather pouch, praying for the chance to give it to her. There was no point in taking it with him.

Dawn was breaking at the flower market but it was far too early for Violette. The old woman on the next stall was already setting up and told him straight.

'She's not been well for weeks. What kept you? That's no way to treat a lady.'

'I have to say goodbye to her. You must, you really must tell me where she lives.'

'Where do you think she is? In a right state thanks to you. Wait here. I'll go and get her.' She saw him perk up, as if ready to follow her, but shook her head. 'No. You stay here. She'll come if she wants to. I can see where you're going. She told me.'

'Ask her to bring Belle.'

'No need for that.'

The woman hobbled off, in no hurry at all, and made him wait twenty minutes for the words he wanted to hear. 'She's waiting on the corner.'

'Thank you, thank you.'

'I'm warning you. She's upset. Be kind.'

A thousand regrets flooded through Arthur's strong and capable body at the sight of her waiting for him, as he had prayed she would. She was on the corner of the street huddling in shawls, one round her shoulders, the other over her head, little Belle sitting neatly at her feet. He kissed her face, her lips, her eyes tenderly, as if she might shatter. That scent again. His heart was pounding against his chest wall as he drew his shivering sweetheart to his warm body. He felt the tap of Belle's paw on his leg, bent down to pick her up and received a hero's welcome. Then he put the dog down again, unworthy of the greeting.

'I love you...Violette ...' he stopped as she pulled her face away from the roughness of his uniform. When he kissed her again there was no life in her. She was not angry, she was heartbroken and he feared for her.

'Have you got our photograph?'

She nodded.

'When I come back it will be you and me.'

He searched his pocket for the soft leather pouch and put the gold ring on the third finger of her icy-cold left hand without ceremony. It was slightly loose, but she clasped her right hand round it and kissed it, a gesture that made them both weep.

He had to ask the question once more. 'Where are you staying? I need to know you're looked after.'

'That's my secret.'

'Violette, I can't write to you. If you're in trouble, any sort of trouble, go to Lady Sylvia. She would want you to. Take these.' He pressed some bank notes into her hand. He had folded them up small. 'There's a one pound note and two ten shilling notes. They're as light as a feather. Sew them into your pocket or the hem of your skirt just in case you ever need them.' He watched her put them in her pocket.

'I'm frightened,' she said, picking up a shivering Belle and snuggling her close to her neck to warm them both. 'I don't want you to go...I'm...I have...nobody except...Thank you, Artie.'

Why was she thanking him? What use was his love to her now? Why war? Why now?

He kissed her long and slow, slow enough to breathe in her sweet scent and taste her tears. Then he bent down to gather the little dog in his arms again, murmuring into the silky ears, 'Good bye, baby Belle, I'm going to miss you.'

Violette pulled something from the pocket of her apron and pressed it into his hand. 'Take this.' Her lip was trembling. 'It may comfort you. *Bon courage, mon chéri.*' Then she was gone.

In the dawning light, a paper, two inches by three, revealed itself to him: a photograph in varying shades of black, grey, brown and yellow of Violette, holding a little dog close to her face. Both were looking at the camera.

PART 3

CHAPTER 28

Belgium, October 1914

The autumn sun shone low on the water as the boat approached land. Waiting down below the men had looked a mixed bunch, but on deck, in orderly lines, preparing to disembark, they were resolute to a man. Arthur fixed his longsighted eyes on the shoreline. A stocky figure, his back strong and his shoulders broad, he made light of the 60lb pack and held his head high. No doubts, no qualms, Arthur was every inch a soldier. He could do this.

Five hundred boots rang out on cobbled streets as they marched. A tangible thrill surged through Arthur's body as he set foot on foreign soil for the first time. French and Belgian women lined the route cheering, smiling, blowing kisses and throwing flowers. Surprise at the welcome and pride in his uniform left him buzzing with excitement.

Roland, marching on Arthur's left, was concentrating hard on keeping pace with his new friend's confident strides. His tall, willowy frame bent under the weight of the pack and his stride lacked definition. There was a sour taste in his mouth from being sick on the sea crossing and his short-sighted eyes squinted in the sunlight behind his spectacles. He searched his pocket for the handkerchief his mother had pressed into his hand when he left, needing to polish his glasses, as he often did when perplexed. No white handkerchief. Disallowed. Could be used to surrender. There was no way back. He had forsaken Cambridge to be reduced to this, the weakest soldier of the motley crew. Misgivings gathered force in his mind with every cheer from the crowd.

It was on the first day of training, when every new man was unknown and unknowing, that the friendship began. They were being put through their paces in a London park, marching every morning and familiarising themselves with the gruesome kit in the afternoons. Roland struggled from the outset, questioning the purpose of every item in the pack; when he first held the truncheon in his hand, his face went white.

'You think too much, that's your trouble,' said Arthur, when Roland visibly wobbled at the bayonet exercises. 'It's just a sack of straw. Imagine it's your friend the Sergeant Major.'

Sixteen mile marches, digging, lifting, climbing, shouting, all the drills demanded of them Arthur did with relish, with enough energy to spare to joke with the men. He seemed to gain physical and mental strength from every raucous laugh. But all were nigh on impossible for Roland, who was left repeatedly stumbling and falling.

'On your feet, Merriman. March!' shouted the Sergeant Major. 'Six miles to go. Get up!'

'I can't.'

'Can't, *Sir*!'

'Can't, Sir.'

'Can't or won't?'

'Can't, Sir.'

'We'll see. You're here to march and fight and march and fight you will.'

Arthur's stomach turned over. He flushed with indignation as he relived the schoolmaster's words. He lunged forward and dragged Roland to his feet.

'You're up. He's up, Sir.'

They marched on side by side and the friendship was set.

No one can foresee the life of a soldier, when every war is different from the last. Throughout the long days and even longer nights, as autumn turned to winter, each man sought his own way of living with the sound of artillery in the distance, the cold, the wet, the waiting. For reasons unknown, they were held back from the front line; their thoughts were all worry and wondering. Some comfort could be found when night fell and hid the bleak surroundings from view. Arthur dropped into a deep and stupefying sleep to find oblivion. Bert played his tin whistle until he was shouted at to give it a rest. Roland pulled out a book to transport himself, by candlelight, on a train across America, travelling east to west in the company of Robert Louis Stevenson. Others smoked, took snuff, moved towards each other or away from each other to close their eyes and dream of home.

'When I get back home,' Bert began cautiously, staring into a starless sky containing no cheer.

'If you get back,' Roland interrupted.

'Thanks, Rolo, let him speak,' Arthur intervened, wanting to hear his old pal from London talk about home. Reminiscing helped at night.

Bert, reluctant to continue now, added lamely, 'They won't believe me when I tell them about all this.'

'I don't believe it myself, but we're doing it, aren't we?' Artie tried to lift the mood.

'I'm glad someone knows what we're doing,' said Roland, who was struck by how many times a day he heard the question, 'What the hell are we doing here?'

Arthur decided to leave Roland out of it. 'What do you miss, Bert?'

'Er...'

'You know the rules. Apart from women.'

'Clean sheets,' said the voice of someone wanting to join in.

'Dry feet,' said another.

'A hot bath.' Arthur had longed for this for weeks.

Bert turned to Roland. 'What do you miss, Rolo? You had everything.'

'My dog, Ruffian,' Roland said without hesitation. 'Reddish brown coat, I've had him since he was a pup. Mud was no problem to him. Every night I imagine him curled up next to me, his rough coat sweet smelling, his breathing a soothing, rumbling snore. He went everywhere with me. I use a spell to conjure him up.'

'What sort of spell?' Bert asked, more comfortable now the talk was not centred on him.

'Doggerel, obviously.' Roland replied.

'You make these words up,' Arthur was convinced of it. 'Let's hear the spell.'

Roland declaimed with some solemnity:

> 'Uffin wee dye,
> Ee eye dine you,
> Agnays chine ways,
> Dim dim, why slagrerprufuff.'

'Eh?'

'That means, in dog language,' Roland declaimed again:

> 'Here and now,
> Beside me sleeping,
> Rough and gentle,
> Friend of mine.
> Strong and fearless,
> Wise and peerless,
> Ruffian, perfect
> Dog, divine.'

'Blimey, Rolo, you've got a way with words,' said Arthur, in genuine admiration.

'I find rhyme comforting.' Sure enough, Roland's mood had lifted a little. He'd been drinking and there was no stopping him. 'I call him Ruff, for short. As in my customary morning greeting, "Woof, woof, Ruff." Your turn, Smartie.'

'I miss climbing trees.' Arthur clung to the memory. 'I've loved it since I was a pup.' He'd been drinking too. 'I find the best footholds and pull myself up, hidden from the ground, up with the birds, out of the mud. Winter or

197

summer, high up is a great place to be.' Arthur settled himself down to listen, his mind clearly still up the tree. 'Over to you, Bert.'

'Fishing. I began to fish when I was with the Scouts. I got a badge for it. Early in the morning is best in summer, when the air is fresh. I sit there all day at the water's edge watching the line, listening to the birds and insects. Time either flies or stands still when you're fishing.' He looked for confirmation from Arthur, but he was fast asleep. 'The day passes in a sort of trance…' Bert was nodding off too.

Roland gasped in disbelief. 'Streuth! That's both of them in the Elysian Fields. Artie in his tree and Bert by the lake. I can't do the simplest things. Oh, God, please, let me sleep.'

Everything at ground level was sodden, but a trillion stars and a new moon were clear in the sky for the first time for weeks. The men were quiet, exhausted from battling against the mud, some grumbling, others lost in thought or sleep. Still no action. Arthur was stretched out, looking up at the brilliance above with his long-sighted eyes, when he heard Roland cursing and rummaging about in his pack.

'Damn and blast.'

'What's up?'

'Trying to light this flaming candle.'

'How long have you been awake?

'About three weeks. Since it started bloody raining.'

'Lights out is lights out.'

'I need to read. To get my head out of this hell hole.'

'Just look up.'

'For what? I see nothing.'

'Yeah, sorry, I forgot. When I see you reading all the time, I forget about that.'

'If it's more than an arm's length away, it's long distance to me.'

'Just close your eyes. The sky's beautiful and there's a thin strip of moon.'

'A crescent moon.'

'That's it. That's the word.' He thought of Garden Crescent, his home since he was born. 'The stars are out in their millions.'

'Sublime.'

'It just looks like heaven to me.'

'Ethereal, unfathomable, innumerable, infinite, divine.'

'Er, yes.'

'Can you see the Pole star?'

'Yep, of course, I can. There it is, right there.'

Now it was Roland's turn to be amazed. 'You know it?'

'I certainly do. I first saw it years ago, out on a boat. Sea fishing.'

'Can you see a white swathe of stars, like a winding road, right across the sky?'

'I can!'

'It's the Milky Way.'

'I know it.' Arthur was back with George, rocking on the dark sea off the coast of Brightsea.

'Millions upon millions of stars. Red, yellow, white, blue, all different distances away from us, some still shining, some burnt out. A million different ages before your eyes.'

'Is this moon shining in England now?'

'If it's a clear night at home they'll see it. Two more

crescent moons to Christmas. It's not shining, you know. It's reflecting the light from the sun.'

'Really?'

'Things are rarely what they seem.'

'What do you think it's made of?'

'They know that already. It's rock.

'Bloody beautiful rock if you ask me.'

'If people ever went there they'd end up fighting over it.'

'I could look at this all day. All night, I mean.'

'Well, I'm going to read.'

'Dora, that's my sister, used to read to me every night, right from when I was young. She called them comfortable words. It got to be a habit. She liked reading and it used to send me to sleep.'

'Well, take your pick. I've got the Bible, Robert Louis Stevenson's journey by train across America or Boswell's *Life of Johnson*, pages in random order.'

'Can you find the one about countenance?'

'I don't need to find that. Numbers chapter 6 verse 24. The Lord bless you and keep you. The Lord make his face to shine upon you and be gracious unto you. The Lord lift up his countenance upon you and give you peace.'

Arthur was surprised how comforting it was to hear these familiar words spoken by a stranger. Nothing had prepared him for the violent changes in mood he was experiencing as a soldier. 'I didn't think war would be like this.'

'Who did? When I decided to leave Cambridge, I thought…I've no idea what I thought.'

'What will you think about when we go over the top?'

'I'll try not to think. That way lies madness. As I can't see anything, I'll walk into an abyss.'

'Here, give me your glasses. I'll put them into your tin box. You don't want these to get smashed as well while you're thrashing around in your sleep.'

'Sleep. What's that?'

'No more reading tonight. Do you know the one: "I will lift up mine eyes until the hills…"?'

'I see no hills.'

Arthur laughed, 'We've got better than that. Stars! Oh, my God! A shooting star! And another! It's incredible.'

Gasps of delight were heard along the trench as hundreds of men looked up in amazement. Roland stared into his blur.

'Keep looking. They often come in clusters.'

'I can't believe what I am seeing. Is it heaven or hell? Can you hear the men cheering?'

'If you believe the soothsayers, shooting stars are a sign of luck.'

'For us and for them,' said the men together.

The sky sustained its comforting magnificence for many hours, as soldiers on both sides took their rest.

CHAPTER 29

London, 31st October 1914

Violette had spent days and nights crying, going over in her mind the unfairness of it all. He had been working since he was twelve years old, he was strong and his country needed him; she had understood that well enough. But the number of casualties was alarming. A notice outside Charing Cross Hospital - QUIET FOR THE WOUNDED - made passers-by speak in a whisper. To have to wait not knowing whether he would come back at all was asking too much. But wait she must.

On the last day of October, Lady Sylvia made contact by means of a note left at the flower market. The envelope contained an order for flowers to be delivered to her house in Chelsea on Monday 2nd November at twelve noon. Money was enclosed. Lady Sylvia clearly wanted no excuses.

When the day came, Violette was outside on the pavement in a state of nervous anticipation, having wanted to speak to Lady Sylvia for a long time. At the first stroke of twelve, she knocked on the front door, flowers in one hand and Belle on the lead in the other.

'Please, come in,' said the elderly maid, who was clearly expecting her. 'May I take your coat?'

'I am delighted to see you, my dear,' said Lady Sylvia,

coming down the stairs dressed in mourning black, her arms open in greeting. They kissed on both cheeks and she bent down to stroke Belle. 'And you too, Belle. I've missed you.' She found it difficult to hide her concern; Violette was so thin. Questions were stacking up in her mind, but she was determined not to interrogate the poor girl. There would be time enough. 'Thank you, Violette. I buy flowers every year on All Souls' Day in memory of my husband Marcus.'

She handed the flowers to the maid and led the way out of the hall to a dining room at the back of the house, where a table was laid with a bewildering array of plates and cutlery on a starched white cloth. 'It's less chaotic here than at Jacob's Hall, because I have staff. They keep everything in order.'

Lady Sylvia's immediate concern was to put Violette at her ease. 'How are you, my dear? Are you well?'

'I have not been well. I ...' It was no use. Tears were so close to the surface speech was impossible.

'Can I help in any way?'

Violette had been waiting weeks for this moment, imprisoned in uncertainty until she was sure. The characteristically warm welcome from Lady Sylvia released her. 'I am having a baby,' she said, through a flood of tears.

'Oh, Violette, what wonderful news,' said Lady Sylvia, handing her a napkin for her tears, her suspicions confirmed.

More tears. *Je suis désolée.* I am sorry. Are you angry?'

'Goodness me! No, not at all. I had been wondering.'

What hugs and kisses abounded as Violette's tears turned

to joy and laughter of relief. Belle was barking and had to be pacified.

'It's time to eat,' said Lady Sylvia, when the maid brought in a tureen of hot chicken soup and a bone for Belle.

'Calm yourself, Violette. All will be well.'

'*Merci, Madame.* Thank you.'

'*Bon appetit.*'

They ate as if to celebrate.

When they were sipping peppermint tea, the conversation turned to practicalities, which had been on Lady Sylvia's mind ever since Arthur left.

'You're wearing a wedding ring, I see.'

'Yes. Artie gave it to me the morning he left. It's loose. I put cotton round it.'

'We'll take that as an engagement.'

'But he's not back.'

'I know. So few are back. But no news is good news.'

'He said he would be back by Christmas.'

'Wars are unpredictable.'

'If I am alone, people will take the baby away from me.'

'What do you mean?'

'I see it every day where I stay. There's a knock on the door. A woman, crying, holding a baby close to her. In the end, the baby is taken.'

'Am I the first to know about your baby?'

'No. A woman where I live knows about these things. She guessed. She tells me to expect the baby in April or May.'

'Does Arthur know?'

This pertinent question released another torrent of tears.

'No.' Violette had asked herself over and over again whether she should have told him the night he left. 'I didn't want to make him stay with me.' There were long silences during this exchange of words, but the tears had stopped. 'And I was not sure.'

Lady Sylvia put her question with the utmost care. 'Would you like to come to live here with me?'

'Is it possible?'

'Yes, it is. It was my good fortune to be married young and a tragedy to lose my husband within a year. We were in love and I regret not a single day I spent with him, so I understand your predicament and find nothing to condemn. It will be best if you stay here until the baby is born.'

Violette was cautious. 'Oh no, I couldn't. I have to stay with Belle.'

'Belle is welcome too,' she laughed, 'it will be a pleasure.'

'Thank you. I will stay until Artie comes home. Then we want to be married.'

'Thank goodness for that!'

'Can you help? I need permission.'

At last! This was the request Lady Sylvia had been waiting for.

'Can you tell me your family name and where you were born?'

Panic turned Violette white. She sprang to her feet and made for the door, with Belle at her heels.

'Stop, Violette,' said Lady Sylvia, rushing to lay a calming hand lightly on her shoulder, 'I am not forcing you to speak. I thought it might help you.'

Violette risked one sentence. 'I have told my story once and I am forgiven.'

Lady Sylvia was aghast at her iron resolve. How was it possible? 'Do you live alone?'

'No. It is a house for women with babies. We are all forgiven there.'

So that was it! Violette, unmarried and pregnant, was living in the house for fallen women behind the market.

'Did you tell them your name?'

'No. I told nobody my name. I chose my name. Violette is my name now. We, we were…' She was beginning to cry.

'Who is we?'

'I was with Belle. We were hiding among big lavender bags all the way from France. Over the sea. I was ten years old. The journey stopped at the flower market and when the driver found us he spoke to a woman on the flower stall next to me and she took me to the nuns.'

'What a journey! Were the nuns kind to you?'

'Yes. I did the cleaning and helped look after the babies that were brought in. I had food there and slept in what they call the dorm. It was horrible; young women were crying all night when their babies were taken away.'

Now that she had started, Violette went on with her story. How the old lady on the flower stall had asked for her help unpacking and arranging flowers and how, after a year or two, she took over stall twenty. At twelve years old, she was in business.

'That's when I first saw Arthur. He came with a note from Kitty. He had to take flowers to 'annover Square.'

'So you knew Kitty before you knew Arthur?'

'Yes. She usually brought the order for the flowers herself.'

Sylvia knew that James had enjoyed a liaison with a woman acquaintance in Hannover Square for many years. Enough was enough. She was more than satisfied all this was the truth. She could not stop herself smiling at the turn of events. 'Leave it to me,' she said happily. 'I will find a way. I think Violette Makepeace the most beautiful name I have ever heard.' Belle's gently rumbling snore helped convince them that all would be well.

Things happened quickly. Lady Sylvia's doctor was called to check on Violette's condition and once the pregnancy was confirmed his advice was simply to keep warm, eat three good meals a day, take regular gentle exercise in the open air and get plenty of rest. All of this Sylvia knew she could provide. The pantry in her Chelsea house was well stocked with bottled fruit and winter vegetables sent up to London once a week by Mr Peck from Essex. The autumn apples lasted through to Christmas once they were picked, wrapped in newspaper and stored on wooden racks in the pantry. Carrots, cabbages, parsnips, leeks, sprouts, swedes, turnips, onions, potatoes: there was never any shortage.

Violette could not believe the luxury of her room at Chelsea. It was on the first floor, overlooking the back garden. Her bed was piled high with layers: a horsehair mattress covered with a feather mattress, a cotton sheet to lie on, then another sheet, two thick blankets and an eiderdown on top. Yet neither Violette nor Belle, who was on a woollen blanket in her basket downstairs in the scullery, was able to sleep. They both complained, Violette politely and Belle by whining all night until Lady Sylvia relented, as she was bound to do. The old basket was left downstairs and a new one provided for Belle upstairs by Violette's bedside so everyone could have a good night's sleep.

The time had come for Sylvia to discuss the matter with her brother James, but enthusiastic as she most certainly was about her plans, she had no idea how they would be received.

'Excellent plan. Let's do it,' he said, without hesitation, when they were talking in private.

'What do you mean, let *us* do it?'

'Don't you see? It would be quite seemly for us both to be legal guardians to Violette, you by caring for her the way you have been doing and I by supporting her financially.' The excitement in his voice was unmistakeable. 'Then both she and the baby will benefit.'

'James, you may feel you have a responsibility to do this, but my wish to be involved in her future comes from the affection I have for Violette and, as I observe, the regard she has for me. For years, I considered all such opportunities long gone.'

'Then we take this on for different reasons,' said James simply, adding that it might be best not to discuss the legal side of things with his wife Alice, at least until he had found the right moment to mention it to her himself. Pleased as he was with the arrangement, he failed to choose the right moment to inform his wife of his decision. Lady Highton was hurt not to have been consulted on so important a matter and told him so.

When everything was in place, Lady Sylvia told Evelina, who told Kitty, who told Dora, who told Rosa, who told Tom. By the time Violette had moved in to the house in Chelsea, everybody was talking about it.

CHAPTER 30

Belgium, November 1914

Fog over the fields, November fog, turned the air thick and
the ground heavy, dispelling all hope of a quick and easy
war. Nothing smelled green any more. Horses struggled
to drag the carts and wheels refused to turn. Men became
indistinguishable in the gloom as they struggled, slipping
and sliding, to keep a foothold in the mud. The fog settled
and would not lift. Fog was in their eyes, their nostrils,
every mouthful of food and drink. They breathed it,
coughed it and smoked it. Day after day it hung there, cold
and damp. Boots were not removed day or night, uniforms
were ridden with lice and the daily wash was a shave in half
a mugful of tepid water. If only the fog would lift.

Garden Crescent, London, November 1914

Dora was sitting with her feet on the fender in front of the
kitchen fire, knitting socks with thick Shetland wool on number
five needles to trap warm air within the stitches. The unthink-
ing rhythm of her fingers helped to soothe her trouble mind.
It was almost dark, but she could turn a heel using four needles
in the half light. She liked to imagine how pleased Arthur would
be to receive the parcel, with salted almonds in a screw of paper

in the toe of one sock and a tangerine in the toe of the other. There was not much news. She had heard about Violette, but it was not her secret to tell. She could tell him about Tinker.

Chelsea, London, November 1914

Life in her new Chelsea home was a constant source of astonishment to Violette. There was a fire in every room from early morning to late at night, hot water gushed from the tap in the bathroom and meals were ready on the table three times a day. She walked with Belle every morning, making sure the route she chose took in her friends on the flower market, and had a rest on the bed every afternoon. Under this strict regime, which Lady Sylvia called 'simple common sense', Violette thrived, becoming plump and visibly expectant. Her spirits were another matter; there was nothing predictable about them, they were either up or down.

'This is to be expected, under the circumstances,' said Lady Sylvia calmly. 'You have much to look forward to and much to fear. Dora knows to contact us as soon as there is news.'

As Christmas approached, Violette began decorating the house with holly, ivy, mistletoe and all manner of blooms provided by her friends at the flower market. But with no word from Arthur, with whom she longed to share her good fortune, she cried in her room every night.

Belgium, December 1914

In mid-December snow fell from a leaden sky. For five days and nights silent flakes dropped and settled on the mud.

The soft blanket, about a foot deep, deadened the sound of the artillery and an eerie quiet spread across the white of No Man's Land. The slush in and around the trench was cursed every minute, day and night.

On the sixth day, under a miraculous winter sky, the men could not help blinking and smiling at the frozen crystals sparkling in the sunshine. Even the night sky dazzled with a million stars. Then the drear returned. It was Christmas, so why were they still there? At morning roll call, the Chaplain read Luke's story of angels appearing to the shepherds, of Mary and Joseph in the stable and the babe in a manger. There was to be a forty-eight hour cessation of hostilities. Peace and goodwill to all men, they called it. In both languages and in all hearts, news of the Christmas truce spread from trench to trench.

As dusk fell and fires were lit, letters and parcels from home were distributed among the men. From London, Manchester, Edinburgh and Cardiff, from farms, seaside villages, cathedral cities and hilltop towns came love and good wishes wrapped up with scarves, mittens, Christmas puddings, rum and cigars, to conjure in the mind bittersweet memories of firesides and faithful dogs at home.

'Read the letter for me, will you, Rolo? I've drunk too much...'

Arthur put the salted almonds away in his breast pocket for later and sniffed the skin of the tangerine for that magic scent, while Roland read the letter aloud:

Dear Artie,

This is my 6th letter to you, which means you've been away six weeks. I hope you can make use of the socks. We hear how difficult it is to keep your feet warm and dry. We're all knitting.

I've looked up the Bible readings for Advent. When the Chaplain reads about watching and waiting, you can think of us watching and waiting for you at home.

We have adopted a kitten, a tabby. Or rather, he adopted us. We put a box down for him in the corner of the scullery but he likes to sit on the top stair and nearly kill us. The first time Mother tripped over him she called out, 'Not on the stairs, you little Tinker.' So that is now his name.

Mother and Dad both send their love,

We all hope you're back in time for Christmas, when Tinker will still be a kitten and will climb all over you.

With love, Dora.

'She writes a good letter,' said Roland, 'I see it all before me.'

For some reason, this reaction pleased Arthur. 'She's always been good at writing. What's in your parcel?' It was time to find out a bit about Roland's family.

'A camera. A VPK. Nobody can accuse my family of a lacklustre sense of humour. They'll put the photographs in an album.'

Hundreds of fires, candles and lamps glowed that night. Every last scrap of paper was unwrapped, string unpicked, photographs kissed and every letter read and re-read. Even

Bert, with no letter to cherish, lay down with a full stomach and his pockets stuffed with sweetmeats that day.

Low and gentle, like a hum, a familiar tune moved on silent feet across the icy expanse under the quarter moon. *Silent Night*. Now the British were singing it too, softly, haltingly, as the words came to mind, or wordlessly humming under their breath.

'*Stille Nacht, heilige Nacht, alles schläft, einsam wacht...*' Roland was singing the German words to himself, gently mouthing them, through one verse and on to the next.

Arthur turned round in astonishment.

'*Stille Nacht, heilige Nacht, Hirten erst kundgemacht,*' eyes closed, body nestling deeper into his great coat, Roland was singing the second verse.

'What's all that?' asked Arthur.

'It's a German carol. My father used to sing it to us.'

'Your father?'

'Yes. He was German. We sang it at Christmas. If Dad could see this bloody war...but he's dead now.'

'Your mother married a German?'

'That's right. Following the example of our good Queen Victoria.'

'So you're half German?'

'Yes. Walter Mann came to England in 1880, met my mother, Helen Merry, then I, Roland Merriman, turned up.' It must have been the drink. Roland rarely spoke about himself but now all the men were staring at him, aghast at the revelation.

'They're thinking of home just like us,' said one, to keep the peace.

'They're thinking we're as mad as they are, more like,' said another.

Arthur's sharp eyes saw lights swaying in the distance. Up on his feet, he set off, lantern in hand, across the snow towards the German side.

'They're coming,' he shouted over his shoulder, still advancing. 'They've got a sign. It's a message.' He studied the words on the placard, sounding the letters out to himself as Dora had taught him all those years ago. 'G-o-tt m-i-t uns. Got mitt uns.' He laughed. 'They've got mittens,' he bellowed back to the others. Then all the men were on their feet trudging together across the frosty ground towards the swaying lanterns of the German army, shouting:

'We've got mittens too.' They were all laughing now.

'What's a mitten in German, Rolo?'

'*Handschuh.*'

'Hand shoe? Yeah, right!'

Even Roland could not resist joining in, following blindly in their wake. '*Gott mit uns.* Can God really be here in this hell?' He looked at his comrades as they ran stumbling, intoxicated, reckless, across the snow towards the other side. 'Peace on earth, goodwill towards men,' muttered Roland. Then his voice sang out: "*God moves in a mysterious way,*" and he laughed with the men at the message.

Friend and foe were but a few yards apart as, lanterns swaying, their footsteps paced the frozen snow. On that patch of No Man's Land, they exchanged handshakes and incomprehensible greetings, and enjoyed much revelling in the spirit of Christmas, under the canopy of the night.

CHAPTER 31

London, January 1915

Throughout the first two weeks of January, Dora was unable to pass the pillar box at the top of the road without thinking of the last two letters she had sent, both of which remained unanswered. The most recent letter from Arthur had arrived mid-December, so Christmas celebrations at home, such as they were, had contained some good cheer. But casualties were high and everyone knew somebody who had lost a loved one. It was only just light when she went to work and dark when she got home, weary, loaded down with a briefcase in one hand and a string bag of fifty exercise books in the other. Like everybody else she talked to, she tried to put her all-pervading low spirits down to the mid-winter gloom.

In the new year, pictures had appeared in the newspapers of soldiers from opposing trenches standing in the snow, laughing and exchanging cigarettes. The politicians were determined to put a stop to it: no more cameras and no more fraternisation. Dora was frantic that the photographs had reached the newspapers but she had no letter from Arthur. Until one morning, when she met the postman on the way to the bus stop.

'Morning, Miss.'

'Good morning,' she replied. 'Have you…?'

'Yes, I have. Wait a minute. I'll find it.'

Her heart thumping, he rummaged in his sack. She saw the bus arrive, the queue diminish and the bus drive off.

'Don't let anyone know I have not put this through your letterbox or I'll lose my job,' said the postman, in all seriousness.

'No, of course not. Thank you so much.' Relief flooded through her the moment she had it in her hand. She read it on the bus and knew it by heart by the time she arrived late for school.

Belgium, January 1915

Shells, grenades and everything that could be thrown across the mud was thrown for three days on end in both directions, bringing hell to earth. Hostilities stopped in the evening, as if by mutual agreement, so both sides could eat before going to meet their Maker the next day. They were surrounded by blood, excrement, vomit and gore, their uniforms a torment of lice; ringing in their ears made them deaf, mad or both and yet they ate. Food was they knew not what, with a tot of rum beforehand and a smoke to finish it off. Boots once removed would not accommodate the same feet again, so the removal of boots was forbidden, an order flouted by any soldier lucky enough to find a pair two sizes bigger than his own. A return-to-Blighty wound was the dream that dogged them all. Horses lay dead on the ground. Rarely did any living creature at mud level look anything but distorted with fear; a bird in flight was the envy of them all.

'If you could have a wish, what would it be?' asked some fellow with a wish of his own.

'Not that again.' It was the voice of someone who had had enough. 'We know. Your wife.'

'You're wrong', said the man with the wish. 'My wish is to see the face of my baby. It must be born by now. "It." Have I got a boy or a girl? Or twins? Or no baby and no wife?'

These words stabbed Arthur in the chest. He had hoped and dreaded in turns that Violette was expecting his baby. He had told Roland about his French girl at home and Bert already knew, of course, and both called him a lucky bastard. That word… If he did not make it home…

'Your best chance of finding out is getting a photograph,' the voice continued, for no reason at all. 'I'll put a bet on you've got a boy.' Talk was a way of passing the time. 'Cameras are easy to get these days. Some of the lads have got a VPK camera in their kit.'

'He's got one,' said Arthur, pointing to Roland. He knew all about Roland's kit, he had tidied it for him often enough.

'Yep. I'm planning to send them scenic views of our holiday abroad.'

'Flippin' 'eck, that'll show them back home.'

'My wish,' said the man with the wife, 'is for a carrier pigeon to take a message home and bring one back immediately.' He knew the joy of a returning pigeon. 'In fact, I'd rather be a pigeon than be stuck here.'

'Toffy, you know, the young officer, told me only yesterday he'd sent a telegraph message to London and got a reply the next day,' said Roland warming to the theme of nonsense.

'What was the message?'

'It's top secret, so don't tell the Huns: SEND REIN-FORCEMENTS GOING TO ADVANCE. Heavily coded, of course. There must have been some mix up in the decoding room back home, because the message print-out read: SEND THREE AND FOURPENCE GOING TO A DANCE. So they sent a reply: HAVE A LOVELY TIME.'

'Where do you get this stuff from, Rolo?' Bert asked.

'Straight from the officer's mouth, so it must be true.'

'What's your wish, Rolo? I need to know,' said Arthur, who enjoyed the rare occasions when Roland waxed lyrical.

'I'd like this lamentably small pile of books to keep replenishing itself with whatever reading matter I fancy.'

'Not books again.' He, whoever he was, had had enough of Roland too.

'There's no point in wishing for peace, is there? Not peace on earth at any rate. That'll last all of five minutes in the eons of time.' Roland was acting volubly for once. 'Why not wish for the ultimate?'

'Ultimate what?'

'The peace of God that passeth all understanding.' That shut them all up for a while.

'If I could fly, I wouldn't be a bloody pigeon,' Artie was thinking aloud. 'If I could fly, I'd be an eagle.' He always did think big. 'So that I could rise over the mountains,' he was looking up, 'through the clouds and over the forests.' It was in his mind's eye. 'I'd fly across lakes, skimming the water,' he was warming to his theme, 'catching fish for my food.' Not one voice interrupted him. 'How wonderful that would be.'

'It had to end with food, eh, Artie?' Bert was impressed, but came out with that.

'Any more where that came from, Smartie?' asked Roland, who had written it down, word for word. But Arthur was asleep. Roland noticed, not for the first time, the soporific effect words could have on his friend. 'Lucky sod,' he muttered, as his night-time panic set in. When sleep eluded him, he faced his demons alone. If he had had his magic box of books, he would have read a play by Oscar Wilde to force a laugh. 'The good end happily, and the bad unhappily. That is what fiction means.' Oscar was no stranger to merry hell.

London, January 1915

Doctor William Bartlett and Lady Evelina were to meet at four o'clock in the tea room of Waterloo Station. She had written to ask for this meeting with little idea what to expect. He was sitting at a table in the corner reading a newspaper when she arrived. She was feeling strangely nervous; no woman of her class should instigate a meeting alone with a man in a public place.

He stood up as soon as he saw her, pulled out a chair and went to the counter to order a pot of tea for two. So far, so good.

'I want to volunteer as a nurse and know nothing about it. What can you tell me?'

William had been working at a hospital in Folkestone since November and had lots to tell: all of it bad. 'Straight to the point, I see,' he said, intrigued by the social situation he found himself in.

'My parents, well, it's my mother mostly, my father is easy to persuade, are not in favour of it, so I'd like to know what I am letting myself in for.'

William was in no rush to reply. He thought of the awful minutes, sometimes hours, before the anaesthetic had its effect, the shuddering, shivering, the natural resistance patients displayed to being interfered with when they were in pain. You had to show dominance to do the job. Even nurses and orderlies had to develop this in whatever way they could or the work could not be done. Only when a patient was under anaesthetic was he able to concentrate fully on the task in hand.

'It might be just the thing for you,' he said. 'It's hard work, that much I do know, but lots of society women are signing up for it and you are fitter than most.'

'It's not the hard work that worries me. I'm not sure I can deal with blood and pain.'

'Nobody can at first. It takes courage, I will say that. The only way you will find out is to try it.'

He was so forthright. Was he challenging her or trying to put her off?

'I feel I have to do something,' she said, rather lamely.

'I know the feeling.'

'Yes, of course, I see exactly. Dora told me you're not volunteering.'

'That's right. Blame me if you like, but I haven't studied all these years to throw my life away when there's a need for doctors. I'd rather save a life. It seems obvious to me.'

'I wouldn't dream of blaming you, William. I would hate it if I were expected to go.' As soon as she said this, a ghastly truth hit home. What if she were forced to go? 'It's something I need to decide for myself.'

'Quite so,' he replied, bringing the conversation to an end by getting to his feet. 'They are training Red Cross nurses at the London hospital in Whitechapel. I'm in Folkestone Hospital if you need me.'

On the train home, it dawned on her that she could no longer live idly at The Lions, neither could she see herself demanding votes for women. It would have to be nursing and she would not be alone. She felt a surge of excitement at the thought. William had not smiled once, nor asked about Dora, nor offered news about his family or asked after hers. If people thought men who had not volunteered were getting off lightly, she would tell them otherwise.

CHAPTER 32

Belgium, January 1915

Arthur walked alongside the mule, gently leading him by the reins, leaning in towards his soft neck; the warm breath of the poor creature by his side was his only comfort. It took three men to manoeuvre the cart through the mud, one at the front and two at the back, pushing sacks under the wheels to stop them spinning. It was all grunts and curses. The task was to load the muddy and bloody wounded onto the cart, turn it around and make for the medical tent; they knew to ignore the dead-eyed dead. Guns that had thundered all day still pounded in his ears and the stench rising from the ground filled his nostrils. It was dark, but the odd flash of shell fire and a few rogue rounds of rifle fire punctuated the eerie quiet. He scanned the wasteland for signs of life.

A nearby moaning put him on the alert. 'Don't go.' Arthur's heart leapt at the voice. There, propped up on the ground, was a figure he knew.

'Bert, is that you?'

'Over 'ere.'

'It's me, Artie.'

'Artie?'

'Yup. What's up?'

'They got me. We're all got. Or dead.'

'Get on that cart and they'll send you home, you lucky bastard.'

'I won't make it home.'

'Don't be daft.'

'I had to leave him.'

'Who?'

'The Officer, the Toff, who joined up with us. He's on the wire.'

'Christ, not 'im. Toffy? Is he out there?' This officer, so young they called him Schoolboy behind his back and Toffy to his face, had such a naturally polite way of giving orders they sounded like suggestions. 'Let's go, boys,' he had said that morning, making sure he was the first over the top.

'Yeah. I couldn't get him. Too heavy. He ordered me back. I had to leave him.'

'Alive?'

'He was.'

'I'll get him. It's Toffy. He's a gentleman. I'll get him.'

'You can't get 'im. He's on the wire.'

'I'll get him. It's what I'm good at.'

'They'll get you too.'

'Where is he?'

'Out there. To the left. Not far, but too far for me.'

'I'll find him.'

'Don't go. We'll lose you too. What's the point?'

'I'm fed up with leaving men to die. If he's alive, I'll get him.'

Arthur found the salted almonds in his pocket, stuffed them into his mouth and chewed for a long time to help his thinking. Then he took a long swig of water from his pocket flask. Dora's words were in his mind. Be brave, Artie. Be brave. He was ready for this and deaf to their warnings. Over the top, elbows and knees on the ground, eyes down, the tin helmet catching the night light, he fumbled his way forwards. Elbow, elbow, knee, knee, boot, boot.

Bert, Roland and the men protested.

'Artie, no!'

'Don't be mad!'

They watched him go, their eyes fixed as he pushed forward, crawling on the mud, trying to find a rhythm.

'What made him do it?'

'A shell'll get 'im,' said Bert, who was watching his every move.

Roland was unable to look and unable to see when he did look, so he turned his attention to Bert. 'He never did think of the consequences, did he?'

'He's stopped.' Bert could see enough to relay the scene in black and white back to Roland. 'He's just catching his breath.'

'There he goes again.'

'He'll get there.'

Men were gathering, by now about a dozen of them, staring into the expanse.

'He's resting.'

'Let's hope he is.'

Through the gloom they saw him reach up to a shape draped backwards over the wire. 'He's there.'

They saw, or thought they saw him drag the man out of his coat.

'Now he's thinking.'

Stock still, eyes glued, they saw Arthur take off his belt, loop it through the Officer's belt and turn to drag him back.

'Christ, he's doing it.'

As if in slow motion, the crawling man moved. Elbow, elbow, knee, knee, boot, boot, stopping, crawling, stopping again, he dragged the dead weight behind him, floundering as he inched his way back. The men muttered as they watched.

'He's got him!'

'But is he alive?'

'It's too late.'

'We've lost him.'

'He's dead.'

'Leave him, Artie. He's gone.'

Dead slow, elbow, elbow, knee, knee, boot, boot, he continued to crawl, when the body behind him twitched and started.

'My God, he's alive!'

They were all on their feet cheering as Arthur came into earshot with his load. Roland, able neither to look nor to see, was searching in his pack for his VPK camera, saying over and over to himself, 'Come on, Artie, come on.'

'He's doing it.'

'Come on lads, you can do it!'

'You're nearly home.'

Over they went. They couldn't help themselves. All the watching men clambered out to drag Artie and his load back into the trench. Roland opened the lens and took his only photograph of the war.

'Artie, you got him!'

'You did it!'

'You got Toffy.'

Happiness burst out against the odds. They propped both muddy men against the wall, shook their hands, welcoming them back from hell to life itself. Neither could speak, so they spoke to them.

'It's unbelievable.'

'You got him, Artie,' said Roland, coming up close, 'You saved his life.'

'You're a hero, Artie,' said Bert, who had revived to see it all. 'You'll get a medal for this. Artie? Speak to me.'

'Yeh,' came the faintest of sounds, more like a breath.

'Good, keep resting,' said Bert. 'You're back.'

'Yeh.'

'You got him.'

'Yeh.'

'Toffy's alive.'

'Yeh.'

'You saved him.'

'Yeh.'

'Have some rum.'

As they tipped Arthur's head forward towards the flask, out gushed a stream of bright-red blood, over Bert, over their coats, over their hands, hot and sticky, ever more of it.

'He's finished,' said one of the men.

'Shut up.'

'You're wounded, Artie. That's good. Back to Blighty. You'll go home. We'll go home together.' Bert was crying now. 'You're a hero.'

'Te…ll…D…D…Dora.'

'What did you say, Artie?'

A ghastly noise, gurgling, rasping, came from Artie's body.

'God, help him,' said Roland, looking up to the heavens, while Bert kept talking.

'We all saw you. Only you could do it, Artie,' said Bert, holding him in his arms. He found his great muddy hand and held that too.

'You'll get a medal. We'll tell everyone.' Bert was desperate now. 'God saw you do it.'

'He's gone,' said one of them.

'No. No! He's breathing. He's strong. He'll come round. Rest your eyes, Artie,' said Roland.

'Tell.. Do..ra….box…under…bed…' Arthur's voice was weak, but he was speaking and Roland heard him.

'Yes, that's a promise,' said Roland. 'And I'll tell her what you've done.'

Roland opened the blood-soaked coat and searched the inside pocket. A wallet. An envelope with a letter, folded. A photograph, brownish and crumpled. It was a young girl, about sixteen, her hair swept high on her head, holding a little dog. Neat writing on the back. *Violette*. He tucked the photograph back inside the wallet and opened the letter.

'Shall I read your letter, Artie? It's from Dora.'

'Yeah.'

Roland's eyes sprang with tears when he saw she had written in capital letters, yet he read in a steady voice:

'FOR MY ARTHUR. THE LORD BLESS YOU AND KEEP YOU. THE LORD MAKE HIS FACE TO SHINE UPON YOU AND BE

GRACIOUS UNTO YOU.' Arthur's face was upturned, his closed eyes, his expression a kind of rapture. He had called out to Dora and she had answered him with comforting words, as she always did.

Roland continued, more quietly now, the words a blessing over his friend:

'THE LORD LIFT UP THE LIGHT OF HIS COUNTENANCE UPON YOU AND GIVE YOU PEACE. WITH LOVE ALWAYS, DORA.'

Arthur's eyes were closed, his breathing shallow and quick. The men rolled him onto his side and put a blanket under his head, hanging on to his breath until his breath was no more.

Bert turned on the Officer. 'He's gone. My big, brave friend has gone. He saved your bastard life, you bastard, Toff.' The Officer slumped over on to his side and fell into the mud. 'He's dead! How dare you die!' He kicked him. 'He saved your life and you bloody died.' He kicked him again and again.

The others tried to drag Bert away but he pushed them off, put his head in his hands. 'Why did he have to die?' he wailed, helpless, hopeless, like a child. 'We were going home, Artie and me.'

'Get on the cart, Bert,' said someone out of the silence.

Bert cried out. 'He's in heaven, I'm in hell.'

'Get him on the cart,' said someone else.

'Don't touch me,' Bert shouted. 'I'm not going without him.'

'We can't take him. He's gone.'

'Take us both or leave us both.'

Two men got Bert onto the cart and after a moment's reflection lifted Arthur up beside him. It would not be the first time a man had died on the way to the medical unit. Bert rocked him in his arms like a baby.

CHAPTER 33

London, January 1915

Tired she may have been, but Dora was almost running home with her heavy load of books. She fumbled with the door key and called out as soon as the door was open.

'Mother, I'm home. Mother! Good news! A letter from Arthur. Came this morning.' She dropped her bags in the hall and just as she was closing the door behind her, saw Mrs Gosling, the next-door neighbour, coming up the path.

'Your mother's not well. Go up to her. I've been to see her but there's nothing I can do. I'm sorry.' She intended no conversation and turned to go.

Dora closed the door and ran up to the bedroom. Her mother lay in her outdoor coat and hat, motionless, face down on the bed. Dora saw it immediately, paper thin, official, on the floor by the bed. A telegram. Rosa moved only slightly in recognition of her daughter's presence. Dora took time to steady herself, went down on her knees and took hold of it. Her eyes scanned the pitiful few words and let it fall. There it lay, untouchable, between them.

London, February 1915

Mourning was a succession of painful minutes, hours, days

and nights spent swallowing food, sipping drinks, sleeping in snatches and waking with a heart as stone. No information and no body. Tom and Rosa scarcely spoke, not wanting to say the wrong thing and having nothing to say in any case. Dora stopped knitting, rarely picked up a book and turned her hand to darning holes in socks and stockings. When that was done, she darned thin patches to prevent holes in socks and stockings. Arthur's letter remained in her coat pocket, with her everyday but not re-read.

Everyone who heard the news was affected, from old Dr Flattery, who had been present at Arthur's birth, to Lord and Lady Highton, Evelina, Kitty and Mrs Brown at The Lions, all of whom had known him as a baby. Evelina, training to be a nurse and busy for the first time in her life, wrote to Dora immediately, urging that to keep busy was the best way forward. It was Lord Highton who told his sister Sylvia, who, when she could postpone it no longer, told Violette. Friends and neighbours came and went, offering to share the burden of sorrow. Tom, lonely in his life and in his grief, continued working. Rosa and Dora both went back to work as soon as they were able and Tom did what he could to help them face the day by making them a cup of tea before he left for work in the morning.

One Sunday morning after church, which had become for her an unsung, spiritless ritual, Dora knew the time had come to hand over the letter. She remembered the joy it had brought her the day it arrived and hoped now that it would ease Tom and Rosa's pain.

'Mother, I have a letter to show you. It's an old letter

from Arthur.' She made her voice matter of fact, wanting neither to cause alarm nor raise false hopes. Rosa started and shuddered, as if for a moment her mind had wandered elsewhere. 'It arrived the same morning as the telegram.' It seemed a lifetime ago. 'I met the postman on the way to school. I've been waiting to give it to you. It might comfort you.'

The weary woman stretched out her hand, then withdrew it, speaking without the strength to move her lips. 'I can't. It's all pain and more pain.'

'I'll put it here for you and Dad to read when you are ready.' She tucked it behind the clock on the mantelpiece. 'It's a fine letter.'

London, March 1914

Roland knew the address from the pile of envelopes Arthur had in his pack, all in Dora's handwriting. He passed the pillar box on the corner of Garden Crescent, holding in his mind's eye a clear picture of Arthur walking this same route, with his strong rhythmic stride, his head held high and his arms swinging. Outside number twenty-four he removed his hat in readiness. Through the glass of the front door, he saw a shadow cross the hall and pause by the bottom stair at his knock. A fair-haired woman, with a woollen scarf around her neck, opened the door. She was clutching something close to her.

'Miss Dora Makepeace?' he asked, his voice soft, educated, tentative.

'Yes.' It was more a noise than a word.

'Roland Merriman. I'm home on leave. I have come to offer you my condolences.'

'Yes.' That noise again.

'I was with Arthur at the Front and I, or rather he and I, would like you to know…' he was still on the doorstep, not sure how to continue. 'We were side by side out there. I'd like you to know how things were for him.'

'Yes.'

He knew from her direct gaze that she was listening. 'May I come in?'

Dora was unsure. She left him standing on the mat in the hall while she went to sit on the bottom stair, still clutching the stone hot water bottle close to her body. He stood in respectful silence for a while, for which she was grateful.

'I promised Arthur I would see you.'

'What did he want me to know?' she whispered.

'That he managed better than most.'

'Mm.'

Roland had envisaged this meeting many times, but her manner was making it difficult.

'He was brave.'

'Mm.'

'He showed no distress or pain -'

'How do you know that?' Anger forced its way out through her tears. 'Why come here and lie to me? No distress or pain? Don't you think it strange that every soldier suffers no distress or pain? It's not true and never will be true.' She stood up, ready to show him out. 'We can guess his end. We've been doing little else.' She stood up to see him out. 'Thank you for calling. Goodbye.'

Rosa, who had been listening from the kitchen, called him back, her hand outstretched. 'Roland Merriman did you say? Please, come in. I want to know how he fared out there.'

Roland followed her, leaving Dora in the hall. 'I was there. Right beside him, day after day.'

Rosa jabbed at the fire with the poker and added more coal with the tongs. 'Dora, put the kettle on. Let's hear what he has to say.'

Roland and Rosa sat waiting in uncomfortable silence for the fire to release its heat. Nobody spoke until the tea was brewing in the pot and all three were sitting at the kitchen table.

'Tell me about my boy,' said Rosa.

Roland welcomed the opportunity of saying more, needing to for his own sake. 'We became friends the first day we met. I've never had a friend like him. He was worth ten of me out there.'

'He was only seventeen,' said Dora bitterly. 'He should never have been allowed to go.'

'He was a man by the time he left and not only in my estimation,' said Rosa. 'I was proud of my son.'

'I have nothing to hide about Arthur. Comradeship is strong out there. All the men rely on it, seek it, treasure it.' Roland was talking confidently now, as if it gave him pleasure to share the good things. 'Artie cheered us all up. We didn't call him Smartie for nothing.' Then he looked straight at Dora. 'He often asked me to read bits from the Bible you and he had shared. It gave him comfort. It helped me too. His faith was there for all to see.'

Dora poured the tea from the pot with unsteady hands. Let them take their own milk and sugar.

Roland sensed they were hanging on his every word. 'He had immense energy and replenished it with deep sleep and as much food as he could get. The last day in action had been long and hard. We were all battered in body and mind. But Arthur had the strength and the will to go out and save a man's life. He kept saying, "I can do this," and would not be dissuaded. He crawled out, taking his time, pacing out every move. He pulled the officer off the wire and dragged him back alive. Half a dozen of us were watching, cheering his every move. He got back exhausted but not in pain; he was looking up, between life and death, as if seeing beyond. And he asked me to do something. That's why I'm here.'

It was Tom, listening at the back door, who now made his presence felt by putting the crucial question. 'When did you see him for the last time?'

Roland sprang to his feet and shook Tom's hand. 'At that moment. Bert was there too. You know him, I expect, Bert from home, Arthur used to call him.'

'Bert Farthing?'

'Yes. Bert took him with him, to the medical unit.'

'This isn't making any sense,' said Tom. 'Who went to the medical unit?'

Roland thought back to that awful day when the two men, one dead, the other sobbing, were lifted onto the medical cart. He chose his words with care. 'They went together. Bert was wounded before Arthur. When the cart came, Bert refused to leave his friend behind.'

Dora shivered. 'So why has he disappeared into thin air.'

Rosa stood up, ready for action. 'Bert saw him last. We need to speak to Bert.'

Roland repeated his words of reassurance. 'Not only Bert. We were all with him when he died.'

Tom, Rosa and Dora all gasped together. 'Died? He's dead? No, please no.'

Roland was stunned. They were in mourning. They knew. His eyes darted from one to the other. Surely, they knew.

Dora explained in a monotone. 'The telegram said he was missing in action, presumed dead. Is he dead or alive?'

Roland looked down to collect his thoughts. His words, when he was able to break the silence, were weighed and measured to contain as much truth and hope as he could muster. 'I saw him taken away by the medical men. You are right. We need to hear it from Bert. He was with him last.'

'I'll get in touch with the War Office,' said Dora. 'Not knowing is agony.'

'Thank you, Mr Merriman,' said Rosa, gesturing to Tom to show him to the door.

Outside on the pavement, Roland realized with relief that the folded sheet of paper was still in his breast pocket. He had cut out the poem *The Soldier* from a January magazine, to offer as a gesture of condolence. Missing presumed dead? Roland had reported the whole incident to his superior at the next roll call, giving full details of Arthur's bravery, how he had crawled out to get the officer, brought him back alive and then the deaths, one after the other. What had he done? He no longer knew what to believe.

Rosa sat up late that night, all hopes and fears renewed. This man knew her son. She picked up the feather duster, flicked it nervously over the ornaments on the dresser and shook it outside the back door. He was brave. He had faith. She moved towards the mantelpiece, eyeing Arthur's letter, tucked behind the ticking clock. He was loved by his comrades. She took it in her trembling hands, sat down before the glowing embers and read:

Dear Dora,

Roland is writing this for me. He's like you with words. I do for him and he does for me. That's how it is out here. We talk a lot. It's amazing how we talk. I'm doing fine here. Thank you for the socks. And for your letters. I can hear your voice in your words. Tinker sounds a right Tinker. Some of the lads struggle out here but not me. I'm strong and I'm doing it. Give this letter to Mother and Dad and tell them not to worry.

I know it's hard for you at home so I'm saying to you what you said to me when I left. Be brave, Dora, be brave.

Love from Arthur.

This was the voice she knew. Her son's voice. On that day of agony, when her baby girl was torn lifeless from her body, he had forced his way into the world. Arthur, her marvellous boy was missing. It ripped her heart out. She shuddered and shivered in the chair. It was dark when she stabbed the dying embers through the grate and went up to bed.

CHAPTER 34

All the sleepless night Rosa was incandescent with rage; Tom could not get near her. It was still dark when she pulled on her hat and coat and left the house, walking so fast she was out of breath in only a few paces. Seething with resentment at the guilt she had carried all these years, she had no idea whether she was talking out loud or ploughing through the words with her body. Why did we get into debt? Why did Tom turn to drink? Why did he take over the household tasks so that I had to ask for a cup of tea in my own house? Shouldn't I have the right to look after my own son? It was a conspiracy. Dora was always taking my place. It's her fault he signed up. I was the last to find out. She swears he didn't consult her. Well, she would, wouldn't she? I have to tell Tom. God help me! 'Almighty God, from whom no secrets are hid…forgive us all that is past. Amen.' Yes, today after church.

Tom found a note in Rosa's handwriting on the kitchen table when he came in from working on the allotment. Growing vegetables was Tom's response to the Kaiser's threat to starve the British people into surrender. Digging the vegetable patch was a quieter place to be alone with his thoughts than in the pub. Work also provided welcome respite from the misery at home. As Manager at the grocer's shop, he was in charge of a new system for collecting and counting the takings. Money taken in payment for goods was placed in a canister and whizzed down a wire to a cashier in the accounts room. The cashier checked the amount, put a receipt and the correct change in the canister and sent it back down the wire to the sales assistant. There was no accumulation of cash on the shop floor, no pilfering from the tills, takings were up and Tom was getting the credit. The note asked him to meet her outside the church after the Sunday morning service. Tom had stopped going years ago, but Rosa still took communion every week.

He was waiting at the lychgate when she hurried out after the Blessing. They walked to the park and found a place to sit, she grateful that the midwinter cold numbed her senses and he searching her face for clues.

'I owe you an apology.' Rosa had prayed for the strength to do this and had found it. 'And an explanation.'

'What is it, Rosa?'

'Do you know, Tom?'

'Know what? Just say it.'

She spoke with a great clutching of her coat, 'Missing, dead or alive, it's time you knew.'

'What? You know what's happened to him?'

'No, I don't. It's not that."

He fixed her with a cold stare. 'What then?'

'Arthur is not your son.'

His iron silence told her he expected more, but when words failed her, he was more than ready to take his turn.

'How dare you tell me he's not my son! I loved him, cared for him, brought him up from the day he was born. My whole life is ruined because my boy is missing.'

'I know, Tom. I see it. I feel it too.'

'Why are you telling me this now?'

'When he was born, I couldn't tell you. I wanted you to love him and needed you to continue to love me.'

'I do love him. Always have, always will. Nothing you say will change that. But you? You stopped loving me.'

Her tears almost blinded her at these words. 'No.'

'You changed towards me.'

'I know.'

'I loved you, Rosa. I loved Dora, Arthur and our baby girl and still you pushed me away.'

'I know.'

This admission turned his rage to tears. 'You know? All these years you offered me no love. Why?'

'I was ashamed.'

'Why?'

'Because I should have told you.'

'Is that all you were ashamed about?'

'What do you mean?'

'Was it your fault?'

Memories of that day had never left her. The images swam before her watery eyes in a surge of shame. Married, with an eight-year old daughter, she had come up in the world since marrying Tom. He was well paid for managing the shop and she was earning more than pin money taking in sewing. It had reached the stage where she could pick and choose what work she took on. One hot day in July, she went into central London on the bus. A trip to John Lewis on Oxford Street was a favourite outing. The haberdashery department on the third floor stocked an enticing selection of buttons, braids, ribbons and fastenings. There was nothing of the same quality in the draper's on the High Street and she prided herself on her eye for detail. That day she walked through town convinced she was in her prime. You get better service if you look the part, she thought, as she entered the shop, enjoying the luxurious scent of perfumes on the ground floor. She did not, of course, buy the evening gown that caught her eye on her way up to the third floor, but she did linger to consider the silk stockings on display at the hosiery counter. When a pleasing selection of buttons, ribbons and threads had been wrapped and paid for in haberdashery, she went once again to hosiery to feel the soft, creamy, featherlight things between her thumb and fingers. Just perfect for hot weather like this, she saw no reason to resist them. Her shopping complete, she stopped for an afternoon pot of tea and a scone in the refreshment hall. It took only a moment to pop into the Ladies' Cloakroom to change into the light summer stockings and slip her feet comfortably into her well-heeled shoes, before gathering up her bags and heading for the bus stop. When she and Lord Highton passed in the street, quite by chance, he raised his hat and they exchanged pleasantries, first about the hot weather, as people with scant acquaintance often do, and then about Evelina and Dora, as both their girls had been born within a year of each other. She was pleased she had taken the trouble to freshen up in front of the mirrors before leaving the store: a dusting of powder on her face, a touch of colour on her lips, a little rouge on the cheeks and a dab of cologne on each wrist. Then, how it happened she had no idea; one thing somehow led to another and before long they were sitting in the garden room of his London club, enjoying a drink, a lemonade for her, always a wise choice on a hot day she thought, and he a wine and seltzer with ice. The situation quite went to her head, as she had never been alone with him before, (and of course never since) and she remembered only…that, my, it was hot and he charmingly suggested…no… in an irresistible way he persuaded her to sip the wine and seltzer and…oh…he could say, and did say, that an unexpected encounter was just that, unexpected, and that on a day like this, a cool drink was just the thing and he ordered another for her. She thought back to that chance, illicit meeting, to the exquisite pleasures of that day, when…it was no good, she just could not, would not admit she had been seduced. She knew it had happened but was unable to say the word, even to herself. God knows she had paid the price for it. Repeated prayers for forgiveness, as we forgive those who trespass against us, had done little to relieve the agony. She, with her dreadful knowledge, and Tom in his ignorance, each had to suffer alone, neither able to stretch a hand out to the other. Was it your fault? Tom's question deserved an answer but how could she explain that she had been …that word again? She could not.

'I made a mistake.' She had searched for the truth, or a truth, and eventually found one. 'I have not known what to do or say about it ever since.' At last she looked him straight in the eyes. 'I am sorry, Tom. I made a mistake.'

'How many mistakes?'

'One! It's the truth, Tom. And years of remorse.'

'You took it out on Arthur. I see it all now.'

'What on earth do you mean?'

'The day he went to school and you hacked his hair short. Why, Rosa, why?'

'Oh, forgive me, Tom!'

'Were you trying to push us all away?'

'Yes. No. It was difficult. I felt undeserving of your love.'

'Have you told anyone?'

'No.'

'Did you tell the man?'

'No.'

'Did you tell Arthur?'

'No.'

'Dora?'

'No. I told no one.'

'Then there's no more to be said.'

No more was said that day or the next. They kept each other company in silence, exchanging occasional glances and perhaps a fleeting touch as he helped her on with her coat or she handed him a bowl of chicken broth across the kitchen table. As the days passed, suspicion, guilt, distrust, were replaced by an unexpected relief, which touched them lightly at first, then settled on them both. When they talked again, it was to comfort each other.

'The day it happened was a day as black as soot. Remorse suffocated me for years,' said Rosa, her words coming more easily now.

'I thought it was the pregnancy that changed you. You nearly died.'

'When our – my - baby girl died it was a like a punishment. My, our, baby boy came into the world against all the odds. I felt he and I had survived for a purpose. I have never been free of the shame.'

'I lost my baby girl. I lost my job and without your love I lost my way with drink. I know all about shame.'

'He's gone. Arthur missing on the battlefield before his eighteenth birthday.'

'Our boy, Rosa. Did you not see how I loved him?'

'Yes, I did. I saw it every day.'

'I have lost him too.'

'Why did we let him go, Tom?'

'He wanted to go.'

'Roland seemed to get to the heart of him.'

'That's easy to do.'

'I believe Roland when he said he saved an officer's life.'

'Probably more than one life.'

'We need to hear from Bert exactly what happened.'

'You're right. That's the best way. We'll ask Dora to write.'

As the days passed, Rosa and Tom looked on helplessly as Dora, excluded from these conversations, suffered alone, lonely, bereft.

Tom felt she deserved an explanation but it was not his secret to tell. He needed Rosa's permission. 'Do you want me to tell Dora?'

'No.'

'I'll tell her that I know and that it is all forgiven.'

'Can you really forgive me, Tom?'

'If you are not to blame, why do you need forgiveness?'

'Thank you. God bless you, Tom.'

'But Dora. She's inconsolable.'

'Knowing will make no difference to her grief. Don't tell her. Please. Not yet. I can't face losing her love.'

'We must tell her one day.'

'Perhaps. Not now.'

'But we must ask her to write that letter.'

Dora's letter to the War Office requesting further information about Arthur's whereabouts brought the same inconclusive response. She was kept waiting weeks to hear the same scant information, that Arthur was missing, presumed dead. Her second letter, asking for the whereabouts of Albert Farthing, informed her that Bert had been taken to a Casualty Clearing Station in Belgium. It gave all the particulars, his army number and the address for further information. Dora wrote to Bert and waited. She was always waiting.

London, March 1915

Neither bud nor bird had sensed the spring when Roland arrived, by arrangement, one afternoon in the last week of March. He had promised to keep in touch when he was on leave and had done so. Dora met him at the front door, ready in her hat and coat to walk to the park to air her grief, which had not abated. Missing, presumed dead meant what it said. It was the day of Arthur's eighteenth birthday but this Dora kept to herself. Roland suggested they went up to Streatham Common, to which she made no objection. During the short, uncomfortably silent bus ride, Roland did his best to ease the way into conversation. 'It's difficult. Nobody knows how to go on.'

Generalisations about other people were of no interest to Dora, but she responded out of politeness. They walked over the Common and up the hill to the Rookery, where they found a wooden seat with a view over land falling away to the west. Roland was grateful for an ear that listened.

'What happened to the hopes and dreams we had before the war? I left them all behind when I was dragged into another world, tested and found wanting. Arthur was far better equipped than most of us out there. His faith was a light that refused to go out.'

His words led her nowhere. She had a cold, gaping hole in her heart where her faith used to be. She said, 'Yes,' and let him continue.

'I kissed the ground when I stepped off the boat in Folkestone. I couldn't face London, so I stopped overnight in Canterbury. There's a place in the High Street, where pilgrims have stayed for centuries. It's a short walk from there to the Cathedral, which is not hard to find because it towers above the city. As I went in through the ancient door and leant against a pillar to steady myself, I felt a welcome in the stone; I was glad to be where I was for the first time in what seemed an eternity. Nobody bothered me. I sat in one of the chapels, turning the pages of the prayer book, its musty smell a welcome memory. Words from my school days jumped out at me, as of their own accord. "I was glad when they said unto me, let us go into the house of the Lord." I went down into the crypt and lit a candle in thanks for Arthur's life. I thought he was dead. Now I can still hope.'

Dora, who was all emptiness, flinched visibly at the word.

'Let's go back,' said Roland, his conscience troubling him on many accounts; not only had he talked too much, he had yet to fulfil his promise to Arthur. It was now or never.

'Arthur mentioned something to me about a box under his bed. He wanted you to know about it. In the event of his death, I mean.' He waited but she made no response. 'I'm not sure whether this is the right time.'

A bird, with something in its beak, hopped into a hedge across the path in front of them. Dora had not the will to acknowledge the tilting of the earth towards the sun. Not the spring. Not the hawthorn. No, not yet.

CHAPTER 35

Folkestone, Kent, April, 1915

Standing on the cliffs at Folkestone looking out to sea, Nurse Evelina Highton found it hard to believe she was in the midst of war. Spring was high in the air, up with the birdsong, and neither the distant rumble of the guns nor the prospect of hours in the treatment room could entirely blot out the glory of the day. She was just finding her feet, nursing in a convalescent home for soldiers in Deal, further up the Kent coast. She had written to William confirming her arrival and thanking him for his help in getting her the position, but opportunities to talk had been few and far between. She was not on duty until the evening but had come over to the Folkestone Hospital in her uniform, in case he had a moment to spend with her. He had been working since November without leave, attending to every injury, imaginable and unimaginable. Off duty and not wearing her uniform, she had not seen him at all.

William was relieved to be working. Anything was better than wasting time in prison, as many conscientious objectors were forced to do. Unshaven, unsmiling, his apron bloodied, he was by the bed of a German casualty, who had turned up on the boat bringing the wounded back to Britain. It happened occasionally. Most of the patients were on the way to recovery, but there was always the odd one unable to pull through. This time it was the German, who had suddenly deteriorated. A letter had been found amongst his few possessions, which William had read, searching for a clue as to a forwarding address.

As soon as Evelina caught his eye, he went over to join her. She was outside the ward with two enamel mugs of tea.

'Tea, Doctor. Hot, with one sugar.'

'Thanks.' He took the mug with hands that were raw from repeated scrubbing.

'Have you got a minute to drink it?'

'Yes. I've finished for the day.'

They sat down together at a small table outside the ward by a door open to the air. He was exhausted and the fresh air was a welcome tonic.

'There's something about working in the evening that I like,' she said.

'You mean you look forward to it?'

'Not exactly. But this is what I came here for. To do my bit.'

William gave a short laugh of derision, 'Me too.'

His mood unnerved her. After three months of punishing training, her hands were rough from constant washing and scrubbing, but she had all the enthusiasm of a newly trained Red Cross nurse. Most of the patients in Deal were on the mend, waiting to be transferred from the convalescent home to the care of their families. It was early days, but so far she was managing.

'There are moments of peace and quiet in the night,

when the patients seem less agitated, more reflective. It's the morphine, probably. They eat, we say prayers, lights go out and they lie there in the dark, listening to the rain and wind. Their thoughts take them home, I suppose.'

'And you play the Lady with the Lamp.'

'That was neither kind, true nor necessary.'

'You're right. I'm sorry.'

'Was it an especially bad day?'

'A normal day.' He sighed. 'Did I say that?'

'You look exhausted,' she said.

'Yup. I've spent twelve hours patching up what can be patched and explaining the consequences of what can't. Then I go to bed and another boatload is on its way.'

'You need some sleep.'

'Yes, nurse.'

'Time off in the day is good, especially at this time of year. The power of the sun works wonders. I was outside today, by the Sally Army tent. Men on their way home were enjoying the April air.'

'April. Yes. We're the lucky ones. To be in England, now.'

'They were listening out for the larks. Or, should I say, some of them were.' Why were they talking like this? She hardly knew him, he was Dora's friend.

His weary mind wandered as he looked at her. How young she looked, how untarnished. Was her hair auburn, brown, golden under that cap? He had forgotten. He wanted to ask but merely said, 'How many patients are there in Deal?'

'Twenty-five or six.'

'And how many nurses?'

'Two VADs, four Red Cross nurses and one Sister.'

'How can seven of you look after over twenty patients?'

'We manage. We share it, working day or night shifts. There are three doctors, two on days and one on nights. I was expecting to do supper trays and bed pans at first, but I'm changing dressings and getting used to the horrors of the treatment rooms. I just hope they don't send me abroad, I'd never manage.'

William had finished his tea and was about to go back to his room for some sleep but delayed a moment longer.

'We have a German patient. Friedemann. His mother lives in London. He's had a relapse and may not last the night.'

'I'm sorry.'

'I feel some sort of kinship. We've both got English and German parents.'

'I'll ask the Sister on duty if I can sit with him if he wakes,' she said, just to please him.

'No, that's not necessary. You've got enough to do in Deal.' But her voice did please him and he leant towards her to take her hand.

'No, Doctor,' said Evelina, getting to her feet.

He laughed at her correctness and felt all the better for it. 'Even on duty, or should I say, especially on duty...' No. Retreat. Turn it around. 'The touch of a hand can work miracles, nurse. Trust me, I'm a doctor.'

'I'd better get myself over to Deal. I'm on duty tonight.'

But Evelina did not leave immediately. She stayed to watch as William went back to the German's bedside. '*Friedemann?*'

'*Ja.*'

'*Ich bin's.* It's William, the doctor.'

'*Ja.*'

William continued in German, the language of his childhood. 'Are you in pain?'

'Yes.'

'Where?'

'Heartache.'

'I understand.'

'I'm a stranger here. My homeland is…'

William could see that time was short and he still needed information. 'Friedemann, the letter you wrote to your mother. I still have it. I will send it to her.'

There was no response.

'Can you tell me her address? Where does your mother live, Friedemann?' He leant towards Friedemann, who could no longer speak, then took his hand, saying slowly and deliberately, in English, the words from his Church of England days: 'O God, give unto thy servant that peace which the world cannot give.' Then he made the sign of the cross on Friedemann's forehead with his thumb, using water from the glass by the bed. 'I ask this in the name of the Father, the Son and the Holy Ghost. Amen.'

Evelina was still outside when William left the ward.

'What were you doing?'

'Saying goodbye.'

'You blessed him.'

'Yes. It was valedictory.'

'But he's the enemy.'

'Was the enemy.'

'Yes. I would like to think…if Arthur were in German hands…'

'Precisely.'

'This war, it's changing everything.'

'Men have a bond.'

Evelina felt she understood nothing, neither how she should behave nor how others behaved.

'It's the rough male kiss of blanket,' said William, immediately regretting it. 'I'm sorry. It's poetry. It happens, believe me. You find out about it at school.'

'I never went to school.'

As soon as she had spoken, she knew she had betrayed herself and William punished her for it. 'I expect it's different with a governess.'

Evelina was defeated and close to tears. Why was he being so difficult?

William regretted outgunning her like this. 'Prayers, poetry, kinship, touch. They help the helpless and they obliterate pain.'

With this she was pleased to acquiesce. 'Yes, they do.'

A more comfortable silence fell between them.

'I need some sleep. Good night, everyone,' said William, past caring how much of their conversation had been overheard.

'Good night, Doctor,' said Evelina, regaining her composure. 'I've got work to do.' Those words thrilled her. In uniform and working at last. On her way out, she paused by the German patient's bedside. 'God grant us a quiet night and a perfect end. Amen.'

CHAPTER 36

London, April 1915

Dora pulled the metal box out from under Arthur's bed. It would change everything. Was this the right time? No. She pushed it back to the exact place he had left it. Not today.

Later that evening she changed her mind. She went into the bedroom and dragged the box out again, this time unlocking it with the little key and lifting out the tray of coins. There was the letter, lying on a pile of bank notes. The words on the envelope chilled her.

TO DORA TO BE OPENED IN THE EVENT OF MY DEATH.

Her mouth went dry. It was his own unmistakeable handwriting. Someone must have written the words for him to copy.

A knock at the front door interrupted the moment. What? At this hour? She put the letter back in the box, locking it again. One more day would make no difference.

Folkestone Hospital, April 1915

Form filling is an important part of any admissions process but sometimes, as on this occasion, there were precious few details to enter: no name, no identification number, no next of kin, just the date of arrival at the hospital. Gently touching his wrist with a professional word of greeting, 'How are you feeling today, soldier-boy? I've come to check your pulse,' the young nurse counted the silently throbbing beats against her watch, when a slight movement of his head made her cry out, forbidden though it was to shout.

'Sister!'

The ward Sister came at a fast walk on her silent shoes. 'Calm yourself, Nurse.'

'This man, he's responding,' she said triumphantly, as his eyelids flickered.

'These things happen, Nurse. Put the details of your routine checks on the notes. First things first. I'll call the doctor.'

'Is he aware?' The nurse squeezed his hand, but there was no response.

'You know the rules; always assume a patient is aware.'

'Yes, Sister.'

When Doctor Bartlett arrived at the bedside, he was not thinking clearly. Exhaustion and a prolonged lack of fresh air conspired against it. He bent over the patient to check his vital functions, then gasped, 'I know him!' He took the man's hand and whispered in his ear, 'Arthur, it's William.' There was a flicker behind the eyelid, but no move of the head towards his voice, no squeeze of his hand.

'We have no details, Doctor,' said the Sister.

William was suddenly on high alert. 'Name, Arthur Makepeace, address 24 Garden Crescent, London. His parents and sister live at that address. He has been reported missing, presumed dead. Here, give me the form, I'll write it all down. Get me some water, would you? I need a drink. Take the details to the office, Nurse, and they will despatch a telegram. Sister, make a telephone call to the convalescent home in Deal and leave a message for Nurse Highton, a friend of the Makepeace family. She can telephone her family with the news.'

'Yes, Doctor.'

William checked his patient thoroughly and set the usual recovery procedures in motion. 'Come on, Artie, you're home now. Relax, deep breaths. You're in England.'

As the good tidings travelled down the wire to London, Arthur lay safe in his place of refuge. Nurses turned him this way and that, checking his reflexes and coaxing nourishment back into him. Evelina requested and was granted twenty-four hours leave from her duties in Deal. She sat by his bedside, watching, waiting, taking notes and keeping Arthur informed about every procedure however small, as if he could hear every word.

The news travelled fast. Evelina had telephoned The Lions and spoken to her father, explaining that the hospital had sent a telegram to the Makepeace family that same day. Lord Highton lost no time in getting Robins to drive him to Garden Crescent. He sat in the back considering the best course of action, knowing that Robins would not speak unless he was spoken to. The car pulled up outside number twenty-four just as the telegram was being delivered. James watched Tom come to the door, take the telegram from the delivery boy and call out to Rosa. The front door closed on the scene. He waited a few minutes, five, or perhaps even ten, before getting out of his car.

'Wait here, Robins.'

'Have you heard?' asked Tom, who answered the knock, expecting he knew not what, but certainly not expecting to see Lord Highton on his doorstep.

'Yes, I've heard. Evelina telephoned. My car is at your disposal,' said Lord Highton, shaking hands with Tom.

'No,' said Rosa, from down the hall. 'We'll go by train.'

'Not at this time of night,' said Tom in dismay.

'Let my driver take you,' Lord Highton insisted. 'Time is of the essence.'

'Thank you, Sir,' said Tom, shaking his hand again. 'We accept.'

'Robins knows the way. Please keep us informed.'

'Yes, Sir.'

'I wish you all well,' said Lord Highton, feeling rather in the way. He told Robins to drive directly to Folkestone Hospital and wait there for further instructions. Then, as there was nothing else to say or do, he returned to The Lions on foot.

Rosa was packing a bag and in no mood to argue. 'What shall we do for money?' she asked, looking in the red tin box on the dresser, where the housekeeping money was kept. 'There's not much in here.'

'I'll worry about that when we get there. Come on, it's time to load the car,' said Tom, taking the bags out. 'Bring some food and something to drink. We don't want to stop on the way. Where's Dora?'

Dora was writing a note to put through Mrs Gosling's door asking her to look after the cat. She had no idea how long they would be away, what to pack or where they were staying. They could use Arthur's money. The clock in the hall was striking midnight when she went into Arthur's room to retrieve the bank notes and the envelope from the box under his bed. Robins held open the car door for her to take her place next to Rosa on the back seat. She travelled all the way to Kent with the money and the sealed envelope containing Arthur's wishes in her sling purse, on her person.

CHAPTER 37

Folkestone Hospital, April 1915

Arthur's return to the world began with a series of involuntary movements. The doctor on duty the next day confirmed responses in the reflexes, but was unsure whether speech and hearing would return.

'Time will tell,' was all he said.

'Do all doctors say that?' asked Evelina, when William was back on duty the next evening. She was wearing her nurse's uniform so she would be allowed onto the ward.

'Yes. The body takes the time it needs.'

'The Makepeace family are on their way, in my father's car.'

'Let me know when they arrive and I'll speak to them.'

'I can't. I have to go back on duty at Deal. I'll come back whenever I can.'

One by one, Rosa, Tom and Dora sat by the bedside in turns. For the half hour each was allowed for visiting, they shared with Arthur their hopes, thoughts and fears. How much he heard remained a mystery.

'He needs to stay here for a few more days at least,' said William, in his doctor's voice, inside the ward. 'Then I'll arrange for him to be transferred to a convalescent home in London. It will be better for all concerned if he's nearer home.'

Outside the ward, he touched Dora on the arm, indicating his wish to spend a few moments alone with her. They found a quiet corner, where he willingly answered her questions as best he could.

'What are his injuries? I see only the bandage on his neck and shoulder.'

'He lost a huge amount of blood and that takes time to replenish. Internal injuries take longer to heal than surface wounds. But he is managing to drink small amounts and there is nourishment in the fluids to build up his strength. Healing demands a lot from the body, mentally and physically. Speech is often the last thing to return.'

'Oh, William. He's alive. I can't believe it.'

'Since I've been here, it may only be a few months but it feels like years, I have seen remarkable recoveries.'

'Thank goodness you're a doctor. You made the right choice. I'm not so sure I did. I feel useless in the face of all this.'

'Dora, I would be pleased for any child of mine to be taught by you. Doctors, teachers, they're both essential. It's good to know in times like these.'

'Yes, it is.'

'I remember jiggling Arthur on my knee when he was a few days old,' he said, these few words of farewell a blessing on their friendship.

Dora decided to return to London by train. She had no wish to stay in lodgings on the coast with her parents, because the noise of the guns over the Channel unnerved her, or so she said. The more pressing reason was that Robins was bringing Violette and Lady Sylvia from London to the hospital that evening and although curious to see Violette in the late stages of pregnancy, Dora was feeling excluded from these hastily made plans. She knew the baby needed a father and Violette needed a husband but Lady Sylvia was organising everything and Arthur knew nothing about it. Visiting was restricted to one person at a time and no doubt Violette and Lady Sylvia would take precedence in the queue. Feeling as she did, home was the best place for her. On the train to London, she thought back to the day Arthur was born, when she had held him, rocked him and learnt the twenty-third psalm by heart.

Was it night or day when Arthur first felt Violette's loving arms around him? *'C'est moi, Artie. C'est vrai. Artie, it's me.'* In the half an hour available to her, she sensed that her presence, her voice and her arms were known to him; there was an awareness without a shadow of doubt. 'You're in England and will soon be home.'

'No, no, no,' said the Sister in charge, not mincing her words at the suggestion that Belle might have a healing influence at the bedside. 'No dogs. Have I made myself clear?'

'I am worried,' said Violette to Evelina, who came to the hospital at every opportunity when she was off duty. 'Artie's parents know about the baby but do they know about our love?'

'They soon will,' said Evelina, with all the authority of a newly trained nurse. 'Babies change everything.'

Evelina was right. The undernourished flower girl Tom and Rosa had seen with Arthur once, or perhaps twice, was now a pregnant sixteen-year-old, glowing with happiness, her hair glossy and her skin soft to the touch when she returned their handshake. Violette won them over in an instant.

'You look so well, my dear,' said Rosa, captivated by the woman Violette had become.

'He proposed on Sandling pier,' she said with pride, holding out her hand to display the gold ring, no longer loose on her finger. 'He gave me this ring the day he left the country.'

Violette produced the precious photograph taken on the day of her engagement. She had been waiting for the right time to show it and that time had come.

'Oh, well I never!' said Rosa, unable to take her eyes off the picture of Arthur helping Violette step down from the charabanc.

'You look very happy, my dear, and you speak beautiful English,' said Tom, pleased with all he saw and heard.

'That's what living with Aunt Sylvia does for you,' said Evelina, taking pride in the transformation her aunt had brought about in Violette. Elocution, deportment, English, written and spoken, French, written and spoken, trips to the theatre, no expense had been spared.

'Lady Sylvia has helped me with everything,' said Violette, 'She is my legal guardian.

'Sshh, my dear, it's nothing. Besides, Lord Highton is your legal guardian too,' said Lady Sylvia, adding, by way of explanation to Tom and Rosa, 'My brother, James, supports me in all I do.'

'I didn't know,' said Rosa, discomforted at knowing nothing about it.

'Rest assured, all will be well,' said Lady Sylvia wisely.

William came straight to the point, as only a doctor might, by asking in front of the assembled company when the baby had been conceived.

'August,' said Violette, to which Lady Sylvia nodded.

'Does Arthur know?'

'No.'

'Go back into the ward, Violette, and tell him. He deserves to know. Doctor's orders.'

Violette approached the hospital bed with all the confidence their secret promises bestowed in her. When she took Arthur's hand in hers, first his eyes, then his head turned minutely towards her as she confided her news to him alone. In reply, he returned her tight grasp.

'Is it time for us to be married?' she asked

'Yes,' it was hardly a word, more a wish. 'Please.'

She kissed him in agreement. *'D'accord, chéri.'*

'Tell everybody he's on the mend,' said William, observing each and every improvement in Arthur's condition. 'There's much to celebrate.'

Over the next few days, Violette kept Arthur fully in the picture by chatting for the full thirty minutes she was allowed by the bedside. 'Remember the day you came to collect the flowers for 'annover Square? I was still in clogs! I took a fancy to you the first time I saw you. The woman on the stall next to me told me you came looking for me a few days later.' She was enjoying recalling it all, her words fluent, still charmingly accented and full of life. 'Our year together in London was the happiest of my life. And Brightsea! I shall always remember Brightsea.'

The half hour visiting slot was nearly up when her waters broke.

'*Mon Dieu!* Help me, please!' she cried out, clutching her skirt, aghast.

'Oh, no,' cried Sister, 'Whatever next? We have enough on our hands. Go over to the nurses' quarters. There should be someone there who has delivered a baby before.'

It was surprising how many VADs and nurses offered to help, all curious to find out exactly what was involved in becoming a mother. Rosa stayed too, praying it would not be twins. Tears, smiles, screams and laughter resounded in the little room for many painful hours before a baby boy was born safe and well, weighing in at a healthy six pounds. When Rosa finally left the scene to return to her lodgings, she was heard to say, 'Thank goodness she had an easy time.'

'Easy?' repeated one of the VADs, who had watched the birth and heard the screams.

Violette dropped asleep with the tiny baby in her arms, singing softly under her breath, for him and for him alone, '*Frère Jacques, frère Jacques, dormez-vous, dormez-vous?*'

'No!' said the ward Sister, when Lady Sylvia asked permission to take the new arrival to Arthur's bedside. 'Whatever next? No babies here. Wait until he's discharged. Off you go, all of you. There's work to be done here.'

It was Lord Highton who picked up the receiver at The Lions. He had been waiting for a call.

'Sylvia? What news?'

'It's a boy. All is well. Violette is tired but everyone is making a fuss of her.'

'That's wonderful news. How is Arthur?'

'Improving by the day. But breathing and talking are still painful for him. He knows he's a father and keeps asking for Violette. They are transferring him to a hospital in London.'

'That's good.'

'Violette is feeding the baby and we're bringing them both back to Chelsea in a day or two.'

'Excellent. Have they decided on a name?'

'Slow down, James. There's a long way to go.'

'He's part of the family when all is said and done.'

'Be careful, James. Think before you speak.'

'Yes, Sylvia, indeed I will.'

Dora was alone in Garden Crescent when the telegram arrived.

++V HAS BABY BOY++STOP++BOTH WELL
++STOP++ARTHUR BETTER STOP++

The last to know. Her most fervent wish had been for Arthur's safe return. So why did she feel so wretched? Why was she the last to know? Dora dragged herself through a full day of teaching.

A letter from William, trustworthy, sensible, reliable William, arrived the next morning by the first post and restored her spirits. She was full of gratitude before she even opened it.

April, 1915

Dear Dora,

I thought you would like a letter from your old friend. Arthur is doing well. We are sending him to a hospital in Streatham. Don't worry when you find out it's the hospital by the Common. He will get better with time, I'm sure of that now.

Before Arthur left England he asked me to help him write a letter and that I did. It is addressed to you. I think it right you know the contents. You'll find it in the box under his bed.

There is much to celebrate. Arthur is alive and has a baby boy. He saved a life on the battlefield and has the love of a beautiful woman.

My thoughts and best wishes are now with you.

William.

The time had come. Arthur's letter, which she had carried, unopened, in her sling purse all the way to Kent and back, was in its place under the bed. She pulled out the metal box, removed the tray of coins and looked once more at the envelope.

TO DORA TO BE OPENED IN THE EVENT OF MY DEATH.

Now she understood the faultless spelling. It was William who had helped him write it. She opened the envelope carefully and read the words slowly, not allowing her eyes to leap ahead.

TO DORA, MOTHER AND DAD.

I ASKED VIOLETTE TO MARRY ME. SHE SAID YES. I SPOKE TO THE VICAR IN BRIGHTSEA. GEORGE KNOWS I DID. HERE IS THE RECEIPT FOR THE GOLD RING I GAVE HER. SHE HAS A PHOTOGRAPH OF US ON THE DAY SHE AGREED TO MARRY ME. PLEASE BE LIKE FAMILY TO HER AND TO BELLE.

ARTHUR MAKEPEACE.

The receipt from Goldsmith the Jeweller, dated 10th September 1914, was enclosed. Dora's heart leapt when she realised the letter had been written before he left for France. He *had* told her first.

There and then she sat down at her writing desk to send the miraculous news of Arthur's return to George in Brightsea and Roland at the Front.

CHAPTER 38

London, May 1915

The British Home for Incurables, an imposing building on the hill by Streatham Common, had been in the newspapers only a few months before, when Queen Alexandra paid a visit to open a special ward for servicemen. The wide mouth of the brass letter box requesting donations pricks the conscience of many who pass by. To Arthur, arriving by ambulance, it was a hospital like any other, but Dora had to screw up her courage to walk through the door of a building whose very name made her shudder.

'It's wonderful to have you back in London, Artie,' said Dora, waiting at the side entrance to greet him as the ambulance drew up.

Arthur was adamant. 'I can walk in myself.'

'Not on my watch you can't,' said the ambulance man, 'orders is orders,' and they carried him in on a stretcher.

'I'm not the only one to come back in a mess,' he said, looking round the ward, where every bed was occupied.

'Not by any means,' Dora replied cheerfully, noticing immediately how much better he seemed since she had last seen him in Folkestone. 'We must count our blessings, you nearly didn't come back at all. Dr Flattery is coming to see you this afternoon.'

'Can we afford him?'

'Yes, we can.' Dr Flattery had waived his fees.

'I can't believe I've got a son.'

'I can hardly believe it myself.'

'I want to see him.'

'Of course, you do. So do I! You'll see him as soon as you can get up. Babies are not allowed on the ward.'

'I can get up.'

'Not yet you can't! Violette is coming to see you tomorrow.'

'What happened to Bert? I can't remember.'

'I wish I knew. Bert's never been much of a letter writer.'

'Bert was with me, but…No. I can't remember.'

'It will all come back to you in time.'

'Roland?'

'You remember him?'

'The best. From day one.'

'That's exactly what he said about you,' said Dora, delighted to hear it.

Arthur was tiring and had slipped from satisfied silence into a sleep so deep he was unreachable. It looked like a coma by the time kind Dr Flattery arrived to give his verdict.

'If you're prepared to nurse him at home when he's discharged from here, I'll take him on as my patient,' he said.

Arthur was wide awake when Violette arrived at visiting hours the next day. She had travelled alone in the back of Lord Highton's car and was bursting with excitement.

'I want to call him Jacques. Do you like it?'

'Yes,' said Arthur.

'It was the first lullaby I sang to him.'

'What was?'

'*Frère Jacques.*'

'Jack it is.'

Arthur stayed four weeks in the Home for Incurables. He kept saying the same thing over and over again. 'I can't remember.' When Dora asked what, he could never elaborate. The ward set aside for wounded soldiers was subdued but every patient had expectations of being discharged, unlike patients in the rest of the building. This hope proved powerful beyond measure. The men were up for part of the day, sitting together, taking a few steps, then a few steps more. There was no talk about the war, as if by mutual agreement; they were all trying to look forward. The lucky ones had visitors.

When it was Tom's turn to sit by the bedside, he told Arthur the sweep had been to clean the chimneys and that Rosa was grumbling about the dust and grime. Arthur could imagine it all, dust sheets over the furniture and the beds stripped in preparation for a big clean. Rosa told him she was waiting for a fine day to put the curtains on the line and mop all the floors.

Then he was home, lying on his bed in the downstairs front room for all to see, his son in his arms. Exertion still made him breathless and caused him chest pain but he was up on his feet for some of the day, saying little, preferring to concentrate on the snuffling, wriggling miracle that was Jack. Violette, who was still living in luxury in Chelsea until they were married, was driven to and from Garden Crescent every day by car. She gazed at Arthur holding their baby boy in his arms with an enduring sense of gratitude and she was full of happy chatter about the places she had visited with Lady Sylvia, who had encouraged outings with her young companion.

'The theatre? Oh yes. Let's go to see *Pygmalion*.' They saw it twice. 'Kew Gardens? It's quite my favourite place and the glass houses are heated. Hampton Court? No, not in winter, it's far too cold. That's a summer outing, and it's best to go there by boat.'

It looked at first as if Tinker and Belle would fight like cat and dog. Tinker considered the whole house his territory and when Belle crossed the threshold, he hissed and arched his back. It took a few days for peace to break out. Tom spent every afternoon after work with Arthur, listening out for clues as to his progress. Or perhaps they shared a companionable silence. If Arthur had tales to tell he told them to his father, who told nobody. In Tom's benign presence, slowly but surely, Arthur got better. Dr Flattery gently reminded Arthur to take things easy and never to smoke a cigarette ever again.

The vicar came to the house to ensure the official side of things would be plain sailing. 'Better late than never,' he beamed, setting just the right tone, determined to find no impediment to this marriage. Even the plan to hold the wedding and the christening on the same day, with only a few minutes between the two ceremonies, he welcomed with equanimity. 'Why not? These are strange times.' The vexed question of the baby's name he resolved to everyone's satisfaction. Rosa had a preference for Jacob, finding Jack rather ordinary and Jacques rather French, until Tom pointed out that the baby had already been called Jacques, Jacob, Jake, Jack, darling boy, *mon ange*, my angel and you little rascal, so it really was of little importance what he was christened.

'Jacques and Jacob are both fine names,' said the vicar. 'Why not register him with both to reflect his heritage?'

As soon as Saturday 26th June was fixed for the wedding, Dora began allocating tasks left, right and centre. Twelve guests were invited, six on each side plus the baby, making a baker's dozen in total. She wrote the invitations by hand, sitting at her writing desk with a well-worn pen nib and a range of coloured inks.

Rosa had her work cut out to make the wedding dress in four weeks from scratch, although her task was made considerably easier by having an unlimited amount to spend on the materials. She and Violette travelled up to town together to choose yards of the finest white cotton, pearl buttons, satin ribbons and threads in the haberdashery department of Selfridge's. Rosa was given permission by Mrs Brown to use the treadle sewing machine in the parlour at The Lions, staying late most evenings to finish the work on time. Lord Highton, who had an account at Selfridge's, insisted on paying for everything and would brook no opposition.

'As legal guardian, it's both my duty and my pleasure to give Violette away, so say no more about it,' was his response to anyone and everyone who questioned it, including his wife.

The conversation he sought with Rosa was considerably

more private, personal, tender even. 'This is indeed a happy time,' he said, reassuringly. 'Who would have thought it?' His manner showed her quite clearly that this could all be managed to everyone's satisfaction.

'Have you told anyone?' asked Rosa, when she heard he was offering to pay.

'No,' said James, the lie coming easily to him. Sylvia was so besotted with Violette and the baby that she would do nothing to upset things.

'That he's yours, I mean.'

'No. There is nothing to tell. Such things can never be verified.'

He was quite definite about it and his words put Rosa's mind at rest for the first time for over eighteen years.

'Have you?' he asked, looking anxious for the first time.

'No.' The truth was good to tell. Tom, God bless him, had not asked that question.

After this short exchange of words, Rosa readily accepted Lord Highton's offer to pay for the wedding as of right, with no regrets. As Violette's legal guardian, it was expected of him.

Poor Lady Highton was left out in the cold, having no particular responsibility on the day, not even to choose the flowers, at which she would have excelled. She could understand why Sylvia might throw her energies into looking after Violette, having no prospect of children or grandchildren of her own, but to involve James was a step too far.

'Sylvia didn't involve me,' said James, refusing to see his wife's side of the argument, 'I offered. Violette needs two legal guardians, one to care and one to pay. Sylvia and I think alike on these things. We are twins, after all's said and done. I am providing an allowance for this young family, because they need it.'

What could she say? Why could he never resist the temptation to help people in trouble? It was a bizarre run of events, to say the least, that James would be walking Violette up the aisle before he had done that service for his own daughter. Even Evelina was proving little comfort these days, away from home skivvying as a nurse and being fashionably vehement on the subject of women's suffrage. She had written to let them know that she was coming from Kent with a doctor friend. A doctor? What sort of friend? Why had he not enlisted?

Replies to the invitations came in, each in its inimitable style. Everyone was willing and able. Or almost everyone. Eva's reply, in purple ink, was the first to arrive.

June 1915, Kent

Dear Dora,

Yes, I'll be there on the glorious day! Or should I say we'll be there? William and I will travel up by train together on the morning of the wedding. We are back on duty the next day so it will be a whirlwind trip. See you at the church. Yes, I'll do something. I'll try to persuade William to say a few words too, but he is exhausted. If only he would laugh!

Love, Eva.

Then came kind words from dear George, carefully written in blue.

                                     June 1915, Brightsea
Dear Dora,

I can hardly believe it. Arthur alive and well and getting married. I'll be there. Violette is the perfect girl for him. He asked the vicar of Brightsea about marrying her last August. This will be my first trip to London. Kitty is meeting me at Liverpool Street Station. I look forward to seeing you at the church at noon on the 26th June.

Best wishes to Arthur and to you,

George

Roland's reply, unexpectedly affirmative, arrived at the last minute. Even the envelope made her long to see him.

                                              Purgatory
Dear Dora,

Miraculous! And I've been granted leave. I'm struggling to believe the news but I know you wouldn't lie to me. Thank you for keeping in touch. Your letters mean so much,

Sincerely, Roland.

There was no reply from Bert.

CHAPTER 39

Jacques let out a louder than usual cry for attention at 5.30 on the morning of the 26th June. As Violette rose from her bed to quieten him, the sheen on the long white gown hanging from the hook on the door caught her eye, causing a collision of nerves and excitement. Sshh…she calmed both herself and her baby with cooing and murmuring noises while she fed him. 'Sshh… Jacques. *Sois sage, mon petit, tu entends?* Be a good boy. All day.' The christening gown, which had been passed down through the Highton family, all lace and not at all boyish, was laid out over the back of a chair.

Preparations were under way in every quarter. The men turning up on the day had only to find a clean shirt and tie, polished shoes and a well brushed suit, yet Arthur struggled. It was the tie that defeated him; he could grasp it, but the injured shoulder refused to take instruction as to which end went over which.

Roland, who arrived immaculately dressed, was overwhelmed to see Arthur with his own eyes and to shake his hand. It was all very strange; they hardly recognised each other out of uniform, standing side by side, breathing English air. Roland was tense, and not at all sure what was expected of a Best Man on the day.

'Just stand by me, Rolo,' said Arthur, reassuringly. 'It's

worked so far. We're still here.' He spoke with unaccustomed slowness, as if his former exuberance was all beyond him.

Dora managed to find a quiet half an hour alone with Roland, in which to fill him in on the details of Arthur's return and slow recovery. Calm and composed as they exchanged greetings, she returned his gaze, quite unable to hide her happiness at seeing him again. Where those thirty minutes went neither of them knew! But she managed to ask whether he would like to sing the second verse of *Drink to me only*. He would. Dora, who made no claims to be anything other than a useful pianist, launched into their first attempt at the second verse of the familiar song with few expectations. His tenor voice, the beauty of the words, her listening ear to his pace and timing took them both by surprise.

'That'll do nicely,' she said, as neutrally as possible.

There was something about her manner that encouraged him to hand over a box wrapped in brown paper and tied with string.

'It's for you, from France.'

'Thank you. Oh, my goodness, is that the time?'

Such things could wait. Roland had two weeks leave.

Kitty was waiting on the platform at Liverpool Street Station at ten o'clock in the morning, when George jumped off the train from Brightsea, bounding with excitement. The summer they had shared many years before, when Kitty had stayed in Jacob's Hall as Evelina's maid, was in both their minds as they exchanged greetings and enthusiasms. 'You look well...The beard suits you! Isn't it wonderful that Artie is home? A baby, fancy that!' and so on. They walked out of the station arm in arm.

'I'm so pleased to be in London, with you,' he said, having to pinch himself to believe how naturally at ease they were with each other.

'I'm so glad I'm in London with you,' she said, proud to link arms with a ship's captain for the day.

'Is there anywhere to get some breakfast?'

'I know just the place,' said Kitty, steering him towards a café she knew well.

'It's going to be a long day. What would you like?'

'Bacon and eggs for me, please. And a pot of tea. I've been up early too.'

'Excellent idea. Add a sausage for me, would you, please?' he asked at the counter.

They travelled to the church on the top of an omnibus so that George could have a smoke outside and get the measure of London. He could not believe the size of the place. 'How far is it? It all starts at noon.'

'I must be there for half past eleven, I'm on duty holding the baby and I've got to put on my glad rags.'

As they walked, George gave silent thanks to Dora, who had taken the trouble many years before to tell him to walk on the kerb side of the pavement when escorting a woman and to change sides, if necessary, every time they crossed the road. Kitty was pleased at his good manners and replaced her arm in his whenever he changed sides. At one change over, her hand moved down to clasp his hand and stayed there.

On the early train from Kent, Eva was rehearsing her

lines. "Let me not to the marriage of true minds admit impediments. Love is not"...

'Surely not,' said William. 'Is that really suitable?'

'No. You're right. It isn't. Oh, heck. What shall I do?'

'I'm not doing a party piece. Dora knows me better than that.'

'She has asked us to make a contribution to the gaiety of the day in whatever way we choose,' explained Evelina, longing to see William relax. 'Laughter is the best medicine, Doctor.'

William was slouching and yawning in his seat, drained of all inspiration, trusting he would be on better form by the time he met Dora. The reception was taking place in the same church hall where they had attended Sunday school, what felt like a century ago.

'You could always recite the periodic table. Just to show willing,' suggested Evelina, provoking no reaction from William, who was asleep when the train pulled in to London.

Dora stood in her long blue cotton frock looking at the church hall with satisfaction. Blue, it was always blue. She was wearing a silver belt around her waist, the beautiful and completely unexpected gift from Roland. The room was far from grand and the shaft of sunlight through the grimy windows revealed dust in the air, but all was ready. The *pièce de résistance,* a wind-up gramophone, brainchild of Lady Sylvia, was in the corner. Tom had been practising operating the thing for days and had a pile of records and boxes of needles at the ready. Flowers decorated every trestle table, sufficient sandwiches had been prepared and bottles of drink supplied, in her opinion, to excess. At one end of the hall, in front of the French flag and the Union Jack, two armchairs awaited the newly-weds, with Jack's cradle on the floor. All Arthur and Violette had to do was sit there, while the guests made merry.

Rosa and Tom were already in the church, sitting in the front pew on the groom's side. Their boy, alive, eighteen years old, a father and about to be married. They struggled to believe it.

A dozen guests had been invited yet more than twice that number were there. How had that happened? The church was nearly full. News travels fast when someone comes back from the dead. Violette had insisted on inviting half a dozen friends from the flower market and they were crowded together at the back. Perhaps everyone had invited an extra guest at the last moment, just as Dora herself had done. There was her friend Celia, for whom teaching was a thing of the past, sitting near the front, clearly expecting a baby, arm in arm with her husband. Dora slipped into the pew just in front of them.

The service was to be short and to the point, without organ music or hymns, on the sage advice of Dr Flattery. Every person in church that day was suffering under the strain of the past months and in the circumstances hymn singing was best avoided. There would be opportunity enough for singing in the church hall afterwards for those who felt up to it.

Arthur and Roland walked into the church and made their way to the front pew almost unnoticed, as if to avoid drawing attention to the fact that truth is stranger than fiction. They had fifteen minutes to wait, sitting side by side; nobody disturbed them.

On the stroke of twelve an expectant hush turned to total silence as Violette appeared at the church door on Lord Highton's arm. The sight of her all in white, with a bouquet of cream and pink roses in her hand, brought the wedding guests to their feet. The gentle swish of her skirt and drag of her train turned every head as the unlikely pair took their slow and dignified steps up the aisle, until she stood in certain readiness by Arthur's side at the altar.

'Dearly Beloved, we are gathered together...' The opening words were as balm on the shattered nerves of all those present. Rosa's eyes sprang with tears. Arthur stood upright enough, at times stumbling over the amount he had to say, causing the assembled company to catch its breath. Violette's vows rang out clearly; she had surely been practising. When the two were pronounced man and wife, the vicar sportingly continued to say the Blessing over the spontaneous applause.

There was much about the marriage service, simple though it was, that reminded Lady Highton of her own wedding day and the memory pierced her heart. *Forsaking all others*...She was aware of her husband sitting stock still in the pew beside her, as if forbidding himself to shift uncomfortably at these words. A feeling of confidence mixed with anger surged through her and she decided to challenge him later that very day, when the words were fresh in his mind. As they moved towards the back of the church for the christening, she felt another pang of regret.

It was hardly her fault they had not had a son and heir. These things could not be arranged at will. The doctors had made that quite clear. She held on to her husband's arm as they gathered around the font.

Baby Jack performed his role to perfection, fast asleep as the service began, punching the air when his godparents, Dora and Roland, were saying their vows, then gurgling appreciatively at the moment when the holy water touched his forehead.

'I baptise thee Jacques Jacob Makepeace,' said the vicar to the babe in Arthur's arms, which set Violette weeping.

The young Mr and Mrs Makepeace walked steadily out of the church into the sightline of Evelina, ready with her Brownie camera to capture a photograph of the newly married couple holding their baby.

'Smile!' she shouted.

'What does Evelina think she's doing?' Lady Highton was looking on in horror, as her daughter took one photograph after another like a hired professional.

'It's too late to worry about that now, my dear,' said her husband.

Whose idea was it to have the Salvation Army Band playing *Love divine, all loves excelling* outside the church? It could only have been Lady Sylvia. The guests and a few passers-by clapped and sang along, la la-ing the tune when words failed them, as the newlyweds led the way into the church hall.

By the time Lady Highton arrived at the reception on her husband's arm, all her indignation had evaporated. It would clearly be a grave mistake to make more of her husband's 'ways' than was necessary. She was feeling that same mixture of pride and satisfaction she had felt all those years ago, when she accepted this handsome man's proposal at the tender age of eighteen. They had lived in comfort ever since. Some of her friends had a wretched struggle keeping their husbands at home, whereas James clearly liked returning to The Lions after business in town. *With my body I thee worship*…It would be unwise to confront him on that aspect of her marriage, as he had on every occasion, suitable and unsuitable, praised her for her beauty, ever ready to show his love for her. 'Oh, darling,' he would say, kissing her tenderly on the cheek, 'it's lovely to be home.' It was the same when they went to Paris. 'How I love being in Paris with you, my dear. I thrill every time I look at you, to know you're mine.' He was unfailingly considerate. 'Why not have a rest this afternoon, before we go to the opera?' He knew how tiring it could be shopping in Paris and deciding what to wear. She resolved to carry on as before, avoiding all unpleasant 'scenes', as he called them. As a result, she breathed more easily for the rest of the day.

James, as self-appointed Master of Ceremonies, proposed a toast to the bride and groom and their baby Jacques, Jack, Jacob or Jake, as he had variously been called since his christening less than an hour before. This was Dora's cue to sit at the piano and play the opening bars of *Drink to me Only*. James, always something of a showman, sang the first verse in his secure baritone voice, with everybody humming the soothing melody and swaying gently to the music. Then he stepped aside, as arranged.

An immediate hush fell as Roland's light tenor voice drew every eye and ear in the room towards him, while the gentle humming and swaying to the romantic second verse continued. 'Who is Roland?' whispered the guests, one to another.

Then it was time for Tom to take over at the wind-up gramophone, filling the room with country dance tunes.

'Kitty, you look wonderful,' said George, taking her hand for the dancing. He had escorted a few girls around the maypole in his time and was determined not to let this particular one go.

'Who'd have thought it?' said Kitty, whose duties were still not over for the day. 'Arthur married before the rest of us. He was a right little rascal growing up at The Lions. There's something to be said for living with hope in your heart.'

'Will you show me something of London?'

'It's a big place.'

'I'm here for two days.'

'We can only do our best. I have a few days off.'

'Well deserved, I'm sure.'

'Kitty, are you ready for *Daisy Bell*?' asked Dora, who had found the music and put it on the piano.

'Why not?' replied Kitty, who had been practising for days. Dora had not been a teacher for nigh on ten years without knowing that rehearsals are essential if a show is to go well. They need not have worried; everybody knew the words to the chorus of *Daisy Bell*.

Then it was Roland's turn to say a few words.

'On this happy day, there is someone missing.' His

tone cast a shadow and a shudder went through the room. Everybody knew somebody who was missing. 'Bert Farthing. Bert from London. Bert with the tin whistle. He became my comrade in arms too. We now know that Bert died of wounds in a hospital in Belgium. He was an orphan, who thought of himself as a nobody. He was wrong. Bert Farthing, was worth a great deal. Comradeship is a seam of gold through the whole miserable business of war and Bert was pure gold. When we thought Arthur's time on earth was done, it was Bert who refused to leave his friend behind on the battle field. Arthur is here because Bert saved his life, only an hour or so after Arthur saved an officer's life. We sometimes hear about a soldier running the wrong way in battle, because he has lost his bearings or his wits. We don't hear enough about the acts of bravery happening every minute of every day in gestures big and small. Neither do we hear much about miracles. We see one before us today. Arthur, my brave friend revived, to be here among us, as we all prayed he would.' Here he paused for the clapping to subside. 'You may know the poem *The Soldier*, by Rupert Brooke, which was read from the pulpit of St Paul's cathedral a few weeks ago. I'd like to read it today not for Arthur, whose time has not yet come, but for the many who, like Bert Farthing and the poet whose work it is, have left England never to return.' The room was heavy with silence as Roland composed himself.

'The Soldier

If I should die, think only this of me:
That there's a corner of a foreign field
That is forever England. There shall be
In that rich earth a richer dust concealed;
A dust whom England bore, shaped, made aware,
Gave, once, her flowers to love, her ways to roam,
A body of England's, breathing English air,
Washed by the rivers, blest by the suns of home.
And think, this heart, all evil shed away,
A pulse in the eternal mind, no less
Gives somewhere back the thoughts by England given;
Her sights and sounds; dreams happy as her day;
And laughter, learnt of friends; and gentleness,
In hearts at peace, under an English heaven.'

The clapping began and would not stop until Roland silenced them with a wave of the hand and retreated to the back of the room, badly in need of a drink. James, by now unsteady on his feet, offered him one and poured another for himself.

'Eva?' said Dora, taking over from James as master of ceremonies. Evelina nodded. She had decided to abandon her Shakespeare and lighten the mood by singing *Waiting at the Church*. She began the verse with great aplomb and a far from genuine cockney accent, encouraging everyone to join in the chorus. That's my girl, thought James, bursting with pride at his modern daughter, doing her bit as a nurse. Lady Highton showed magnanimous forbearance, wincing only at her husband's over-loud: *"My wife won't let me!"* Drink had got the better of him again.

'A song for Jacques,' cried Dora, deciding to risk an unrehearsed rendering of *Frère Jacques* as a round. She hit middle C on the piano, comfortably low, and started things off by singing the opening bars and inviting a group on her left to join in, then she brought in the next group two bars later and eventually had the whole room either singing in very English-sounding French or humming and ding dong dinging in wonderful harmony.

'She's a marvel,' said Roland, to nobody in particular as he fetched another drink for himself and poured a glass of champagne for Dora.

Somebody had set the gramophone going again and dancing jumbled about in the room as more people joined in than the space could comfortably accommodate. Some, like Tom and Rosa had not danced for years. Dr Flattery courteously led Lady Sylvia to the dance floor, with little idea what was expected of him. He took the view that his primary purpose was to steady his partner while she danced.

'It's been a long while...' mused Lady Sylvia, in whose eyes Dr Flattery could do no wrong. He had taken care of Arthur without charging a fee ever since he had arrived in London. She wondered where he got his money from.

Dora and Roland were chatting together in unaccustomed poses, he bouncing Jacques up and down on his shoulder and she taking a hearty swig of champagne, which she allowed herself only because her piano playing was finished for the day. Dora was delighted with everything, her new silver belt and the company of this man surprised by joy. The gathering was going with a swing, no mean achievement in the midst of war.

Only William was out of sorts, preferring to sit on the side lines, painfully aware of Dora with Roland. He had seen and heard more about this bloody war from his patients than most people in the government. 'They won't be writing poems like that much longer, when the truth gets out,' he said to Eva, who had crossed the room to sit next to him. William felt a surge of gratitude when she laid her hand on his arm, as if to urge him to cheer up and join in the fun.

Lady Highton was watching from across the room. What are you thinking of Evelina? It won't be long before somebody gives him a white feather.

'Everybody out!' The Mothers' Union, a babble of babies, toddlers and chattering women, was clamouring to get in.

'What a commotion! See what you've let yourself in for, Arthur,' said Tom, whose turn it was to hold Jacques.

'More by accident than design, but that's always been his way,' Roland added, knowing full well that Artie would not be returning to the Front. 'We don't call him Smartie for nothing.'

Arthur had uttered few words that day, but he managed a private exchange with George. 'Those days out on the fishing smack. I'll never forget them. And the nights. It was the first time I really looked at the night sky.'

'The stars are always with us. You just have to wait for the weather.'

Arthur was reminded how little he had to say to George for him to understand. 'How are the pirates?' he asked, smiling spontaneously for the first time for what felt like a lifetime.

'Alive and well. Come and see for yourself.'

'I will. I've dreamt about Brightsea often enough.'

A motor car, with Robins at the wheel, was waiting to take the bride, groom and baby back to Chelsea.

'Shall we walk, Mrs Makepeace?' asked Arthur, disregarding the difficulties of walking in a wedding dress with a train and a baby crying to be fed.

'Not bloody likely,' replied Violette, rather unexpectedly playing to the gallery with an expression from her Drury Lane days. Then she climbed into the car to a round of applause.

CHAPTER 40

Those inclined to speculate on the whereabouts of young Mr and Mrs Makepeace in the months after the wedding would do well to eavesdrop on conversations which took place between their family and friends a few days after the ceremony. Plans were made, some cast-iron, others as gossamer.

Arthur and Violette were all set to move with baby Jack to Jacob's Hall.

'I've dreamt about it often enough,' he kept saying, as if going there was the only way of convincing himself that a land of fresh air, seagulls and boats really did exist. 'Besides, I'd like to introduce my wife and child to the Reverend Drinkwater and give him a piece of my mind.' Arthur was recovering.

'We'll have to learn to swim, *mon petit*,' said Violette, her eyes fixed on Jacques as she rocked him in her arms.

'It will be so good for Arthur and Violette to be out of London in a place of their own,' Lady Sylvia confided to Dr Flattery. 'Don't you agree, John?' They were on first name terms.

'I certainly do, Sylvia,' he replied, strategically agreeing with everything she said. 'Sea air does wonders for convalescents.' He persevered, knowing it was her wish to get away from London and spend the summer painting in

Cornwall. 'In fact, sea air does us all a power of good, whatever our age or state of health.' He longed to retire and accompany her and she knew it.

'Kitty is keen to join them as maid of all work,' Sylvia went on. 'She will love the arrangement, I'm sure.'

Kitty did love it and so did George when she told him.

'You're coming to live in Brightsea? At Jacob's Hall? To help Artie and Violette?' he asked, in disbelief.

'Yes, yes and yes!'

'Can you still swim? And row? You used to be good at it.'

'I won't have time for all that. This little family is going to be a right handful.'

'I'll make sure we have time together. I'm going to show you off all over town.'

Tom declined a well-paid, full-time position on offer at the Lions. He neither wanted it nor needed it. His many years of experience as Manager of the grocer's shop in the High Street had paid off. Trusted for his fairness, always the first to arrive and the last to leave, he was Senior Accounts Manager with four branch managers under his direction. His latest responsibility was to install the new cash system in all four shops, a task well within his capabilities. More significantly, his hours were of his own choosing. 'Good news,' he said to Rosa, as they walked arm in arm on Streatham Common. 'They have offered me a car. I'll use it for work during the week but come Saturday afternoon and Sunday it's all ours! How do you fancy a day out to Box Hill?'

'Steady on, Tom. Box Hill yes, but don't you think you should learn to drive first?'

'That's not going to take me long.'

They were walking to The Home for Incurables, to post an envelope through the brass donations box in the wall. They had so much to be thankful for. Rosa had been asked to continue working afternoons at The Lions and had accepted, much to Lady Highton's relief. With Mrs Brown at the end of her working life and Kitty off to Brightsea, The Lions was seriously understaffed. 'We're happier now than we've been for years,' said Rosa. 'Thank you, Tom.'

Tom was full of optimism. 'We're both working, Dora's working, Arthur's recovering, Violette is blossoming and Jack is doing all the things babies do. Let's hope this war ...'

'Not today, Tom. No war talk today, please.'

Eva and William returned to Kent with a friendship that offered them both some distraction from their gruesome work. But sensible, reliable William had changed. Exhausted and angry, his spirits continued to sink and refused to rise. He had never intended to be an army doctor but under the circumstances he could neither complain nor resign. Evelina was unused to being out of London and once the initial satisfaction of being part of the nursing team had worn off, she felt disillusioned, worn out and unsettled. She had money to spend and time off duty but no idea what to do with them. What did people do in Kent? She soon realised that William, whose spare time was taken up with political meetings, did not have the answer. Or none of his answers made sense to her. Besides, was he reliably hers? She defended him fiercely whenever her mother showed her dismay at the friendship by saying, 'Mama, William saves lives every day at the hospital,' but she was seriously considering returning to London as Lady Evelina and all that entailed. Come on, Eva, use your privilege, your energy and your brain to fight for what you believe in. But how? When? Where? And what did she believe in?

Lord and Lady Highton carried on as they always had done. He liked pleasing women but most of all he liked to please his wife, which he did in a thousand considerate ways. She found comfort in her marriage but could not stop worrying about her daughter's prospects.

'If only Evelina would marry,' she said. 'She'll have everything she wants when she marries.'

James looked askance at his wife but decided against a discussion on the merits of marriage.

'Don't look at me like that, James. We have much to be grateful for. Please respect the old ways. Till death us do part.'

He tried, but found himself more in tune with the new age, driving his car at top speed, enjoying his confusion of roles as business man, husband, father, legal guardian to Violette and honorary grandfather to Jacques. Yet he was, in his way, also deeply concerned about his daughter. He hoped this nursing experience would make her realise how restricting it was for a woman to work. Why did they all want to work? Was it even possible to work, support charities, bring up children, be a good wife and run a household? He secretly wished, along with his wife, that Evelina would acknowledge her title and put it to good use.

It will come as no surprise that Dora and Roland reflected on their futures with caution. He went to see his parents but was back within a day or two, eager to spend the few remaining days of his leave in Dora's company.

'You certainly look happier than when I first came to Garden Crescent,' he said, as they walked on Streatham Common.'

'Don't remind me. I am sorry I was so unwelcoming. I'm glad you came to the wedding.'

'I wouldn't have missed it for the world,' said Roland, irresistibly drawn to her now her grief had lifted. 'To see you playing the piano, drinking champagne, laughing and dancing.'

'It's true. It was a happy day. I'd forgotten what it feels like.'

'This war has unbalanced every one of us. We all come back changed, if we come back at all. I had a friend in Cambridge, twenty-five years old, brilliant, amusing, as clever as Socrates. He's gone, and left no trace.'

'When will it all end? It's been going on almost a year.'

'We ask that every day out there.'

'I wonder what Jack will be doing when he's twenty-five,' said Dora, in an attempt to lighten the mood.'

'In 1940? Who knows?'

'You're right. Anything can happen. Hasn't this wedding proved it?'

'Tell me, Dora, what are your plans?' He, unable to make plans of any sort, asked this simple question with intent, as if he wanted to know her innermost thoughts. He stopped walking to hear her reply.

'I have no plans,' she admitted, somewhat discomforted, preferring to walk as she spoke. 'But I wonder whether I'm cut out for teaching. It's a daily grind. Did you see Celia at the wedding, glowing with happiness? She says she prefers mopping the hall floor on her hands and knees to standing in front of a class of children.'

'Do you feel the same?'

'No, not quite. I enjoy it but it's hard. Besides, I don't have that choice. The war has put everything on hold.'

All at once he knew what he had to say. He stood still again and opened his mouth to speak, his heart pounding with the exhilaration of the moment... but was this the right moment?

'Will you write to me?' he asked, looking straight into her eyes. Her letters to Arthur had touched him and now she was close and confiding he was captivated.

Dora felt the thrill of his look. Letter writing was a pleasure, but was it worth the pain of waiting for a reply? Arthur's letters had been a lifeline, even though she knew someone had written them for him. That someone was Roland.

'Yes, I'll write,' she said, slipping her arm through his and leaning against him as they walked. Oh, the relief and joy in both their hearts, as they paced the well-trodden path together.

He squeezed her arm, his mind made up. He would write and ask her.